Captain Picard . . . In His Own Words!

The Cardassians' weapons banks erupted at us with renewed fury. The *Daring* shivered and jerked sideways under the force of the attack. A console exploded, sending out a shower of sparks.

I felt a hand clutch my shoulder. "Get us out of here," Red Abby demanded of me.

Then the Cardassians struck again. I was flung out of my seat. The next thing I knew, I was dragging myself off the deck, a ringing in my ears and the taste of blood in my mouth.

My comrades had been tossed about as well. One by one, they began to stir, to show signs of consciousness.

Red Abby cursed and looked to Worf. "Report," she rasped, her blue eyes glittering as they reflected a sudden burst of sparks.

"Shields are down," the lieutenant told her, blinking away smoke. "Weapons are disabled. And the engines are offline—impulse as well as warpdrive."

"I looked at the viewscreen. The Cardassian warship wasn't firing on us any longer. But then, it didn't have to.

We were dead in the water.

STAR TREK
THE NEXT GENERATION®

THE CAPTAIN'S TABLE

BOOK TWO OF SIX

DUJONIAN'S HOARD

JEAN-LUC PICARD

AS RECORDED BY
MICHAEL JAN
FRIEDMAN

THE CAPTAIN'S TABLE CONCEPT BY
JOHN J. ORDOVER AND DEAN WESLEY SMITH

POCKET BOOKS
New York   London   Toronto   Sydney   Tokyo   Singapore

This book is a work of fiction. Names, characters, places and incidents are products of the author's imagination or are used fictitiously. Any resemblance to actual events or locales or persons, living or dead, is entirely coincidental.

An *Original* Publication of POCKET BOOKS

POCKET BOOKS, a division of Simon & Schuster Inc.
1230 Avenue of the Americas, New York, NY 10020

STAR TREK is a Registered Trademark of Paramount Pictures.

A VIACOM COMPANY

This book is published by Pocket Books, a division of Simon & Schuster Inc., under exclusive license from Paramount Pictures.

ISBN: 0-671-01465-X

First Pocket Books printing June 1998

10 9 8 7 6 5 4 3 2 1

POCKET and colophon are registered trademarks of Simon & Schuster Inc.

Printed in the U.S.A.

For Jason, Roni, Jesse, and Dana,
who love to go a-wanderin'

DUJONIAN'S HOARD

Madigoor

CAPTAIN JEAN-LUC PICARD looked around at the thickening fog and decided he would never reach his destination.

In the pea soup that surrounded him, every building looked like every other. Floating street illuminators were few and far between. And as Madigooran cities were known to have their deadlier sides, he wasn't at all comfortable not knowing where he was going.

Turning to his friend and colleague Captain Neil Gleason of the *Zhukov,* Picard shrugged. "Maybe we ought to turn back," he suggested. "Return to the conference center."

"Nonsense," said Gleason, his face covered with a thin sheen of moisture, his blue eyes resolute beneath his shock of thick red hair. "We can't turn back. We're almost there."

Picard cleared his throat. "Forgive me for sounding dubious, Neil, but you said the very same thing ten minutes ago, and—unless I'm mistaken—ten minutes before that."

Gleason stopped and clapped his colleague on the shoulder. "Come on, Jean-Luc. I've never attended a more useless excuse for a conference in my life. Trade routes, transitional governments, border disputes ... it's enough to make me wish I'd become an engineer."

Picard had to agree.

A year earlier, the Federation had signed its treaty with the Cardassian Union, with each side ceding certain planets to the other. After that, matters along the border had gotten complicated rather quickly.

For one thing, the Maquis had entered the mix, using guerrilla tactics to make it known they weren't going to accept Cardassian rule—treaty or no treaty. Like it or not, that compelled Starfleet Command to formulate a whole new line of policy.

Hence, the strategic conference on Madigoor IV, which Picard and Gleason had been asked to attend. But in its first day, the conference had dealt little with practical matters—such as where and how the Maquis might strike next—and more with a host of attendant political considerations.

"We owe ourselves a little relaxation," Gleason insisted with a smile. "A little diversion, if you will. And there's no place in the galaxy as diverting as the Captain's Table."

"Yes," Picard responded. "You told me. A pub to end all pubs."

"An understatement, I assure you."

The captain ignored the remark. "At which point, if you'll recall, I said my pub-crawling days were well behind me."

"That's right," Gleason agreed. "And I told you *this* pub would make you change your mind."

Truth be told, Picard had had another reason for trying to decline his friend's offer. He'd had a lot on his mind lately—an *awful* lot—and he still needed to sort it out.

However, there had been no arguing with the man. So Picard had accompanied him—a decision he was rapidly beginning to regret.

Looking around again, all he could make out were vague shapes. Fortunately, none of them were moving, so there was no immediate danger. But the fog was getting denser by the moment.

"I'm sure you're right," he told his companion reasonably. "I'm sure this Captain's Table is a perfectly wonderful establishment. But if we can't find the place . . ."

"Oh, we'll find it all right," Gleason assured him. He frowned and peered into the fog. "It's this way," he decided, though he sounded even less sure of himself than when they'd left the conference facility. "Yes, this way for certain, Jean-Luc."

And he started off again. With a sigh, Picard followed.

But after another ten minutes, they still hadn't gotten where they were going. A little exasperated by that point, the captain took Gleason by the sleeve of his civilian garb.

"Listen," he said, "this is absurd, Neil. At this rate, we'll be wandering these streets all night."

Gleason scratched his head and did some more looking around. "I just don't get it," he replied at last. "Last time, it seemed so close to the conference center. And now . . ."

"That was a year ago," Picard reminded him. "Maybe it's closed down in the interim. Or moved."

Gleason didn't say anything, but his look admitted the possibility his friend was right.

"At any rate," said Picard, "this is looking more and more like a wild-goose chase. And as someone who has actually chased a wild goose in his youth, I can personally attest to the fruitlessness of such an endeavor."

Clearly, Gleason wasn't as sure of himself as before, but he still didn't seem willing to admit defeat. "Look," he sighed, "maybe if we just go on a little farther . . ."

Having reached the end of his patience, Picard held his hand up. *"You* go on if you like. I'm going to call it a day."

Of course, he was so lost at that point, finding the conference center would be no mean feat. But at least he knew the place still existed. That was, unless the Madigoorans had hidden it as well as they'd hidden Gleason's pub—which seemed fairly unlikely.

Gleason squinted into the fog. "It's here somewhere," he insisted. "I could've sworn it was . . . " Suddenly, his face lit up. "Right there!" he announced triumphantly. And he pointed.

Picard followed the man's gesture. Through the concealing, befuddling fog, he could make out a whimsical sign handpainted in bright colors. In flowing Madigooran characters, it read *G'kl'gol Ivno'ewi.*

Gleason translated. "The Captain's Table." He held his arms out like a performer seeking applause. "You see? I told you I'd find it."

"So you did," Picard conceded.

Funny, he thought, how that sign had seemed to loom up out of nowhere. Looking at it now, he didn't know how he could have missed it.

"Come on," Gleason told him, tugging at his arm.

They crossed what appeared to be a square and reached the door beneath the sign. It was big, made of dark wood and rounded on top, with a brass handle in the shape of a mythical, horned beast. All in all, a curious entrance—even for Madigoor, which had its share of antique architecture.

Without a moment's hesitation, Gleason took hold of the handle and pulled the door open, allowing a flood of noise to issue forth from inside. Then he turned to his colleague with a grin on his face.

"After you, Jean-Luc."

Picard took Gleason up on his offer. Tugging down on the front of his shirt, he went inside.

His friend followed and allowed the door to close behind them. "Well?" Gleason asked over the sounds of music and clattering glasses and conversation. "What do you think of it?"

Picard shook his head. After hearing his colleague's description of the place, it was hardly the sort of ambiance he had expected. The place wasn't a pub at all, was it?

Rather, it was reminiscent of a French country inn, from the elegant but faded wallpaper to the violin melody coming from somewhere to the ancient hearth blazing in the far wall. There was even an old French nation-flag, hanging from the smoky, dark rafters.

Also a stair, off to the side and just past the bar, that led upstairs to another floor. No doubt, the captain mused, there were rooms to let up there, for those who had drunk a bit more than their fill.

Tables stood everywhere, a veritable sea of them, each illuminated by an oil lamp in the center and liberally stocked with half-empty wine bottles. And there was hardly a vacant seat to be had, except in the farthest reaches of the place. Nearly every table was surrounded with guests, some sitting and some standing.

Picard couldn't help but remark—if only to himself—on the assortment of species in evidence there. He had run into almost every kind of being in known space at some point in his career, and he was hard-pressed to think of one absent from the proceedings. In fact, there were a fair number of patrons whose like he'd never even heard of.

As he continued to examine the place, something caught his eye. A display case, actually, with—unless his eyes were failing him—something remarkable inside it.

Something *quite* remarkable.

"Jean-Luc?" said Gleason.

"Just a moment," the captain replied.

He wound his way through the closely packed crowd, drawn by his curiosity. Moments later, as he stopped in front of the display case, his initial conclusion was confirmed.

There was a bottle inside the case. And inside the bottle was a model of a Promellian battle cruiser—much like the one he had built as a boy, which stood now in his ready room on the *Enterprise.*

Picard had never seen another such model in all his travels. It was hard enough to believe another child somewhere in the universe had been so fond of Promellian ship design. But the chances of that child being inclined to build something in a bottle . . .

He shook his head. It staggered the mind.

Yet here it was, an exact replica of his boyhood trophy. The captain turned to comment on the coincidence. "Look at this, Neil. I—"

But Gleason was gone.

Picard looked about, imagining his fellow captain had merely strayed in another direction. Toward the bar, perhaps. But the longer he looked, the more certain he was that Gleason was nowhere to be found.

Now, that's strange, Picard thought. Gleason was so eager to show me this place. Why would he bring me in and then abandon me?

The captain didn't wish to jump to any unfounded conclusions. However, it occurred to him he knew almost nothing about this establishment. The hair prickled on the back of his neck.

If Gleason *had* somehow fallen victim to foul play . . . perhaps someone he'd met here on a previous occasion and offended . . .

Picard stopped himself. You're overreacting, he thought. A massive conspiracy aside, the place was too crowded for Gleason to have been shanghaied without witnesses. And not every bar was a playground for kidnappers and cutthroats, despite his experiences to the contrary.

He'd simply give his friend a chance to turn up, which he would no doubt do in the fullness of time. And in the meantime, Picard would take a closer look at the bottled ship.

As he did this, Picard found himself marveling at the model—at both the care that had gone into its construction and the choices that had been made. For instance, the method used to put the metal hull joints together.

They weren't glued, as one might have expected. They were fused—just the way *he* had done it. In fact, if he hadn't known better, he would have suspected the thing had been taken from his ready room and placed here only a few hours ago.

An unlikely event, the captain conceded. A ridiculously unlikely event. Still, the resemblance was—

Suddenly, he saw something out of the corner of his eye. Something shiny. And it was flying in his direction.

Whirling, he snatched at it—and found himself holding a foil by its leather-wrapped pommel. For a moment, he stared at it, for it was clearly an antique—six hundred years old if it was a day. Then he looked up to see how it had come hurtling his way.

There was a man standing not twenty paces away, carving the air between them with a twin to the foil. He was human, about Picard's height, with a roguish mustache and the fine, worn clothes of a swashbuckler. No doubt, one of those who fancied period styles.

The man smiled. "En garde, mon ami."

The captain held a hand up for peace. "Excuse me," he said with the utmost diplomacy, "but I think you've mistaken me for someone else. I didn't come here to duel with you."

"Ah," said the man with the mustache, "but I believe you have."

"Jean!" came a deep, commanding voice.

Picard whirled. Unless he was mistaken, the summons had come from the direction of the bar. Sure enough, the bartender seemed to be looking in the captain's direction.

He was a tall, heavyset human-looking fellow with long, silver hair and a starched white apron. His gaze looked sharp enough to cut glass. Not unlike his tone of voice, it carried something of a warning.

"Are you speaking to me?" Picard asked, wondering how it was the man knew his name.

"I'll have no bloodshed here," the bartender insisted. "Not like the last time, Jean."

The *last* time? the captain wondered. There hadn't been any last time. Not for him, at least.

"You needn't worry," the swashbuckler said. He inclined his head to the bartender even as he pointed his blade at Picard. "There will be no dire injuries tonight. Only a few welts in the name of fun."

Abruptly, Picard realized the swashbuckler was called Jean, as well. And with narrowed eyes and rippling jaw muscles, the man was advancing on him, his point extended.

The assembled patrons pushed a couple of tables aside and scurried out of the way. They seemed eager for a little entertainment, and the swashbuckler seemed only too happy to give it to them.

Under most circumstances, the captain would have declined. After all, he stood a chance of getting hurt, and in a strange milieu at that—and he still didn't know what had become of his friend Gleason.

However, the challenge, delivered so recklessly, had stirred in him an emotion he thought he'd suppressed long ago—the bravado of a young cadet. Besides, the swordsman had said he intended no serious violence. And if it were welts he was eager for, as he had

8

announced . . . Picard smiled. He would do his humble best to oblige the man.

"Well?" asked the other Jean, stopping a couple of strides from the captain. "Will you fight me?" He tilted his head slyly. "In the name of good fellowship if for no other reason?"

Picard chuckled. "In the name of good fellowship . . . why not? The game is one touch. Agreed?"

His adversary grinned broadly. "Let us make it first blood."

The captain frowned. He was somewhat less comfortable with that approach, but he agreed to it.

"First blood, then," he said.

They raised their swords and advanced on one another. Before Picard knew it, he was engaged in a storm of clashing blades.

The captain's opponent was clearly an expert with the foil, flicking it about with deadly accuracy. But Picard was no novice, either. He had studied in some of the most famous fencing dens on Earth, under some of the most exacting masters. Before long, he proved himself equal to any assault his adversary cared to mount.

Then, after about thirty seconds or so, the fellow's attacks began to speed up. It became clear to the captain that his opponent had been testing him to that point, gauging his skills. And now, having educated himself on that count, mustached Jean was beginning to fence in earnest.

Still, Picard kept up with every cut and thrust. He foiled every attempt to bind his blade. And all the while, he looked for an opening, an opportunity to beat his opponent with minimal risk to himself.

But then, was that not what fencing was all about? Anyone could become a swordsman on the physical plane. But the mindgame, the contest of wills and wits . . . that was another matter entirely.

Picard barely noticed the cheering of the crowd. He was too intent on keeping up with the play, too focused on seeking a weakness he could capitalize on before his opponent discovered one in him.

Their blades whipped back and forth as if they had a life of their own. It was lunge and parry, counter and retreat, over and over again. Each exchange was a thing of beauty—even to Picard himself, though he had little time to appreciate it.

And then he spotted his opening. The other Jean, a little fatigued perhaps, had lowered his blade a couple of inches. Picard pretended to launch an assault on the fellow's shoulder.

Seeing it, the other Jean reacted, bringing his weapon up to fend Picard off. But the captain's true target wasn't Jean's shoulder at all. In midlunge, he dropped his blade and came in under his opponent's armpit.

Not hard enough to hurt him, of course, but hard enough to pierce his white, ruffled shirt and break the skin beneath it. After all, the game *was* first blood.

"Alas!" Picard bellowed suddenly, commiserating with his adversary as fencing tradition demanded.

The other Jean took a step back and raised his sword arm. Clearly, the fabric of his shirt had been pierced. And there was a bloodred mark just to the side of the hole.

Eyeing Picard with a mixture of disappointment and admiration, the fellow hesitated for a moment. Then he brought his blade up to his forehead and swept it down smartly in a fencer's salute.

"You've won," the other Jean conceded.

"So it appears," Picard replied, returning the salute with one of his own. "But it was well fought."

His opponent nodded. "I thought so, too."

A hearty cheer went up from all assembled, shaking the very walls of the place. And before it died, someone had thrust a glass of wine into the captain's hand. From the background, he could hear the stirring strains of ancient France's national anthem.

As the patrons of the Captain's Table clinked their glasses and put their own words to the music, Picard wondered at their careless enthusiasm. What kind of place *was* this? he asked himself.

He had a thought. A very disillusioning thought, at that.

Could this be his old nemesis Q at work again, showing off his vaunted omnipotence for some purpose the captain couldn't begin to fathom? He searched for Q in the crowd, but couldn't find him.

Suddenly, the captain felt an arm close around him like a vice. He looked up into dancing eyes and a dense, white beard and for a moment—just a fraction of a second—imagined he was face-to-face with Santa Claus. When the stranger laughed, filling the room with his mirth, it didn't do anything to dispel the illusion.

"Why, you're more solid than you look," the big fellow guffawed. He thrust a meaty paw at Picard. "Name's Robinson, lad. Just Robinson. It's a pleasure to make your acquaintance."

The captain took the man's hand and found his own enveloped. "Jean-Luc Picard. The pleasure is mine."

"There's a lad," Robinson rumbled. He pulled the captain in the direction of a table in the corner. "Come and say hello to my friends. They want to meet the man who bested the best sword-fighter in the place."

The best? Picard considered the inn in a new light. Did that mean there were *others*?

A moment later, he was deposited in a chair. Looking around, he found himself in the company of Robinson and his friends. The big man introduced them one by one.

The tall, slender being with the green skin and the white tuft atop his head was Flenarrh. The muscular Klingon female was named Hompaq. Bo'tex was the overweight, oily-looking Caxtonian nursing his over-sized mug of ale—and exuding an unfortunately typical Caxtonian odor. And Dravvin was the heavy-lidded Rythrian with the loose flaps of skin for ears.

"And this is Jean-Luc Picard," Robinson announced. "Master swordsman and captain extraordinaire."

Taken aback, Picard turned to the man. "How did you know I was a captain?" he asked.

Robinson laughed and slapped Picard on the back, knocking him forward a step. "Didn't anyone bother to tell you, lad? We're *all* captains here, of one vessel or another."

Picard looked around the table. "I didn't know that," he said. And of course, he hadn't.

"That was some duel," Bo'tex remarked, changing the subject a bit. "Best I've seen in this place in quite a few years."

"Admirable," agreed Flenarrh, placing his hands together as if praying. It gave him an insectlike look.

"Here," said Hompaq, pouring a glass of dark liquid into an empty glass. "There is only one drink fit for a warrior."

Picard recalled his tactical officer's dietary preferences. He couldn't help wincing as the glass was placed before him.

"Prune juice?" he ventured.

Hompaq's eyes narrowed. "Of course not. It's blood-wine—and you'll find no better on Qo'Nos herself!"

"Not everyone *likes* bloodwine," Dravvin noted, his voice as dry and inflectionless as the other Rythrians of Picard's acquaintance.

"He will like it," the Klingon insisted. She thrust her chin in Picard's direction. "Drink!"

He drank—though perhaps not as much or as quickly as Hompaq would have preferred. To be sure, bloodwine was a powerful beverage. The captain didn't want to be caught at a disadvantage here—especially when his comrade was still missing.

"Excuse me," he said, "but has anyone seen a fellow named Gleason? He's human, a bit taller and broader than I am, with bright red hair turning gray at the temples."

His companions looked at one another. Their expressions didn't give Picard much hope.

"I don't think so," Bo'tex replied, speaking for all of them.

"Worry not," Robinson assured Picard with the utmost confidence. "People have a way of appearing and disappearing in this place. Your friend'll surface before long." He sat back in his chair, as if preparing himself for a good meal. "What's important now is the storytelling contest."

Picard looked at him. "Contest?"

Robinson nodded. "Indeed. We have one every night, y'see." He eyed the others with unmitigated glee. "This evening, we're out to see who can tell the most captivating tale of romance and adventure."

"Yes," Bo'tex confirmed. "We were just about to begin when you and Lafitte started flashing steel."

Picard looked at him. "Lafitte?" he echoed. And now that he thought about it, the bartender had called the man . . .

"So?" Hompaq rumbled, interrupting Picard's thoughts. She leaned across the table toward Bo'tex, accentuating an already ample Klingon cleavage. "You have a story for us, fat one?"

The Caxtonian's complexion darkened. "I'm afraid I'm not much of a storyteller," he demurred. "The . . . er, exigencies of command haven't left me much time to perfect that art."

"Rubbish and nonsense," Robinson boomed, dismissing the idea with a wave of his hand. "You always use that excuse. But captains make the best storytellers of anyone, and Caxtonian captains are no exception."

"If that's so," Bo'tex countered in a defensive voice, "why don't you get the ball rolling for us, Robinson? Or is it possible you haven't *had* any romantic experiences?"

Robinson shot the Caxtonian a look of reproach. "As it happens, Captain Bo'tex, I've had not *one* but *three* great loves in my life. All of them transcendent beauties, and educated women to boot." He cast his eyes down and sighed. "One died young, bless her soul. The second died in middle age, just as I was about to propose marriage to her."

"And the third?" the Rythrian inquired.

Robinson's features took on a decidedly harder line. "She died not at all," he said.

But he didn't go on to say how that could be, or what effect it had on him. And since no one else pressed the man for an explanation, Picard thought it best to keep silent as well.

Robinson turned his gaze on Bo'tex again, obviously not done with him. "And what of you, sir? Is it possible any female could stand the unwholesome smell of you?"

Bo'tex smiled a greasy smile. "I'm not smelly at all— at least, not to other Caxtonians. In fact," he went on, waxing poetic, "my full-bodied scent is actually a pheromone bouquet unequaled on my homeworld. I've often got to fight females off with a stick."

Dravvin closed his eyes. "Somehow, I'm having difficulty conjuring that image in my mind."

"You're not the only one," said Flenarrh.

Hompaq spoke up. "I once had a lover," she growled.

"Oh?" said the Rythrian. "What happened to him?"

The Klingon grinned fondly, showing her fanglike incisors. "I had to gut him, the mangy targ. But he'll always live in my heart."

Dravvin rolled his eyes. "Delightful."

Hompaq eyed the Rythrian with undisguised ferocity. "You mock me?" she rasped, challenging him.

Dravvin was unflustered. "Me?" he said dryly. "Mock you?"

It wasn't exactly an answer. However, it served the purpose of keeping the Klingon in her chair while she pondered it.

Suddenly, a half-empty mug of ale slammed down on the table, causing it to shudder. Picard turned to see its owner—a short, stocky alien with mottled, gray skin and tiny, red eyes. The fellow leaned in among them, between Bo'tex and Robinson.

"Kuukervol," Flenarrh sighed.

"That's right," said the newcomer, who seemed more than a little drunk—though not so much so he hadn't caught the gist of their conversation. "Kuukervol, indeed. And I've got a story that'll make the heartiest of you quiver and the weakest of you weep for mercy—a tale of blood and thunder and love so powerful you can only dream about it."

The assembled captains exchanged glances. Picard noted a certain amount of skepticism in their expressions.

"He was on his way to Rimbona IV . . ." Hompaq growled.

". . . minding his own business," Bo'tex continued, "when he ran into a Traynor Disturbance. Level one, perhaps a little more."

"Enough to rattle my sensor relays!" Kuukervol protested.

"And necessitate repairs," Dravvin amplified.

"There he was," said Hompaq. "Blind on his port side, vulnerable to enemy attack and the vagaries of space . . ."

". . . except he *had* no enemies," Bo'tex noted, "and he'd already stumbled on the only real vagary in the sector. Nonetheless . . ."

". . . I hurried desperately to make repairs," Kuukervol pointed out, "when who should show up but . . ."

". . . a Phrenalian passenger transport," Dravvin added. "And lo and behold, it was headed for Rimbona IV just as he was."

"Of course," Hompaq said, "it wasn't going to stop for him."

"It was full!" Kuukervol declared. "Full to bursting!"

"So it was," Dravvin conceded. "Which is why it could rescue neither our friend nor his crew. However, its commander promised he would alert the Rimbonan authorities to Captain Kuukervol's plight."

"Which he did," said Robinson.

"And they would have arrived just in the nick of time," Bo'tex gibed eagerly, "had they seen any reason to effect a timely rescue—or indeed, effect a rescue at all."

"Unfortunately," Dravvin went on, "there was no discernible danger to ship or crew."

"No *discernible* danger," Kuukervol emphasized. "But the *un*discernible lurked all around us!"

"Under which circumstances," said Flenarrh, "Captain Kuukervol and his courageous crew had no choice but to take matters in their own hands—and repair their sensor relays on their own."

"At which point," Hompaq chuckled, "they went on to Rimbona . . ."

". . . warier than ever . . ." Kuukervol said.

". . . and," Dravvin finished, "arrived without further incident."

The newcomer's mouth shaped words to which he gave no voice, as if he hadn't spoken his fill yet. Then he gave up and, wallowing in frustration, took his half-full mug and wandered away.

The Rythrian looked pleased. "I think we've taken the wind out of his sails. And good riddance."

Robinson made a clucking sound with his tongue and turned to Picard. "The poor, benighted sot tells the same story every night. Except for a few middling changes, of course, so it'll fit with the evening's theme."

Flenarrh smiled benignly. "If we've heard him tell it once, we've heard it a hundred times."

"Come to think of it," said Bo'tex, "we never did get to hear the juicy part. I wonder . . . would it have been the Phrenalian commander who served as Kuukervol's love interest? Or perhaps he would have singled out some member of his command staff?"

"The possibilities boggle the mind," Dravvin observed ironically.

"Minds being boggled," said a voice from over Picard's shoulder. "Sounds like my kind of place."

Picard turned and saw another fellow coming over to join them—one dressed in a navy blue pullover with a white symbol on the upper right quadrant. He had dark hair with hints of gray and a goatee to match. Also, something of an antic sparkle in his greenish brown eyes.

"Ah," said Robinson. "The Captain of the *Kalliope*."

The newcomer smiled. "Good to see you again, Captain Robinson. What's it been? A year or more?"

"Time has little meaning in a place like the Captain's Table," Robinson replied. "How's your wife? And the little ones?"

"Not so little anymore," said the Captain of the *Kalliope*. "The big one's trimming the sails now and his brother's taking the tiller." He glanced at Picard. "I wondered if you would drop in here someday."

Picard looked at him. The fellow seemed awfully familiar, somehow. Picard tried to place him, but couldn't.

"Have we met before?" he asked the Captain of the *Kalliope*.

The man shrugged. "In a manner of speaking. Let's just say your fame has preceded you." He raised a mug of dark beer until it glinted in the light. "To Jean-Luc Picard, Starfleet's finest."

The others raised their glasses. "To Jean-Luc Picard."

Picard found himself blushing. "I'm flattered."

"Don't be," said the Captain of the *Kalliope*. "These guys will drink to anything. I learned that a long time ago."

The others laughed. "How true," Hompaq growled. "Though I am not, strictly speaking, a guy."

Bo'tex snuck a sly look at her bodice. "It appears you're right," the Caxtonian told her.

Her eyes narrowing, Hompaq clapped Bo'tex on the back, sending him flying forward across the table. "How clever of you to notice," she said.

As Bo'tex tried to regain his dignity, the Captain of the *Kalliope* sat and winked at Picard. "Some group, eh?"

The fellow reminded Picard of someone. It took him a moment to realize who it was. Riker was a little taller and more sturdily built, but otherwise the two had a lot in common.

Picard nodded. "Some group."

"Now, then . . . where were we?" Robinson asked.

"A tale of romance and adventure," Flenarrh reminded him. "And we still haven't got a volunteer."

"Don't look at me," said the Captain of the *Kalliope*. "You know I can't tell a tale to save my life."

Flenarrh looked around the table—until he came to Picard, and his eyes narrowed. "What about you, Captain? You look like a fellow just steeped in romance and adventure."

Robinson considered Picard. "Is that true, Captain? Have you a tale or two with which to regale us?"

Picard frowned as he weighed his response. "In fact," he said, "I do. But it's one I would rather keep to myself."

His companions weren't at all happy with that. Dravvin harrumphed and Hompaq grumbled, both clear signs of displeasure.

Robinson leaned closer to Picard. "Come, now," he

said. "We're all friends here. All *captains,* as it were. If you can't share your tale with us, who the devil can you share it with?"

Picard looked around the table. Normally, he was a man who kept his feelings to himself. Nonetheless, he felt remarkably at ease in this place, among these people. He drummed his fingers.

"All right," he said at last. "Perhaps I'll tell it after all."

Robinson smiled. "Now, there's a lad."

"A warrior," said Hompaq.

Indeed, thought Picard. And he began weaving his yarn.

The Tale

MY STORY BEGINS a couple of months ago. I and my ship, the fifth Federation vessel to bear the name *Enterprise,* were performing a routine planetary survey when we received a communication from Starfleet Command.

It was an eyes-only communication—which meant I needed to receive it in private. Leaving my first officer in charge of the bridge, I repaired to my ready room.

As it turned out, the communication was from Admiral Gorton—a very likeable fellow with whom I shared an interest in equestrian sports and French wines. I asked him what I could do for him.

Gorton frowned, making the lines in his weathered face seem deeper than usual. "Normally," he pointed out, "Starfleet doesn't ask its captains to search for missing persons. In this instance, however, I'm afraid I've got to make an exception."

I leaned back in my chair. "Very well, then. I take it there is something unusual about this missing person?"

"There is indeed. His name is Brant, Richard Brant. Ring a bell?"

I thought for a moment. "Wasn't there a Richard Brant aboard the *LaSalle?* Its first officer, as I recall?"

"You memory is as good as ever," Gorton confirmed. "For reasons of his own, Brant resigned from Starfleet almost a year ago. His intention was to charter expeditions to exotic destinations."

"And?" I prodded gently.

"He dropped out of sight about a couple of months ago, as far as we can tell. At first, we suspected he had been abducted by the Maquis, since his expeditions took him into the vicinity of the Badlands."

"The Maquis haven't engaged much in kidnapping," I noted.

"True," said Gorton. "That doesn't seem to be the way they normally operate. Still, we couldn't rule it out as a possibility. Then, less than a week ago, Command received word that the Maquis had nothing to do with Brant's disappearance."

"You have a lead on him, then?" I asked.

Gorton nodded. "We've learned that Brant was seized by mercenaries in the Caliabris sector."

I was puzzled. "Mercenaries? What would they want with him?"

"Jean-Luc," said the admiral, "have you ever heard of something called the Hoard of Dujonian?"

I nodded. After all, I had been a student of archaeology since my days at Starfleet Academy.

"The Hoard," I said, "was part of a treasure unearthed on Cardassia Prime some two hundred years ago, when the Cardassians excavated a series of large Hebitian tombs."

For those of you unfamiliar with the Hebitians, they were the cultural ancestors of the Cardassians—a peaceful and spiritual people who are said to have loved justice and learning.

It seems that wasn't all they loved. Their burial

21

chambers were magnificent vaults, filled from wall to wall with priceless, jeweled baubles.

But it wasn't merely the *quality* of their gems that made some of the Hebitian artifacts so priceless.

"One variety of jewel unearthed with the treasure was called glor'ya," I continued. "It was found to have properties similar to dilithium, but vastly superior. Cardassian scientists saw in it unlimited potential, certainly with regard to propulsion capabilities—but also when it came to weapons design."

"Exactly right," said Gorton. "Then you must also know the rest of it—how, according to legend, a twenty-second-century Cardassian named Dujonian managed to steal all the Hebitians' glor'ya-encrusted artifacts and hide them somewhere off-planet."

"Nor was he ever heard from again," I mused, "so the truth of the matter could never be proven, nor Dujonian himself taken to task for his actions."

However, I was unaware of any link between Brant and the Hoard. I said so.

Gorton frowned. "Our source tells me these mercenaries believe Brant can lead them to Dujonian's treasure trove."

I grunted softly. "Why would they believe this?"

The admiral shook his head. "We don't know. Maybe they unearthed a clue to the Hoard's location and it led them to the Caliabris sector."

I saw the connection. After all, the *LaSalle* had done considerable work in that part of space. "In that case, Brant's knowledge of the sector would have been invaluable to them."

"Exactly," said Gorton. "Or maybe the mercenaries simply got wind of something—a clue that told them Brant had located the Hoard. In any case, the man was abducted."

"And you want him found," I concluded, "and rescued—before these mercenaries can find the Hoard and make use of the glor'ya in it."

"Or even worse," said Gorton, "sell it to the Cardassians."

"Who would employ it," I responded, "to make their warships even more dangerous than they are already."

The admiral nodded. "That's our concern. Of course," he went on, "there are several agents we could have assigned this task, but you're the only one with any real archaeological background. You'll need it to verify if you actually encounter the Hoard."

"I understand," I told him.

Gorton regarded me. "At this point, I'm sorry to say, I don't have much else in the way of hard information. I can only point you to the source I mentioned—the one who reported Brant's abduction in the first place."

He suggested I go undercover to make the contact, so as not to compromise our informant. I agreed that I would do that.

"Good," he said. "I'm transmitting all pertinent information on him. Needless to say, you'll have to use discretion in sharing what I've told you with your officers."

"Needless to say," I echoed.

The admiral smiled grimly. "Good luck, Jean-Luc. And godspeed."

"Thank you," I told him.

Then he ended the communication. His image vanished from my monitor, to be replaced with the starred symbol of Starfleet.

I pondered the task Gorton had set for me, leery of entering a situation I knew so little about. All sorts of questions came to mind, none of which was the least bit trivial.

What if Brant's kidnapping were not what it seemed? What if, far from being their victim, he had joined these so-called mercenaries of his own volition? Indeed, what if Brant's disappearance had nothing at all to do with Dujonian's long-lost treasure?

With luck, I would have some of the answers before long. Without luck, I would be operating at a considerable disadvantage.

Abruptly, a beeping sound told me there was someone at the door to my ready room. "Come," I said, inviting him or her in.

As the door slid aside, I saw that it was William Riker, my executive officer. He looked curious.

"Something interesting?" he asked, a boyish smile on his face.

"I should say so," I replied. And I described my assignment in as much detail as possible.

After all, I trusted the man implicitly. Given the option, there was nothing I would have considered keeping from him.

Before I had finished briefing him, the boyish smile vanished. After all, Riker was rather businesslike when it came to my welfare, and had been from the time we first met. It's the mother hen in him.

"You're not going alone?" he asked. It wasn't really a question. At least, not in *his* mind.

"I hadn't really thought about it," I answered.

"I'd go with you," he said, "except one of us should stay on the *Enterprise*. Just in case."

"Agreed," I told him. It was common sense.

Riker frowned. "You'll need someone tough and adaptable. Someone who's gone undercover before."

There was one obvious choice. I spoke the man's name.

My first officer nodded. "He's the one."

"All right," I said at last. "I'll ask him to come along. But that's it, just the two of us. I don't want to be too conspicuous, Number One."

My first officer sighed good-naturedly. "I'd prefer

more, sir. You know that. But Lieutenant Worf is worth several ordinary officers."

I found myself hard-pressed to disagree.

As it was still very early in the morning, I found Worf in the ship's gymnasium, teaching his Mok'bara class. As Hompaq can attest, Mok'bara is a ritual Klingon martial-arts form designed to enhance one's agility in hand-to-hand combat.

Though there were no other Klingons on the ship besides Worf, the class had become a popular one. On that particular day, I saw my Betazoid ship's counselor and my human chief medical officer among those striving to achieve perfection under my Klingon lieutenant's watchful eye.

When I entered the room, Worf hesitated, his expression one of concern. But with a gesture, I assured him there was no urgency to my visit. I would stand there and watch while he completed the morning's exercises.

Nor did I mind in the least. Mok'bara was as elegant a discipline as any I had encountered, and I had encountered my share.

That said, I had no desire to take part in it myself. When it came to exercise, my tastes at the time ran more toward horsemanship and fencing. They still do, as you have seen, in part, for yourselves.

When the ritual exercises were over, one of Worf's students—a young woman—asked him about a particular maneuver. Apparently, it was a method of dealing with an attack from behind.

With a patience he seldom displayed in other circumstances, the Klingon showed the woman how to turn her attacker's wrist and grip it just so. Then he came around behind her and let her attempt the move on him.

It worked like magic. The woman performed the maneuver as Worf had indicated, turning, twisting and throwing her hip out—and the Klingon went spinning to the mat.

Of course, I had to wonder how much of the Klingon's fall was involuntary and how much of it an attempt at encouraging his disciple. Still, it was an impressive display.

The woman thanked Worf and withdrew, enlightened by his lesson. I must say, I was enlightened a bit as well. Even if I was not a practitioner of Mok'bara, I was intelligent enough to pay attention when there was something valuable to be learned.

Worf's class didn't last much longer after that. As his students filed out, muscle-sore but exhilarated, I approached him.

"You do not come down here often," he noted.

"That's true," I said. Lately, I had gotten in the habit of taking my exercise in the holodecks. "And as you seem to have guessed, this isn't just a casual visit. I have need of you, Mr. Worf."

My tactical officer looked at me, his very posture an assurance that he would do whatever I asked of him. Klingons place a premium on loyalty, as Hompaq will confirm—and Worf was no exception.

"When do we leave?" he asked.

I hadn't yet told him we would be working undercover. I hadn't even said we'd be disembarking from the *Enterprise.* He just seemed to know.

"As soon as I can make arrangements," I replied. "It all depends on when we can find a ship headed for the Caliabris sector."

His brow furrowed. "Why the Caliabris sector?"

"Allow me to explain," I said.

In the next few minutes, I briefed him on our mission, and he absorbed the data dutifully. But the particulars mattered less to him than the fact that there *was* a mission.

"I will be ready," he told me.

And of course, when the time came, he was.

With the help of Starfleet Command, Worf and I obtained passage on a Thriidian freighter bound for the Caliabris sector.

As far as the Thriidians were concerned, my companion and I were just two of the many characters who spent their lives drifting from one end of known space to the other, taking work where they could get it. The fact that Worf was a Klingon drew a few extra stares, but I had anticipated that and accepted the risk before we set out.

Certainly, there were those in the galaxy who harbored a burning hatred for Worf's people. However, we didn't run into any of them on the freighter. In the end, we reached our destination on time and without incident.

Soon we found ourselves in orbit around Milassos IV, a backwater planet on the fringe of the Caliabris sector. Our informant, an Ethnasian named Torlith, was there to meet us at our prearranged beam-down site—a clearing in the fragrant, blue-green forest that surrounded that world's largest city.

Ethnasians were broad, slow, and ruddy-skinned, with black eyes and a collection of equally black spines projecting from their lumpy skulls. Torlith was even broader and slower than most of his species, but his wits were quick—and to Starfleet Command, whom he served as an invaluable conduit of information, his wits were all that mattered.

"Captain Picard?" said Torlith, his eyes gleaming darkly in the light of three full moons, the shadowy foliage an eerie backdrop behind him.

"I'm Picard," I confirmed. I indicated my security chief with a tilt of my head. "And this is Lieutenant Worf."

The Ethnasian regarded the Klingon and nodded.

Then he turned back to me. "You know," he said, "as long as I've worked with Starfleet, I've never met a starship captain."

"Well," I replied, not much interested in his assessment, "you've met one now. Shall we go?"

Torlith chuckled at my eagerness. "Of course. I've got a hovercar parked less than a kilometer away. And I've booked some lodgings for you, as I was instructed. If they're not to your liking——"

"They'll be fine," I assured him. "But if it's all the same to you, I'd prefer to go straight to the tavern."

The Ethnasian dismissed the notion with a wave of his pudgy hand. "The one I spoke of won't be there until later. A couple of hours, at least."

"That's all right," I told him. "I want to get the feel of the place before she arrives."

Torlith may not have thought that was necessary, but he acquiesced quickly enough. "The tavern it is," he said, and led Worf and myself in the direction of his hovercar.

The Ethnasian was true to his word. His vehicle was less than a kilometer's walk from our beam-down site, concealed from the casual observer by a thicket of leafy branches.

Looking around, however, I saw no freshly cut stumps, no sign of phaser burns on the surrounding flora. By that sign, I decided Torlith had used this place for his business dealings before—and I didn't imagine all of them had been on behalf of Starfleet.

His hovercar was efficient, if noisy. It took us out of the forest and into the city—if one could call it a city. More accurately, it was a maze of haphazardly erected edifices, altogether without reason or focus. None of the buildings was remarkable in any way, either by virtue of its size, its shape, or its appearance.

My first officer would no doubt have called the place "a dive." However, it was the logical and seemingly unavoidable starting point of our search for Richard Brant—and, if the legends were true, for a good deal more.

Landing his vehicle in an open lot designated for such a use, the Ethnasian led us through the city's winding streets. They started out deserted but became increasingly more populated as we went on.

Most of the faces we encountered were those of the native Milassoi, a towering but pale and ultimately fragile-looking species who wore dark robes and hoods. However, there were at least half a dozen other spacefaring races present as well, humans sprinkled among them.

Finally, we came to the tavern in question. Torlith led us inside, making his way through the crowd until he found an empty table in the back. Then he sat and gestured for Worf and myself to do the same.

It was nothing like the Captain's Table. The place was dark, rough-hewn, almost cavelike in its appearance, with vials full of Veridian glow-beetles providing the only real illumination.

On the other hand, none of its patrons seemed daunted by the lack of artifice. In fact, they seemed to like it just fine.

A moment after we sat down, a serving maid approached us and asked for our preferences in libations. It took only a couple of minutes for her to bring the order to the bar and return with our drinks.

As I sampled my synthehol, I took quick stock of those around us. The crowd was what one might find in a great many other "watering holes" I had encountered—noisy and full of furtive glances, but basically harmless.

"I see no particular danger," Worf confirmed.

"Nor do I," I returned. "Still, the evening is young."

Suddenly, Torlith grabbed my arm. "It's her," he said. And he jerked his spiny head in the direction of the bar.

I peered at the crowd, but didn't see whom he was talking about. "Where is she?" I asked.

The Ethnasian jerked his head again. "Keep looking. She's on the other side of that Moqausite."

A moment later, the Moqausite moved—and I saw her. At first, it was only her back I spotted, with her red hair cascading down it. Then she turned around and I got a glimpse of her face.

Her eyes were a languid blue, her lips full and expressive, and she had a spray of girlish freckles across the bridge of her chiseled nose. It was the visage of a poetess, perhaps, or a dreamer. She didn't at all look the part of a veteran transport captain.

"That's our woman?" I asked our informant, unable to quite keep the incredulity out of my voice. "Are you certain?"

"Absolutely," said Torlith.

Worf scowled. "You said she would not arrive until later."

"She doesn't," said the Ethnasian, "usually."

I watched her move among the other denizens of the tavern, all of whom were male. She was slender and graceful, yet sturdy in a way. After a while, she joined a longhaired Orion and a wiry-looking human—a man with a scar across the bridge of his nose.

Part of her crew? I wondered. They didn't seem to show any particular deference to her.

"What's her name?" I asked.

"They call her Red Abby," Torlith told us. "If she's got another name, she doesn't use it."

Worf leaned closer to the Ethnasian. "And she was your source with regard to Brant's kidnapping?"

Torlith nodded. "Of course, she didn't say how she knew, but she seemed pretty certain of it. She's put out a call for experienced hands—so she can follow in what she says are Brant's footsteps."

Interesting, I thought, continuing my observation of the woman's interactions at the bar. Interesting indeed.

"And where do these footsteps lead?" the Klingon demanded.

"How should I know?" Torlith replied in an attempt at humor. "Red Abby's the one who's shipping out, not me."

It was fairly obvious the woman was seeking the same treasure as Brant's abductors. I said as much. "Why else go after him?"

"As you say," our informant agreed, "it seems pretty obvious. In any case, you've got a golden opportunity on your hands."

"What's that?" Worf asked.

"Just say you've heard she's looking for a crew. If you're lucky, Red Abby will sign you up and take you right to Brant—and maybe the Hoard of Dujonian, to boot."

My companion eyed Torlith. "If we're lucky," he echoed.

The Ethnasian nodded again. "Yes."

"And why are you not offering to sign up yourself?" Worf inquired. "Are you not eager to make yourself rich?"

Torlith laughed. "Because, if you must know, Klingon, I don't believe in the Hoard. I think it's a one-eyed sailor's tale, made of wind and weather and not much else."

"Of course," I interjected, "none of that really matters—at least with regard to our mission. The important thing is that we find Brant and extricate him from his captivity."

"If he *is* a captive," Worf reminded me.

"Yes," I said. "If."

"Of course," Torlith agreed. "Brant's your objective." His black eyes slid slyly in my direction. "But be honest, Picard. In the back of your mind, where you're more man than officer, aren't you hoping Red Abby's got a line on the Hoard after all? And maybe, just maybe, you'll have a chance to lay your eyes on all that treasure?"

I was honest, as he'd asked. "I don't deny it. But my mission remains the same, treasure or no treasure." I glanced at Worf. "Let's get going. We've a new captain to meet."

My officer grunted at the irony and got to his feet. I did the same. Together, we made our way to the bar. We hadn't gotten more than halfway before Red Abby noticed our approach.

Her companions noticed it, too. The Orion made no move, but the human's hand drifted to his belt, beneath which he probably had a weapon.

"What can I do for you gentlemen?" the woman asked us.

Her voice, like her appearance, was smooth and even a little seductive. But her tone was that of a business-woman.

"We've heard you're looking for some experienced hands," I told her. "My name's Hill. My friend here is called Mitoc." They were names I'd made up during the hovercar ride, mine inspired by a fictional detective I had come to admire. "We'd like to sign on."

Red Abby eyed me. "Even though you don't know where we're headed? Or what the dangers may be?"

I shrugged as if such matters didn't faze me. "It won't be the first time," I said. "Or the last."

Red Abby turned to Worf. "You say you're experienced? Then tell me where you've served."

My lieutenant thrust his bearded chin out. "I have served on several Klingon trading vessels," he answered. "Unfortunately, you would not know them. I also worked the *Coridanni* and the *Jerrok Mor*."

The woman nodded judiciously, then turned her gaze on me. "And you?" she demanded. "Where have *you* served?"

"On the *Jerrok Mor,* as well," I said. "Also the *Nada Chun,* the *Ferret,* and the *Erron'vol.*"

"As what?" she asked.

"You name it," I told her. "Helmsman, navigator, engineer."

"A jack-of-all-trades," she concluded.

"Something like that."

"The rest of that saying is 'master-of-none.'"

I chuckled a little. "That part wouldn't apply, then. I'm good at what I do. *All* of it."

She regarded me a moment longer, then turned back to Worf. "And you, Mitoc? What are *you* good at?"

"I can also perform several different functions," he said. "However, my specialty is tactics and armaments."

Red Abby raised an eyebrow. "Really. Then you know how many prefire chambers are in a Type II phaser?"

"Four," Worf answered without hesitation.

She grunted. "I'll take your word for it. Personally, I don't know anything about phasers and I couldn't care less—as long as the damned things work when I need them to."

"Then we're hired?" I asked.

Red Abby considered me. "As soon as my officers check your references. As it happens, I know Captain Goody rather well. I'll want to ask him about your tour on the *Ferret* personally."

"I'd expect no less," I assured her.

Of course, both Worf and myself had been careful as to which ships we mentioned. The *Erron'vol* had been destroyed in a spatial anomaly the week before, about the same time the *Ferret* was caught smuggling weapons to the Maquis—so neither of their captains would be available to refute our stories.

In the same vein, the captains of the *Coridani,* the *Jerrok Mor,* and the *Nada Chun* were all retired Starfleet personnel. Starfleet Command had told them enough to make them useful to us, but not so much as to leave our mission open to discovery.

In short, Red Abby would find our references impeccable. That is, if she even bothered to check, which I suspected she would not.

"One more thing," she told us.

"And that is?" I asked.

The woman seemed to look inside me with her soft, blue eyes. "Have you got any enemies I should know about, Hill? Anyone at all?"

I pretended to think for a moment. Then I shrugged. "None that come to mind," I said.

"And you?" she asked Worf.

He curled his lip. "None who still live," he told her, giving her an answer worthy of a Klingon.

Red Abby nodded, then turned to me again. "See me tomorrow night, same place. If everything checks the way it should, you'll ship out with me the following morning."

"The sooner, the better," I said.

Unexpectedly, she smiled at that. It was a stern smile, without any humor in it. "Always," she replied. Then, having dismissed us, she resumed her discussion with the Orion and the man with the scar.

Exchanging glances with Worf, I headed back to our table, where our contact had been waiting for us. His eyes crinkling at the corners, he asked, "So? Are you gainfully employed?"

"I suspect we are," I replied.

Madigoor

"AND WERE YOU?" asked the Captain of the *Kalliope*, leaning forward in his seat at the Captain's Table. "Employed, I mean?"

Picard nodded. "We were. And as I would find out later, I had been right about Red Abby checking our references. She hadn't bothered."

Dravvin's eyes narrowed with interest. "And you took off the morning after you signed on, as this Red Abby said you would?"

"Yes," said Picard. "We beamed up to her ship, the *Daring,* along with a number of other recruits."

"What kind of ship was she?" asked Bo'tex.

"An old Ammonite vessel," Picard replied, "sleek and black, with a few worn spots on her hull showing her age. Nonetheless, she was in good working order for a ship of that age. Red Abby had added some improvements to her as well, particularly in the areas of propulsion and armaments."

"To her credit," Hompaq remarked.

"In any case," Picard continued, "neither we nor any

of the other newcomers to the Daring were apprised of our destination. As I understood it, only three people on board had that kind of knowledge."

"Presumably," said Robinson, "the ones Red Abby felt she could trust."

Picard nodded. "One was her first officer, the Orion we had met. He called himself Astellanax. The second was the human with the scar, who went by the name Sturgis and served as her navigator. The third was a half-Romulan, half-Bolian named Thadoc, who helmed the vessel."

Flenarrh rubbed his hands together thoughtfully. "A half-Romulan, half-Bolian, you say?" He smiled. "I don't believe I've ever seen a joining of those particular species."

"What did he look like?" Hompaq asked.

Picard recalled Thadoc's features. "Like a hairless Romulan with blue skin and a subtle ridge running down the center of his face. But his demeanor was strictly Romulan."

"Relentless," Robinson observed.

"Relentlessly *efficient*," Picard noted. "Red Abby couldn't have asked for a more capable officer."

"And the other two?" asked Flenarrh. "What were they like?"

Picard shrugged. "Sturgis didn't say much, so it was difficult to tell—though I had a feeling he would as soon have cut my throat as looked at me. Astellanax, on the other hand, was as talkative as most Orions, and what he talked about most was the *Daring.*"

"The ship?" asked Hompaq.

"Yes. He said he had never served on a vessel so quick and responsive." Picard looked around the table. "Of course, he had never been on the bridge of a Galaxy-class starship."

Hompaq regarded him. "But you must have had *some*

idea of where you were going. You could see the stars, could you not?"

"Not well," Picard told her. "Once we left Milassos Four, we assumed a pace of warp six or better. But Lieutenant Worf and I could glean enough to determine our general heading."

Robinson's eyes seemed to twinkle. "And that was?"

"A portion of the Caliabris sector sandwiched between the Cardassian Union and the Romulan Empire, though claimed by neither. I knew little about it," Picard conceded, "as the Federation had not charted its worlds. But I had a feeling I was going to find out."

"What about the rest of Red Abby's crew?" asked Bo'tex. "Were there any Caxtonians aboard?"

Picard shook his head. "Most of the crew was either human, Andorian, or Tellarite, though there were more than a few Ferengi and Yridians present as well . . . and a Pandrilite named Corbis, with whom Lieutenant Worf had—shall we say—a small difference of opinion."

"Do I detect a note of sarcasm?" asked Dravvin.

"Judge for yourself," Picard said.

The Tale

HAVING BEEN AMONG the last to sign on with Red Abby,
Worf and I were given the graveyard shift. That meant we
had some time on our hands. Several hours' worth, in
fact.

If we spent it apart from the rest of the crew, Red Abby
would surely hear of it—and begin to wonder what we
were up to. So rather than arouse her suspicions—or
anyone else's, for that matter—we opted for a public
venue in which to while away the hours. Since the ship
boasted no lounge or recreation areas, the only choice
left to us was the mess hall.

It was a severe place, as gray and dimly lit as any of the
corridors, and devoid of observation ports. That and its
location on the ship led me to believe it hadn't always
been a mess hall, but a storage area of some kind.

The place stood in stark contrast to the lounge on the
Enterprise. Still, the trio of replicators behind a rounded,
gray rail seemed to be in working order, and the chairs,
though flimsy-looking, appeared to be reasonably comfortable.

There were several other crewmen already occupying the mess hall, seated at one table or another. Obviously, they were graveyard-shifters as well, and they'd had the same idea we had as to how to pass the time.

Approaching the replicators, Worf and I each took a tray from a stack in a recessed compartment. I ordered a ham-and-egg sandwich, an old favorite from my boyhood on Earth, then found a seat at an empty table and waited for Worf to join me.

Unfortunately, Worf's replicator wasn't working as well as he had hoped. As we would learn later, it simply wasn't programmed for a great variety of Klingon dishes. After making several attempts, the lieutenant rumbled deep in his throat and reached for the replicator I'd used.

The result was the same. Refusing to believe he couldn't have his heart's desire—a plate of rokeg blood pie, as it turned out—Worf reached for the third replicator. However, by then, a Pandrilite had come up behind him for a second helping and was reaching for the same set of controls.

As you may have guessed by now, this Pandrilite was Corbis, of whom I spoke. If I told you the fellow was big, it would be an understatement. He stood a head and a half above my security officer, and Worf was not puny by any means.

In any event, in reaching for the replicator, my lieutenant inadvertently upset Corbis's tray. Before the Pandrilite could react, his plate slid into his chest and deposited the greasy remains of a stew.

With a curse, he righted his tray and the plate slid back. But by then it was too late.

Corbis looked down at his tunic, where the stew had left a dark, oily stain. Then he looked at Worf.

"What are you, blind?" he rumbled with a voice like thunder. "Who's going to clean this tunic?"

The Klingon shrugged. "That is your problem. You

would not have soiled yourself if you had not been so eager to grab for more food."

"I soiled *myself?*" the Pandrilite echoed, towering over Worf. "It was *you* who pushed my tray over."

"I pushed *nothing,*" the Klingon insisted, his lips pulling back to show his teeth.

"You're a liar," Corbis grated, leaning forward so his eyes were only inches from Worf's. "You shoved my tray and you'll clean my tunic—or you'll take your next meal through a tube."

I had overheard everything, of course. At first, I let it go, thinking the incident would blow over. But when I heard the Pandrilite's threat, I knew I had been overly optimistic.

Getting up from my seat, I hurried over to intervene. In the process, I saw a couple of Corbis's friends rush over, as well. One was an Oord, judging by the tusks protruding from either side of his mouth. The other was a rather husky Thelurian, his facial markings an angry green.

It was a disaster in the making. However, I intended to head it off. After all, I had negotiated treaties between entire species. Surely, I thought, I could make peace between Worf and a Pandrilite.

I was mistaken, of course. It wasn't the first time, and, sadly, it would not be the last.

Worf, I must say, was showing admirable restraint. At least, by Klingon standards. His eyes narrowing, he said, "I would advise you not to make threats you cannot carry out."

"Oh, I can carry them out all right," Corbis replied— and flung the remnants of his meal in the direction of Worf's face.

The lieutenant must have been expecting it, because he ducked. Instead of hitting him, the Pandrilite's tray went hurtling across the room and struck a bulkhead, then clattered to the floor.

Arriving just in time—or so I thought—I interposed myself between Worf and Corbis. "Gentlemen," I said, "this is a simple misunderstanding. I'm sure if we cool down for a moment, we can settle everything."

The Pandrilite looked at me for a moment, as if trying to decipher my existence. Then he drove his fist into my face, sending me hurtling like his tray—except not quite as far.

As I regained my senses, I saw Worf had not taken kindly to the battering of his commanding officer. Hauling off, he drove a blow of his own into the center of Corbis's face, snapping the man's head back and sending him staggering over the replicator rail.

Unfortunately, the Pandrilite's friends had entered the fray by that time. Spinning Worf around, the Oord head-butted him between the eyes. Dazed, the Klingon was an easy target. The Thelurian took advantage of it by planting his fist in Worf's midsection, doubling him over.

By then, I was on my feet again. As the other diners roared encouragement at us, I charged the Thelurian and shoved him into a bulkhead as hard as I could. Then I turned toward the Oord—just in time to see him lunge savagely for my throat.

Sidestepping his rush, I chopped at his neck as he went by. It had some effect, but not nearly as much as I'd hoped. Then again, Oord are known for their ability to endure punishment, and I'd probably missed the nerve bundle I was aiming for anyway.

Suddenly, I was grabbed from behind and dragged over the serving rail. Rather than resist, I flipped backward and caught my attacker by surprise, sending him crashing into the wall behind him.

Twisting to free myself, I saw it was Corbis. Before he could react, I struck him once in the belly and a second time in the jaw. The crowd bellowed its approval.

But Corbis was a Pandrilite. Even my best blow couldn't have incapacitated him, especially in the cramped quarters of the serving area.

He tried to respond with a pile driver of his own, but I vaulted over the rail again and he connected with nothing but air. Unluckily for me, he followed me over the rail.

Corbis swung his fist at me and I ducked. He swung again and I ducked a second time.

I thought to sweep his legs out from under him when something—or rather, someone—hit me from the side. We rolled a couple of meters together before we could even begin to disengage.

I was about to lash out at my attacker when I was realized it was Worf. Apparently, one of his opponents had sent him flying in my direction.

"Are you all right?" I asked.

"Yes," he said. "You?"

"I've been worse," I told him.

And that was all the time we had for conversation because our enemies had come together and were headed straight for us. What was worse, we had precious little room to maneuver, thanks to the tables wedged behind us.

There was no shortage of chairs either. But that wasn't a problem. Far from it, in fact. With one mind, Worf and I reached back and grabbed the nearest chairs to hand. And as our adversaries closed with us, we swung at them for all we were worth.

There was a great clatter and cry, in the course of which I believed I had connected with my target. Nonetheless, something barreled into me, sending me hurtling end over end across the table in back of me. In fact, over *several* tables in back of me.

As I struggled to my feet, reluctant to let Worf carry on the battle all alone, I caught sight of a leather boot.

42

Looking up, I saw that it belonged to the captain. Red Abby was glaring down at me.

"That's enough!" she snapped, her voice like a whip.

Suddenly, everything stopped. Looking back toward the replicators, I saw that Worf and the Oord were locked in midstruggle. Slowly, their anger wilting under Red Abby's scrutiny, they let each other go.

A moment later, Corbis and the Thelurian got up from the floor. They looked bruised. The Thelurian was bleeding from a broken nose.

I got to my feet. I was bleeding, as well, I realized, from a cut across my cheek. I looked at Red Abby, then the rest of the diners, whose enthusiasm for the brawl had cooled considerably.

Red Abby turned to me. "I don't like fighting on my ship," she said. She eyed Worf and then the Pandrilite and finally his friends. "I don't care who was right and who was wrong. If there's a repeat of this, I'll jettison the lot of you into space. Do I make myself clear?"

"Eminently," I said.

After all, there was a mission at stake. I was willing to swallow my pride, to do whatever was necessary to see it to a successful conclusion.

For Worf, it was a little harder. But he managed to appear humble nonetheless. "It will not happen again," he vowed.

Red Abby extracted the same kind of promise from Corbis and his friends, though the lot of them had to be seething inside. Then she turned and left the mess hall.

In her wake, things returned to normal. Tables and chairs were righted and the crew sat down to eat. The only exceptions were the Pandrilite and his allies. They chose to leave instead—but not before Corbis shot us the dirtiest of looks.

As Worf and I took up positions on the replicator line, our meals having been casualties of the altercation, I leaned in to whisper a warning to my officer. After all, the Pandrilite and his comrades didn't seem eager to forgive and forget.

"We'll have to keep an eye on Corbis," I told him.

Worf nodded. "I agree."

However, Corbis would soon be the least of our worries.

Madigoor

Dravvin shuddered. "Nasty, those Pandrilites."

"They can be," Picard replied. He thought of Vigo, who had served under him on the *Stargazer*. "On the other hand, I had a Pandrilite weapons officer who was gentler than you could ever imagine."

Robinson grunted. "Not when it came to the enemy, I trust."

"No," Picard conceded. "Not then."

"I knew a couple of Pandrilites once," said Bo'tex. "Twin sisters. Lovely creatures, too. They had an intriguing little stage show on a station called Mephil Trantos . . ."

Hompaq held her hand up. "Spare me, Caxtonian."

Bo'tex fell silent. However, he looked as if he would have dearly loved to say more.

"Captain Hompaq is quite right," said Robinson. "This table is no place for the tawdry and the tasteless. At least, not tonight it's not. Until the sun comes up—or suns, as the case may be—we're dealing exclusively in remarks of delicacy and refinement."

The Caxtonian looked contrite. But he also looked as if he would speak of his Pandrilites if only someone would let him.

"I've never actually seen a Pandrilite," said the Captain of the *Kalliope*. "Are as they as big as people say they are?"

"Probably," Dravvin replied.

"They're not only tall, you see," said Flenarrh, "but also extremely muscular. However, the most impressive thing about them is their diet."

Picard recalled Vigo's favorite dish. "That officer of mine used to like something called *sturrd*."

Flenarrh nodded. "I've seen it. It looks like a pile of fine sand mixed with shards of broken glass."

The Captain of the *Kalliope* made a face. "Sounds appetizing."

Dravvin cast a sidelong glance at Hompaq. "Appetizing is in the eye of the beholder," he noted. "Even Pandrilites like their food *cooked*."

Taking the bait, Hompaq curled her lip at him. "Klingons prefer to cook their *enemies*."

Picard knew it was a joke. So did the others, he imagined. Still, Dravvin looked too disgusted to come up with a reply.

"Now, then," said Robinson, "let's not get too far afield. Our friend Picard was regaling us with a tale, remember?"

"That's right," said Bo'tex, leaning forward with curiosity.

"Tell me," Flenarrh asked the captain, "what did you mean when you said Corbis would soon be the least of your worries?"

Picard smiled sympathetically. "That would be getting ahead of myself."

The Tale

As Worf and I were newcomers to the *Daring,* I had expected Red Abby to relegate us to scut work—running diagnostics in engineering, perhaps, or safety-checking the ship's half-dozen life-pods. Apparently, that was not to be the case.

When the duty list was posted, we found that we had been assigned to the *Daring*'s bridge. Exchanging looks, Worf and I said nothing. We merely made certain not to be late.

When we arrived on the bridge, a place marked by gray-and-black metal bulkheads and pale green lighting globes, we saw Astellanax occupying the rounded captain's chair. Red Abby herself was absent, no doubt getting some rest.

The Orion turned to me. "You, the jack-of-all-trades. You'll be manning the helm." He glanced at Worf. "And I'll need you at tactical. Any questions, either one of you?"

We shook our heads from side to side. "No questions at all," I said, for the sake of clarity.

Astellanax nodded. "Then get to it."

I felt strange assuming any other post but the center seat. After all, it had been more than twenty years since I served as anything but the captain of a spacegoing ship.

Nonetheless, I did as I was bidden.

As I approached the helm, Thadoc unfolded himself from behind his console. "She's all yours," he told me. Then he added, in a decidedly more sober tone: "Treat her right."

"I have every intention of doing so," I assured him, and sat down in the helmsman's place.

Sturgis, who was sitting at navigation and showed no sign of leaving, cast a wary eye at me as I joined him. I mumbled something. He mumbled back. It was the extent of our camaraderie.

Worf's position was behind mine, so I couldn't watch as he acclimated himself to the ship's weapons control console. It was just as well. I had my hands full getting to know the *Daring*'s helm.

Still, I took note of two officers whom I had not yet met. One was the operations officer, a blond man with a boyish smile and a long, ornate earring—though it wasn't of the Bajoran variety. I would learn later that the fellow's name was Dunwoody.

The other officer, a dark-haired woman, was at the bridge's engineering station. Her name was Sheel—a Trill, as I would also learn, though not the joined kind.

We soared through subspace at warp six, the stars streaking by us, all periodic system checks coming up negative. In short, the *Daring* was in admirable working order.

It wasn't until near the end of our tour, when the captain and her morning-shift personnel came out onto the bridge, that we hit our first snag. What's more, it had nothing to do with the workings of the ship.

Our first hint of it was when Sturgis scowled at his

navigation monitor, where long-range sensor scans were reflected. "Captain," he said, "sensors show something dead ahead."

"Something?" Red Abby echoed.

The man's scowl deepened. "Ships," he said. "Five of 'em."

The captain came over and peered at Sturgis's board. "Let's see them," she said, her voice cool and even.

A moment later, the image on the viewscreen changed. It showed five specks. And though I couldn't see them very well, their precise positioning confirmed they were spacegoing vessels.

"Increase magnification," Red Abby ordered.

The image changed again. We were no longer looking at a collection of specks. They were ships, as Sturgis had indicated, though no two were of the same design.

Pirates, I thought. It was the inescapable conclusion.

Worf and I traded looks. This was precisely the sort of obstacle we had hoped to avoid. After all, we were only pawns on this chessboard, subject to the whims of our captain and her newfound adversaries. And with their superior numbers, those adversaries had us at a distinct disadvantage.

Red Abby cursed beneath her breath. "Battle stations. Raise shields. Power up the phasers."

Our communications officer turned in his seat. "They're hailing us," he told the captain.

Red Abby glanced at him. "On screen."

A moment later, the image of a swarthy, heavily bearded human appeared on the viewer. His thick, unruly hair, shot through with strands of silver, was bound at the nape of his neck in a tight braid.

I recognized him. His name was Marrero Jaiya, a key figure in the Maquis rebellion. I'd clashed with him on two separate occasions, more to his chagrin than my own.

Apparently, he'd abandoned his post among the Maquis since our last encounter. Otherwise, he wouldn't be pirating in this sector—or holding up our vessel at the point of his phasers.

Turning to Worf, I saw his Klingon brow furrow at the sight of Jaiya. When he shot a glance at me, there was a warning in his eyes—one I had no trouble at all understanding.

If the pirate recognized either one of us, our cover was blown. We had to make sure that didn't happen. And as there was a good chance we were both on screen, we had to slink *off*-screen before disaster struck.

"What do you want of us?" Red Abby demanded of Jaiya.

Little by little, Worf and I made our way toward the periphery of the bridge. Nor did the former Maquis seem to notice.

"You've got a big, beautiful vessel there," he told our captain. "We could find a thousand uses for a vessel like that. Maybe a million."

"No doubt you could," Red Abby replied tautly. "I hope you get your hands on one someday."

"Actually," Jaiya said offhandedly, "we were thinking we might get our hands on one *today*. That is, if you were inclined to be . . . how can I put it? Generous as well as realistic."

Red Abby shook her head. "I'm not very generous. Any of my men will tell you that. But when it comes to realism, I'm a past master."

Worf and I kept moving, inch by careful inch. And still no reaction from the pirate. Finally, we removed ourselves to a position from which we didn't think we could be spotted.

"I see," Jaiya said. "Then you'll stand down your weapons and drop your shields, so we can inspect our new vessel."

"I'll do nothing of the kind," Red Abby replied evenly.

"But you're outnumbered," he pointed out. "And outgunned."

"And I've got a big, beautiful vessel, remember? One you wouldn't covet unless you appreciated its tactical capabilities—which are more than enough to send your people to their respective makers."

The pirate looked at her for a moment. "You know, I'd heard you could be stubborn on occasion."

"You heard right," Red Abby assured him.

"Even when the odds are five-to-one?"

"All that means," she said, "is I've got five times as many targets to choose from."

"I see," Jaiya responded. "Then, as they say, the ball is in my court. Do I wish to mar that beautiful vessel by blowing big, ugly holes in her hull—and perhaps take a few lives into the bargain? Or do I grant you safe passage for the time being?"

"That's the choice," Red Abby agreed. "But as you consider it, consider something else as well. If the situation becomes a violent one, your vessel will be the one I'll go after first."

The pirate's eyes narrowed slightly. "A threat?"

Our captain smiled grimly. "A piece of information I thought you should have. Certainly, if our positions were reversed, *I'd* want to have it."

"I'll take that into account," said Jaiya. And without another word, his image vanished from the screen, to be replaced by the forbidding spectacle of the five mismatched fighters.

Astellanax looked at Red Abby, the muscles rippling in his temples. "What do you think they'll do?" he asked.

She shook her head. The bravado she'd displayed for the pirate seemed to melt away before my eyes, revealing the worried creature underneath.

"I don't know," Red Abby answered at last.

She was being honest, of course.

As you all know—as *any* captain knows—it's impos-

51

sible to determine an adversary's intent without reading his or her mind. One can guess, perhaps even point that adversary toward a particular logical progression. But one can never say for sure.

For what seemed like an eternity, the pirates hung there in space, neither attacking nor retreating. Sheel muttered something under her breath. Dunwoody drummed his fingers on his console.

And still the pirates didn't make a move.

Then, all of a sudden, Jaiya's ship peeled off. The other vessels followed him, one after another. And in seconds, they were gone.

Sturgis turned to Red Abby. "You did it, Captain."

She nodded. "He believed me when I said I wasn't going to give up without a fight. The only thing he was going to win was a cloud of space debris, and it would have cost him a few ships to obtain it."

I glanced at Worf as we yielded our posts to Thadoc and the morning shift. The lieutenant was smiling. But then, he was a Klingon, and they appreciated bravado almost as much as a good battle.

"Resume course," Red Abby said. "Steady as she goes, Mr. Thadoc."

"Aye, Captain," the helmsman replied, working his controls.

I regarded Red Abby. Until that point, I had thought of her mainly as a means to an end, and not a particularly pleasant means at that. But after seeing her stand up to Jaiya and his pirates, I was forced to look at her in a new light.

I was also very much relieved. Had the pirates boarded the *Daring* as they had threatened to, Jaiya would almost certainly have recognized Worf and myself. And he wouldn't have hesitated for a moment to make the most of such valuable captives.

Worf and I entered the lift at the rear of the bridge and let its doors close behind us. As I programmed the mechanism for the deck where our quarters were located, my lieutenant turned to me and smiled. It was the same smile I had seen on his face a few moments earlier.

"She has the heart of a warrior," he said.

"Red Abby?" I responded, though I knew whom he meant.

"Yes," he said, his grin widening. "Red Abby."

I found myself forced to agree.

Worf and I went straight from the lift to our sleeping quarters. After all, we were rather weary by that time, not having slept since our departure from Milassos IV.

As captain of the *Enterprise,* I enjoyed an entire suite of private quarters. Not so on the *Daring.* Worf and I shared a single cabin with the same black metal bulkheads and green lighting globes that we had seen on the *Daring*'s bridge. The place held six bunk beds and a replicator.

As it would turn out, the beds were never in use at the same time. At least half of our roommates were always on duty or about the ship at any given moment—so though our accommodations were rather cramped, they never became crowded enough to seem intolerable.

That first morning, Worf and I had the place all to ourselves. We shared a bunk bed, I above and he below. I slept well, but not long—five hours at most. And yet, my lieutenant was already awake when I opened my eyes.

We didn't discuss our mission, on the off chance we were being watched via some shipwide surveillance system. I didn't believe that was the case, but there was no reason to take chances.

Instead, we talked about breakfast. We didn't wish to draw any more attention to ourselves by getting involved in another brawl, but the thought of eating in our quarters was unappealing. In the end, we decided to revisit the mess hall.

Luck was with us. Corbis wasn't present, nor were his

comrades, the Oord and the Thelurian. And though there were some other tough-looking crewmen seated here and there, they didn't make the slightest move to cross us. Perhaps word of our prowess had gotten around.

Or, more likely, word of the captain's wrath.

However, as we took our places in the replicator line, a voice cracked like a whip. "Hill," it snapped. "Mitoc."

It was Red Abby.

I looked up at the intercom grid. "Here, Captain."

"I want to see you," she said. "Both of you. In my quarters. Now."

Her tone spoke clearly of her impatience. Exchanging glances with my lieutenant, I wondered what had irked the woman.

"We're on our way," I assured her. Then Worf and I left the mess hall and took a lift to the appropriate deck.

The Klingon scowled as we emerged from the lift compartment. "I do not like this," he said under his breath. "Why would Red Abby have summoned us and no one else?"

"There's only one way to find out," I told him.

True enough.

Following the corridor, we came to the captain's quarters. A moment later, the door whispered open and we went inside.

The place was made of the same gray and black metals we had seen on the bridge and in our own quarters—except here, there were no green globes to provide illumination. Instead, Red Abby had fitted the floor and ceiling with plain, white lighting strips.

The furnishings were simple as well, constructed of a hard, gray material with which I was not familiar. There was a bed, a desk, and a couple of chairs, nothing more.

Red Abby herself was standing in the center of the room—but she wasn't alone. First Officer Astellanax was with her. So were Sturgis and Thadoc.

As the door closed behind us, I focused my attention on the captain. "Here we are," I said.

She nodded. "I can see that."

Suddenly, all three of her officers pulled their phasers from their belts. In accordance with what had obviously been a prearranged command, they trained them on us.

Apparently, Worf's instincts had been accurate. Unfortunately, I had waited too long to heed them.

I eyed Red Abby. "What's all this about?"

"Who are you really?" she asked me. She glanced at my lieutenant. "And who's your friend?"

"What do you mean?" I inquired.

Red Abby frowned. "When I was speaking with those pirates, I noticed you two moving away from me . . . as if you didn't want to be recognized. That's not the behavior of men who have no enemies."

The situation could have been much worse, I thought. It seemed I had a chance of salvaging it if I worked quickly.

"All right," I said reasonably. "You've got us. But it's no big deal. We were Maquis operatives for a while—until we had a run-in with some of our comrades in the movement."

"A run-in," she echoed.

"That's right. It was purely a philosophical rift—no treachery involved on either part. Still, the Maquis know we could give them away. They'd sleep better at night if they could do away with us."

Red Abby weighed my "confession." Then, without warning, she pulled out her phaser, took a step forward, and pressed its barrel to my forehead.

For a moment, I thought she would activate it. At that range, almost any setting would be a kill setting. I could see Worf out of the corner of my eye, restraining himself as best he could.

Then Red Abby lowered her weapon. A moment later, she signaled for her officers to do the same.

"Get out of my quarters," she told us. "And if I find out either of you has lied to me again—about this or anything else—I'll kill you just as quickly as the Maquis would."

I assured her she wouldn't have occasion to do that. And taking Worf by the sleeve, I escorted him out of the captain's quarters.

It had been a close call for us. Nor would it be the only one we would have to endure.

Madigoor

Bo'tex chuckled. "And what would you have done if this Red Abby of yours had sniffed out the truth?"

Picard shrugged. "At that point, I suppose, there wouldn't be much I *could* do—except, perhaps, accept my fate."

"And what would that have been?" asked Dravvin.

"Yes," said Flenarrh, "what indeed? Would Red Abby have shot you in the brain, as she threatened?"

Hompaq looked at him disdainfully. "You heard Worf's assessment of her. The woman had the heart of a warrior. How could she have done otherwise?"

Robinson eyed Picard with a sly grin. "Well, Captain? Care to resolve the matter for us? Would she have shot you or not?"

Picard smiled back at him. "You asked for a proper story, did you not? As I recall, that requires me to reveal everything in good time—and nothing before that time."

Robinson laughed. "Touché, my friend. By all means, proceed, and rest assured we'll vex you no more."

Picard accepted the promise in the spirit it was offered—a rather ironic one, he thought—and moved on.

"For a time," he related, "the *Daring* proceeded through the void without obstacle or incident. However, Red Abby continued to keep the details of our destination to herself."

"No doubt, a frustrating situation," Bo'tex commented.

"As you say," said Picard. "However, Worf and I trusted we would soon have the information we required. All we would have to do is play our parts and the pieces would fall into place."

Robinson harrumphed. "The best-laid plans of mice and men."

Dravvin looked at him. "I beg your pardon?"

"They oft go astray," Robinson explained, completing the saying.

"How right you are," Picard told his fellow human.

"And what made them go astray on the *Daring?*" asked the Captain of the *Kalliope*.

Picard smiled a tight smile. "A Galor-class warship."

"Galor-class?" Hompaq repeated. Her eyes narrowed beneath her brow ridge. "You ran into the Cardassians?"

Picard grunted. "Much to our chagrin."

The Tale

THE DAY AFTER Red Abby's reprimand, I took charge of the helm again—despite whatever suspicions our captain may still have harbored about me. Perhaps she just wanted me where she could see me.

In any case, the first task I set myself was to conduct a long-range sensor sweep. Mind you, I never thought it would turn up a Cardassian warship. I only wanted to see if Jaiya and his pirates were still on our trail.

Imagine my surprise when I saw something bigger and a lot more dangerous than Jaiya. The vessel was at a considerable distance, but it was clearly keeping pace with us.

"Cardassians," I announced. "One ship. Galor-class."

Sturgis switched to long-range sensor capability and studied his monitor. "Hill's right," he confirmed.

Red Abby straightened in the captain's chair. "On screen."

Sturgis ran his fingers over his controls. A moment later, the viewscreen filled with the sight of the warship.

It looked like some great, tawny predator savoring the prospect of a kill.

And the kill it was savoring, no doubt, was *us*.

Red Abby bit her lip, none too happy with the spectacle. "Hail them," she said at last.

At the tactical station, Worf complied with the order. The seconds ticked off slowly.

"No response," he told the captain.

"Keep trying," Red Abby insisted.

I didn't like the odds. The *Daring* was an able ship, but not a fighter. On the best of days, she was no match for a Galor-class warship. If the Cardassians decided to attack . . .

And then, it was no longer a matter of *if*.

"Captain," Worf called out suddenly. "The Cardassians are accelerating to warp eight."

For a moment, I imagined he was speaking to me. Then I remembered where I was and what station I held there.

"Full power to the shields," said Red Abby.

Sturgis muttered a curse at navigation. "They're powering up their weapons batteries," he reported.

Our captain eyed the enemy vessel as it loomed larger and larger on our viewscreen. "Ready phasers," she said.

"Ready," Worf replied.

"Target and fire," Red Abby barked.

The Klingon did as she said. Our phasers lashed out furiously at the Cardassian vessel, but her shields appeared to be a match for us. I glanced at Sturgis's monitors.

So did the captain.

"Not much effect," the navigator told her.

Worf made a sound of disgust. "They're returning fire!"

The viewscreen confirmed his warning. We held on to our consoles as the Cardassian's weapon batteries raked us with a blinding barrage.

The *Daring* shuddered and bucked with the impact, but not so badly that anyone was hurt. Recovering quickly, I glanced again at Sturgis's monitors to see how severely we had been damaged.

"Shields down forty percent," he reported.

Red Abby turned to me, the glare of the viewscreen glinting in her eyes.

"Evasive maneuvers, Mr. Hill. And for all our sakes, I hope you're as good as you claim."

I hoped the same thing. After all, it had been a long time since I'd done any tactical piloting, and I wasn't nearly as intimate with this ship as I would have liked.

As I directed the *Daring* into a sudden, gut-wrenching turn, sending a couple of my comrades tumbling out of their seats, the Cardassians unleashed another energy barrage. This time, they missed.

It seemed I had gotten us one step ahead of them. It was a step I was reluctant to relinquish.

With that in mind, I whipped the *Daring* about in the opposite direction. The move elicited cries and curses from my shipmates, but this time they hung on. Again, the Cardassians attempted to skewer us on their beams. Again, they fell short.

However, I couldn't elude them forever. It was only a matter of time before I made a fatal mistake—or they anticipated our next move and made us pay for it. With this in mind, I gambled everything on a single maneuver.

It was one that had originated in the skies over Earth's European continent some four hundred years earlier, in a conflict called World War One. The idea was to loop over and back behind one's pursuer, instantly transforming oneself from hunted to hunter.

In the *Enterprise,* the move would have been a difficult one. And the *Daring* was by no means as quick or maneuverable as the *Enterprise.* Still, I felt compelled to try it.

"Hang on!" I bellowed.

Suddenly, I brought our nose up and accelerated, straining our ship's inertial dampers to their limit. I was thrown back in my chair with enough force to rattle my teeth.

The deckplates screamed as if with a human voice, but I showed them no mercy. In for a penny, I thought, in for a pound. I pulled us up and back into the tightest arc the *Daring* could handle.

On the viewscreen, a shower of stars plummeted past me. For a moment, I lost all sense of up and down. My stomach flip-flopped and I experienced a brief but awful moment of vertigo. As I mentioned earlier, this was definitely *not* the *Enterprise*.

Through it all, I kept my eye on my controls. When the Cardassians tried to shake us with a course change, I compensated. Jaw clenched, fighting inertia, I reached out and activated the starboard thrusters.

We were on their tail. At least, all my instruments indicated as much. But I wouldn't be satisfied until I saw the back of the Cardassian loom up on the screen in front of me.

Another few seconds, I told myself. Just hold on. Another few seconds and we would know if our effort had paid off.

Abruptly, I saw what I was so desperately looking for. The Cardassian warship fell into view, filling our screen with its nearness, its nacelles spilling streams of photons on either side of us.

We were so close to the enemy, we could almost see the seams in her hull. For the first time in our encounter, we had the upper hand. Immediately, I leveled us off.

Nor was our captain slow to recognize her advantage. "Fire!" cried Red Abby, her eyes alight.

Our phasers stabbed at the Cardassians. And this time, at considerably closer quarters, they had more of an effect. The enemy's shields began to buckle under our barrage.

"Keep firing!" Red Abby snarled.

The Cardassians fled, executing some evasive maneuvers of their own. But I maneuvered right along with them, keeping them in our sights so Worf could worry their hindquarters.

The *Daring*'s weapons batteries were hardly up to Starfleet standards, but the lieutenant didn't seem perturbed in the least. His aim was unerring, his timing impeccable. In a matter of seconds, he had knocked out one of the warship's shield generators—and was going after the other one.

Then the tide turned.

The Cardassians' shields jumped to full strength again, no doubt drawing on energies from less crucial systems. Once again, our beams spattered harmlessly before they could do any damage.

I engaged the port thrusters, knowing what was coming next. But, despite my best efforts, I was too late.

The Cardassians' weapons banks erupted at us with renewed fury. The *Daring* shivered and jerked sideways under the force of the attack. A console exploded, sending out a shower of sparks. Smoke filled the bridge.

I felt a hand clutch my shoulder. "Get us out of here," Red Abby demanded of me.

Then the Cardassians struck again. I was flung out of my seat. The next thing I knew, I was dragging myself off the deck, a ringing in my ears and the taste of blood in my mouth.

My comrades had been tossed about, as well. One by one, they began to stir, to show signs of consciousness. All except Sheel, whose head lay at a fatally awkward angle at the base of a blackened console.

Red Abby, who was only a few feet away from Sheel, crawled over and checked the woman's neck for a pulse. Apparently, there wasn't any. The captain cursed and looked to Worf.

By then, he had regained his post.

"Report," she rasped, her blue eyes glittering as they reflected a sudden burst of sparks.

"Shields are down," the lieutenant told her, blinking away the smoke that wafted around him. "Weapons are disabled. And the engines are off-line—impulse as well as warp drive."

"What about life supports?" asked Red Abby.

Worf consulted his monitors. "They still function," he concluded. Then he added, "For now."

I looked at the viewscreen. The Cardassian warship wasn't firing on us any longer. But then, it didn't have to.

We were dead in the water.

Madigoor

"BUT WHY DID THEY attack you in the first place?" asked Hompaq.

"I wondered that myself," said Dravvin.

"Did they suspect you of aiding the Maquis?" asked Bo'tex.

Flenarrh grunted. "Perhaps they were asserting a right to territory beyond the borders established by treaty."

Robinson nodded. "Perhaps."

"Unfortunately," said Picard, "I was destined to wait some time before I received an answer. At the moment, my comrades and I were more concerned with the Cardassians' intentions than their motivations. And since they weren't making a move to destroy us . . ."

The Captain of the *Kalliope* shook his head. "They had decided to board you," he concluded.

Picard smiled. "That was our guess as well."

The Tale

RED ABBY TOOK IN everyone present with a single glance.

Her hair was wild and fiery amid the spark-shot smoke, her eyes slitted with desperation. She had to know there was little chance of winning this encounter, but she was still determined to try.

"We can't let them take the bridge or engineering," she told us adamantly. "Any other section, but not those. Then we'll still have a shot at getting out of this."

"I'll head for engineering," Astellanax volunteered. "They'll need someone to give orders down there."

"I'll go with you," said Sturgis.

The captain nodded. "Take Hill and Dunwoody too. The rest of us will try to hold things together up here."

Brushing aside a loose strand of hair, she looked up at the intercom grid. "All personnel, listen up. We've taken a beating and we're expecting a visit from the Cardassians. For now, find yourself a place you can defend and keep your head down."

Assad, a broad, dark-haired man, chose that moment to speak up. "Captain," he said, "the Cardassians can beam us *off* the *Daring* as easily as they can beam themselves *on.*"

It was true, of course. But I knew the Cardassians. The one thing they would *not* do is bring an armed enemy onto their vessel.

Judging by the look Red Abby shot at Assad, she knew the Cardassians, too. "Next time I need someone to state the obvious, I'll know whom to call on." She turned to Astellanax. "Get a *move* on."

As the first officer started for the turbolift, I cast a glance at Worf—a warning not to do anything I would consider foolhardy in my absence. After all, I needed him more than ever if we were to complete our mission. But I knew my admonition would carry limited weight with him.

The Klingon held only one thing higher than his sense of duty, and that was his warrior's code of honor. If the situation became such that he could survive only through cowardice, he would simply choose not to survive.

With this grim thought in mind, I followed Dunwoody into the lift. Then Astellanax slammed his fist into the appropriate stud on the control strip and the turbo-compartment took us down to the engineering level.

"I've fought the Cardassians before," the Orion told us, though he declined to say where. "They're merciless. We've got to be merciless as well."

I agreed with the sentiment—up to a point. Still, I wasn't going to take part in a bloodbath if I could help it. I set my phaser on stun.

A moment later, the lift doors opened. Astellanax stuck his head out cautiously, scanning the corridor in one direction and then the other. Satisfied it was safe— at least for the time being—he gestured for the rest of us to come after him.

We proceeded in the direction of engineering. As the newcomer in the group, I brought up the rear.

It gave me a chance to watch the others in action. Astellanax and Sturgis looked ahead and behind at every step. They seemed to know all too well what they were doing.

Dunwoody, on the other hand, was something of a novice at this sort of thing. I made a mental note to stay clear of him if and when we ran into the Cardassians.

Moving cautiously, we took a couple of minutes to cover fifty meters of winding corridor. As we approached an intersection, we heard what sounded like the scrape of footfalls up ahead. A second later, it was followed by the rasping of furtive voices.

Those of our crewmates? Or the enemy? We all wondered the same thing.

His back to the wall, Astellanax began inching toward the intersection. Sturgis came next. Dunwoody and I followed. None of us dared even to breathe, lest we give away our presence there.

Abruptly, the Orion—whose hearing was more acute than anyone else's in our party—stopped and turned to look at us. "Those aren't Cardassians," he said. "They're human."

Accelerating his progress, he peeked around the corner and confirmed his observation for himself. Breathing a sigh of relief, he went out into the intersection and signaled with his phaser.

When I followed, I saw a woman, an Yridian, and a Ferengi at the far end of the corridor. I recognized the Ferengi as someone I'd seen in the mess hall, just before our conflict with Corbis.

Our comrades looked surprised to see us. But for some reason, they didn't seem relieved. Suddenly, I realized why that might be. The insight sent chills up and down my spine.

I searched their faces more closely. The five of them seemed tense, fearful, as if they perceived a danger more urgent and immediate than the general threat of invasion.

Almost as if they had already *encountered* the enemy . . . as if he were close enough to shoot them in the back if they didn't obey his commands.

"Commander Astellanax," called the Yridian. "I'm glad to see you."

"And we, you," the first officer replied. "Didn't you hear the captain when she told you to take cover?"

"Yes," the woman said. "We did. In fact, the three of us were on our way to a cargo bay to do just that."

Her voice trembled ever so slightly. Perhaps I wouldn't have heard it if my suspicions hadn't been aroused already, or if I hadn't been human, too. But I *did* hear it—and I could delay no longer.

Without a word to any of my fellow bridge officers, I moved past them. And not only them, but the crewmen we'd encountered. To forestall the questions I knew would follow, I held up my left hand. Then I planted myself against the wall, took a breath, and waited.

I expected the Cardassians to burst out of concealment at any moment, eager to spring their trap. They didn't disappoint me.

Aiming carefully, I took out the first one with a beam to the center of his chest. As he went sprawling, a second one appeared and took hasty aim. Fortunately, he managed only to sear the bulkhead above my head. And he never got off a second shot because I shot first.

But there were other Cardassians behind them. They poured out into the corridor like locusts—nearly a dozen of them—firing their lethal beams at anything that moved. And since we had orders to reach engineering, we stood our ground and fired back.

The corridor became a lurid, screaming vision of hell, lances of seething energy crisscrossing madly in midair. My back pressed against the wall, I fired this way and that, trying to make out my nearest adversaries between flashes of fire.

Then, just as I was spearing one Cardassian with my phaser beam, I saw two more coming at me. Both of them had me in their sights and there was no time to beat them to the punch. So I did the only thing I could think of—I threw myself at them.

Not at their weapons, of course, because that would have spelled disaster. Rather, I launched myself at their ankles, hoping to knock them off their feet in the manner of an ancient Terran bowling ball.

I was fortunate. They missed me and went down in a heap of tangled limbs. But my phaser was kicked out of my hand in the process, leaving me a lot more vulnerable than I had planned.

As the first Cardassian tried to get to his feet, I planted my hands on the deck and lashed out with my foot, knocking him unconscious with a blow to the head. Then I hurled myself onto the other Cardassian.

He turned out to be a more formidable opponent than I had expected. First, he snapped my head back with a teeth-rattling blow to the jaw. Then, reaching for my throat with both his hands, he squeezed my windpipe until he had cut off my air supply.

I tried to wrench his hands away, but it was no use. He was too strong. As I felt myself blacking out, I struck him in the face.

A second time.

And then again.

The third blow was the charm. It loosened his grip on me, enabling me to suck in a desperately needed draft of air.

Turning the tables on the Cardassian, I hit him in the throat with the heel of my hand. And as he gasped for air, his eyes popping as if they wished to escape their sockets, I knocked him senseless.

That accomplished, I cast about for my fallen

phaser—and found it less than a meter away. I was just about to close my fingers on it when a boot came down on my hand rather painfully.

Suppressing a yelp, I looked up and saw a Cardassian soldier aiming his weapon at me. This time, it seemed there would be no escape. But no sooner had I thought that than a bright red beam punched my enemy in the chest, sending him hurtling into a bulkhead.

I sought out the source of the beam and saw it was Dunwoody who'd rescued me. But there was no time to thank him for it. Grabbing my phaser, I looked around for a target.

Only a couple of Cardassians were still standing. And as I watched, Astellanax and Sturgis made short work of them. The skirmish over, an eerie silence filled the corridor.

Of the dozen or so Cardassians who had attacked us, none moved. But we had taken casualties, as well. The Ferengi was staring at the ceiling, his eyes no doubt fixed on some celestial treasury. The woman was dead, too, her chest a smoking ruin.

I regretted what had happened to them. Nonetheless, the rest of us still stood, and our goal hadn't changed.

"Come on," said Astellanax. He glanced at the Yridian. "Pick up a weapon and let's go."

"Go where?" asked the Yridian.

"Engineering," the first officer told him.

Without further explanation, Astellanax took the point again, advancing to the intersection of the two corridors and looking about. When he saw the way was clear, he went on.

As before, we were right behind him.

Madigoor

"STIRRING," SAID DRAVVIN.

"I daresay," Robinson added.

Hompaq didn't speak. She just growled deep in her throat.

The Captain of the *Kalliope* looked at her. "You disagree?"

The Klingon eyed him. "A warrior does not set his phaser on stun. A warrior sends his enemies to their deaths."

Picard returned her gaze evenly. "Perhaps. But I do not fancy myself a warrior, Hompaq. Nor would it have furthered my mission to destroy every Cardassian I laid my eyes on."

"Nonetheless," said Flenarrh, "you were fighting for your life. A stunned enemy is one who can rise again and prove your undoing."

"True," Picard conceded. "But I was willing to take that chance."

"And this Dunwoody," said Bo'tex. "It turned out you were wrong about him. He saved your life."

Picard smiled. "He did indeed. But again, I find I'm getting ahead of myself. As I was saying . . ."

The Tale

The Tale

WE NEGOTIATED THE CORRIDORS of the *Daring*, phasers at the ready, on the alert for the enemy. But, initially at least, all we encountered were a couple more strays.

One was a tall, slender Bajoran named Murrif, who looked uncomfortable holding a phaser—even more so than Dunwoody. The other was an Oord, though not the one who had stood by Corbis in the mess hall.

"Have you seen any Cardassians?" asked the Oord.

Astellanax nodded. "We got the best of the encounter. But there are bound to be more of them around."

"What about the captain?" asked Murrif.

"She's defending the bridge," said the first officer. "Or anyway, she's supposed to be. Our job's to get to engineering."

"And get there we will," Sturgis added.

There were nods all around. As wary as ever, we resumed our journey. After a while, the Yridian came up beside me.

"I didn't want to fool you," he told me.

"No?" I replied.

"It turned my stomach," he went on. "But the Cardassians said they would kill us if we didn't cooperate."

I glanced at him. "And now two of you are dead anyway."

"I'm alive," he pointed out.

I frowned. But all I said was, "Yes. You're alive."

As I turned away from him, I heard a curious sound—as if someone were pushing metal over metal. It seemed to be coming from the stretch of corridor directly behind us.

I whirled. At the same time, a half-dozen Cardassians dropped from the ceiling, where they had slid away a series of access plates. Even before they landed, they began firing their weapons at us.

"Back here!" I shouted to my comrades, pushing the Yridian in one direction as I threw myself in the other.

A couple of directed-energy beams sliced past us. Someone screamed, though I didn't see who it was.

Then Astellanax and the others fired back, and the battle was joined in earnest. The air around me shivered and seethed with barrage after deadly barrage. One even came close enough to blind me for a moment.

As my eyes cleared, I leaned as far into the curvature of the bulkhead as I could and picked out a target. Doing my best to ignore the chaos all about me, I took aim and fired.

My beam hit the Cardassian square in the center of his chest. It knocked him off his feet and sent him skidding backward down the corridor. But no sooner had he fallen than another came forward to take his place.

Then that one fell, too, spun about by a blow to his shoulder. A third took a shot to his midsection and rolled over, clutching himself. The tide of battle seemed to be turning in our favor.

Unlike the prior combat, this one never devolved into a hand-to-hand struggle. We simply fired and fired some more, and kept firing until none of the Cardassians were left standing.

In the strange, dense silence that followed, I surveyed the corridor. Two of my comrades had been hit by enemy fire. One was the Oord, who had sustained only an injury to his shoulder.

The other was the Yridian. In his case, the damage was a bit more serious. Moving to his side, I closed his gaping, dead eyes with a sweep of my hand. Then I glanced at Astellanax.

The first officer didn't say anything. He just walked over to the nearest Cardassian, who happened to be still breathing, and picked him up by the front of his uniform.

"I want to know one thing," he said evenly. "Why didn't you just materialize behind us? Why did you have to try to take us from above?"

The Cardassian looked at him. For a moment, I thought he would give Astellanax an answer. Then he spat in the Orion's face.

Astellanax let him slump to the floor and wiped the spittle from his cheek. Then he took aim at the Cardassian and killed him.

"Obviously," said the first officer, "the enemy is having trouble beaming men aboard the *Daring*. My guess is the captain has found a way to resurrect our shields."

"It's possible," Sturgis remarked.

"Or," I said, "we managed to disable the warship's transporters when we fired on her."

Astellanax looked at me. "I'd like to think so."

Then he made his way down the winding corridor again, this time with a bit more haste.

Madigoor

Dravvin held up his hand. "A question, if I may."

Picard nodded. "Go ahead."

"You didn't seem very happy with the Yridian. I take
it you didn't approve of his decision to survive at the
expense of others?"

"That's true," Picard replied. "I *didn't* approve. Mind
you, I think one should do whatever one can to keep
body and soul together, but I stop short of endangering
the lives of others."

"I agree," said Robinson. "If you've got coin, buy
what you like. But don't reach into someone else's
pocket."

The Captain of the *Kalliope* stroked his beard thoughtfully. "Then, in the Yridian's place, you would have
refused to cooperate? Even at the expense of your life?"

Picard shrugged. "I might have given the appearance
of cooperation—so as to make myself useful at a later
time. But I would not have cooperated with the Cardassians in fact."

Bo'tex laughed a hearty laugh. "You wouldn't make a very good Caxtonian, Captain Picard."

"Nor a very good Yridian, apparently," said Hompaq.

"Would he make a good Klingon?" Flenarrh asked.

Hompaq grunted. "A Klingon would not have allowed himself to be captured in the first place."

Picard couldn't help but chuckle at that.

"In any case," he continued, "we pressed on. And, as luck would have it, we reached the engine room without further violence."

The Tale

THE PROBLEM, AT THAT POINT, was getting inside the place.
After all, the doors to the engine room were closed, and
the last thing we wanted to do was blast our way in.

Under normal circumstances, we could have contacted
the engineering staff via ship's intercom. However, the
Cardassians were no doubt monitoring for such messages.

Fortunately, Astellanax carried a portable communications device that could interface with the workstations
in the engine room. Pulling it out, he tapped out a
message and waited.

A message came back. Those in the engine room
wanted to know how they could be sure of the first
officer's identity. They suspected the Cardassians had
captured Astellanax and were using his device to try to
gain entry.

The Orion frowned and tapped out another message.
It wasn't a sentence, as it turned out. It was some sort of
code—one that someone in the engine room was capable
of recognizing.

A moment later, the doors slid apart, revealing a by-now-familiar gray and black decor. The engine room contained a surprising number of working consoles, all of which reflected the pale green glare of the bulkhead globes.

However, there was no one at the consoles that we could see—no one to greet us or ask us in.

Astellanax seemed undaunted by the fact. He started for the entrance—until I grabbed him by the arm.

"Wait a minute," I whispered. "What if this is a trap like the other one? What if the enemy is waiting for us inside?"

Murrif seemed less than impressed with the possibility. "If it's a trap," he said, "they don't seem very eager for us to enter it. The engineers made us give them the password, didn't they?"

"It could be they're just playing their parts," I pointed out.

"It could be," Astellanax echoed thoughtfully. "But our people weren't under any pressure to respond to my signal. It's not as if the Cardassians would've known I was sending it."

I bit my lip, wishing there were a way to allay my fears. "I don't suppose there's a countercode?" I asked.

The first officer looked at me with just a hint of a smile. "Next time," he said.

"I've got an idea," said Dunwoody. "I'll go in and check things out. If there's a problem, you'll know it."

"What if they threaten your life?" asked Murrif.

Dunwoody eyed him. "They'll have to make good on their threat. I'd die before I'd let them use me the way they used the others."

Sturgis glanced expectantly at the first officer. "Sounds like a plan to me," he said.

Astellanax considered the offer—as well as the man who had made it. "All right," he said at last. "Go ahead, Mr. Dunwoody. And good luck."

With that wish on his side and little else, Dunwoody made his way down the corridor and walked through the open doors into engineering. He turned to someone we couldn't see, waved, then turned back to us.

"It's all right," he called. "There's no one here but—"

Before the fellow could get the next word out, a couple of Cardassians materialized behind him. Sensing that something was amiss, he whirled and fired his phaser at them.

One Cardassian went sprawling, propelled by the force of Dunwoody's beam. But the other invader was already taking aim at him.

"Watch out!" I cried, and fired.

It wasn't the cleanest shot I had ever made, but it had the desired effect. The Cardassian spun about, his weapon falling from his hand.

Cursing, knowing how close he had come to death, Dunwoody leveled his phaser at the Cardassian—but his hand was trembling so badly, his beam missed by several inches. It was only with his second shot that the man hammered his adversary senseless.

Suddenly, the Oord bellowed a warning. Turning, I saw a group of Cardassians materializing in the corridor behind us.

"Quick!" Astellanax cried. "Into the engine room!"

But there were Cardassians materializing there as well. I saw Dunwoody retreat from my view, presumably to join a clutch of engineers already holed up behind their consoles.

I hesitated just long enough to consider our options. The Orion's advice still seemed to make sense. Engineering remained a key to control of the ship—and it was easier to defend than an open corridor.

Firing at the Cardassians behind me to keep them at bay, I made for the open doors of the engine room. So did Astellanax, Sturgis, and Murrif, and with equal haste.

Only the Oord stayed behind. Battered shoulder and all, he stood his ground, giving the rest of us time to escape.

It was a suicide stand—the Oord had to have known that. But he stood there anyway, firing his phaser with deadly accuracy into the oncoming ranks of the enemy. As we charged into engineering, I heard a sound that could only have been the Oord's body hitting the deck.

At that point, I was too much in the thick of the conflict to mourn my comrade. The engine room was full of Cardassians—perhaps twenty in all, none of them eager to give up their foothold. They sent a barrage at us that should have dropped us all in our tracks.

As it happened, it only dropped one of us. An energy beam hit Murrif square in the face, breaking his neck with its force—and his momentum slid him into an unmanned console.

I knew from watching Dunwoody that at least some of the engine room's defenders were to my left. As I returned the Cardassians' fire, I retreated in that direction. Then I picked a spot between two workstations and dove full length, hoping to make it to cover before our adversaries' volley could tear me apart.

Directed energy beams crisscrossed in the air around me, scalding it with their passage. But none of them hit me. I landed, rolled, and felt myself grabbed by several pairs of hands.

I looked up into the faces that went with them. To my relief, one of them was Dunwoody's.

"Glad you could join us," he quipped, though the sheen of sweat on his face belied the casual tone of his remark.

"Not half as glad as I am," I replied.

I glanced about. Astellanax and Sturgis had made it as well, joining the handful of engineers and assorted crewmen holed up there already. We exchanged the grateful looks of men who had risked their lives together and emerged from the experience unscathed.

The Cardassians chose that moment to send a barrage into the workstation I was hiding behind. There was a wretched whining sound and a geyser of sparks, but my comrades and I remained unharmed.

Hefting my phaser, I peered across the engine room at the enemy. What I saw was not encouraging.

The Cardassians were continuing to beam reinforcements into the place. If the captain had discovered a way to befuddle the enemy's transporters for a time, that time was now past.

It made me wonder if the Cardassians had taken the bridge. It made me wonder if they were assuming control of the *Daring* even as we risked our lives to save her. It made me wonder what had become of Worf, though my lieutenant had proven himself a difficult man to stop.

And it made me wonder if they had killed Red Abby.

It cut me to think so. Despite her avarice, the woman had shown herself to be a brave and able commander— one of the few I had met outside Starfleet. She had won my respect.

And perhaps something more, though I was reluctant to admit it at the time—even to myself.

At any rate, I had no way of knowing Red Abby's fate—or Worf's, for that matter. All I could do was fire away at the Cardassians in their increasing numbers, hope we could hold them for a while, and watch faithfully for a window of opportunity.

It came, all right. But not for *us*.

Up until then, the workstations in front of us had been our salvation, protecting us from the increasingly fierce attacks of the enemy. In a single moment, they became our greatest danger.

One by one, they began to blow up. With a sinking heart, I realized the Cardassians had taken the bridge after all. And they had found a way to overload the circuitry in the workstations.

The result? Chaos.

Half of us bolted like rabbits driven from their warren—only to be cut down by the invader's relentless barrage. I and some of the others stayed where we were, continuing to fight from cover as long as we could.

Unfortunately, there was no pattern to the explosion of the engineers' workstations—or at least, none I could discern. No doubt, the Cardassians meant it to be that way. I remember wondering whether the console in front of me would be the next to blow up.

Then I didn't have to wonder anymore.

Madigoor

"IT EXPLODED?" asked Robinson.

Picard grunted. "Right in front of me."

"But it didn't kill you," Bo'tex observed.

"Obviously," said Dravvin.

"I was lucky," Picard told them. "All I suffered was a few burns. However, the force of the explosion was enough to knock me out."

"Then what?" asked the Captain of the *Kalliope*, obviously caught up in the particulars of the tale.

"I regained consciousness perhaps half an hour later," Picard replied. "I found myself in the *Daring*'s small, gray transporter room with a Cardassian energy rifle in my face. But it was only one of a dozen carried by a contingent of stony-faced guards."

"You were alone?" asked Flenarrh.

Picard shook his head. "There were some forty of us being held there."

"Forty survivors," Robinson mused.

"Precisely," said Picard.

"What about Worf?" Hompaq demanded.

85

"To my immense relief," Picard told her, "Worf was among that number—though the Cardassians had opened a dangerous-looking gash in his temple. Looking around, I saw Astellanax, Sturgis, and Thadoc as well. Also Corbis, and his friends the Oord and the Thelurian. And Dunwoody, though he was holding a limp and painful-looking arm."

"And Red Abby?" asked Robinson.

Picard nodded. "Our captain was there, too, though I didn't notice her at first. She was kneeling, tending to one of the wounded. Though she had been bruised and battered as badly as any of us, she managed somehow to maintain an air of defiance."

Bo'tex smiled. "I see where this is going."

"So can I," said Dravvin.

"This woman inspired you," Bo'tex speculated. "She gave you hope in the midst of despair."

"And when the Cardassians let their guards down," said Dravvin, "you attacked them and freed yourselves."

Picard chuckled grimly. "Had you been there, you would have known an uprising was an impossibility."

"Indeed," said Flenarrh. "Charging your captors would no doubt have cost you dearly."

"I believe so," Picard agreed. "And even then, we would not have gained anything. We would still have had to escape our cargo bay."

Flenarrh leaned forward. "And with the *Daring*'s transporters under the Cardassians' control, they could have beamed in all the reinforcements they required."

"Aye," said Robinson. "Or beamed out you and your comrades, one at a time. The Cardassians held all the cards."

"Still," Hompaq snarled, "if it had been me in that cargo bay, I would have gone for a Cardassian throat." She glared at Picard. "And if I had died, at least it would have been a warrior's death. Only a coward allows himself to be herded like a pack animal."

Picard, of course, knew a few things about Klingon ethics. He had, after all, been the Arbiter of Succession—the man who picked Gowron as the leader of the Klingon High Council.

"Only a fool wastes his life on a useless gesture," he told Hompaq pointedly. "I had a mission, remember—a duty to Starfleet. In order to fulfill that duty, I had to survive my captivity."

Hompaq bared her teeth, less than thrilled with Picard's tone. For a moment, he thought she might pull a concealed weapon—or at the least throw herself across the table at him. In the end, however, she made a sound of disgust and stayed in her seat.

Not that the Klingon was fearful of facing him. Quite the contrary. Rather, it seemed to Picard, she had a healthy respect for the establishment in which they were seated.

For the Captain's Table.

"As I was saying," Picard continued, "we may have thought about an uprising, but we didn't attempt one. We simply waited, exchanging grim glances, until the Cardassians received an order via the ship's intercom."

The Tale

I UNDERSTOOD ENOUGH Cardassian to make sense of the order. Apparently, my fellow prisoners and I would shortly be beamed to the enemy's warship. It was better than being destroyed out of hand, I thought.

A moment later, my comrades began to disappear, two and three at a time. Corbis and his friends were among the first to go. Worf, Thadoc, and Sturgis came soon after. I myself was among the last.

We materialized in a place not unlike the one we had left. Of course, the bulkheads around us were of a decidedly darker hue, and the recessed lighting gave off a smoldering, orange glow, but it was clear we were in a cargo bay.

A *Cardassian* cargo bay. It was a chilling thought, to say the least.

Once all of the prisoners were assembled, a stocky Cardassian officer entered the bay with something like a tricorder in his hand. Glancing at it, he scanned our ranks until his eyes fell on our captain, who endured his scrutiny with a scowl.

The Cardassian pointed at her. "You," he said in a tongue she could understand. "Come with me."

Astellanax and some of the others looked ready to intervene. Obviously, they didn't like the idea of leaving their captain alone in the hands of the Cardassians. For that matter, neither did I.

Abruptly, the issue became an academic one. The officer pointed to Astellanax as well. "You will come, too," he said.

Then he eyed the rest of us and glanced again at his handheld device. After a moment's consideration, the Cardassian picked out Worf, Sturgis, Thadoc, and myself, and informed us that we would be accompanying him.

We didn't know on what basis we had been selected— though I might have ventured a guess—but we didn't argue with the decision. When the officer left the cargo bay, we left with him, flanked by a pair of armed guards.

The Cardassians escorted us down a corridor to their version of a turbolift. The door irised open and we went inside. Then the officer punched in a destination code.

Unfortunately, I couldn't see it from where I was standing. A few moments later, the lift stopped and the door irised open again, allowing us to enter a dimly lit corridor.

I looked right and then left. To my right, the corridor wound out of sight. To my left, it ended in a rather ornate egress.

Only then did I realize where we were headed.

Remember, the Federation had been at war with the Cardassians years earlier. In the course of that war we had taken some of the enemy's ships. Though I hadn't personally toured one of those vessels, I had seen the schematics disseminated by Starfleet.

That's how I knew we were headed for the bridge. But for the life of me, I couldn't see what purpose our presence there was meant to serve.

The six of us were herded in the direction of two ornate doors. Just before we reached them, they parted for us. As I had predicted, the warship's bridge was beyond them, as dark and smoldering with orange light as the rest of the vessel.

Like the other Cardassian bridges I had seen, this one had five stations—two forward, two aft, and a massive-looking captain's chair. Graphics in gold and electric blue gleamed at us from tactical screens situated on every bulkhead.

My attention was drawn to the viewscreen, which was considerably smaller than that of a Starfleet vessel and oval in shape. It gave us a view of the *Daring* as she hung in space, her port nacelle and parts of her hull charred beyond recognition.

I glanced at Abby. She seemed transfixed by the sight. You all know what she was feeling, I imagine. Certainly, I did. She was, after all, the captain of that crippled vessel.

The gul in charge of the warship turned and took note of our arrival. He was a tall, almost gangly specimen, with the self-assurance bordering on arrogance that I had come to associate with Cardassian leadership.

"I see everyone has arrived," he said. He turned to Abby. "As you will note, your bridge officers are all present—at least, insofar as our sensor data could identify them. In general, we took pains not to kill any more of your people than we absolutely had to."

"That was generous of you," Abby replied, no doubt meaning to inject a note of sarcasm.

But her voice was hollow, drained of energy. Of course, a stun blast would have had that effect on even the strongest victim.

The Cardassian smiled. "I am accustomed to being addressed by my name and title. From now on, you will call me Gul Ecor whenever you speak to me. Is that clear, human?"

Abby frowned. "It's clear."

"It's clear, *what?*" asked the gul.

The woman's eyes blazed with hate, despite her fatigue. "It's clear," she said, "Gul Ecor."

The Cardassian nodded, then glanced at the viewscreen. "Unfortunately," he remarked, "I can't treat your ship as I have your crew. It would serve as a marker with regard to our encounter here, and that might cause me problems in the future."

He gestured to his weapons officer, whose fingers flew over his controls. A moment later, the Cardassian looked up.

"Ready, Gul Ecor."

Ecor paused a moment, as if to build up the drama. Then he made a gesture of dismissal. "Fire."

Suddenly, a pair of disruptor beams shot across the viewscreen, stabbing the *Daring* in her aft quarters. The ship buckled and blackened under the barrage. Then there was a blinding burst of white light—the kind that might be created by an exploding warp core.

As it subsided, we could see that the *Daring* was gone.

I turned to Red Abby. Her eyes had become ice chips and her features had gone as hard as stone. But to her credit, she didn't look away from the *Daring*'s demise. She stared at the Cardassian viewscreen without flinching, as if trying to etch the moment in her memory.

I empathized with the woman. I had never seen a ship under my command so completely destroyed, though I had seen one wrecked so badly I was forced to abandon her.

But that is a tale for another time.

"Unfortunate," said Gul Ecor. He gazed at Abby with hooded eyes.

"Isn't it . . . Captain Brant?"

Brant? I thought.

That was the name of the man Worf and I were searching for. Clearly, Ecor had some inkling as to Red

Abby's objectives. That wasn't good news for her—or for myself and Worf either.

However, the Cardassian had made a mistake. Brant wasn't Red Abby's name. I looked at her, then at Ecor, then at her again. I waited for Red Abby to point out the gul's error.

But she didn't. She just stood there, looking more wary than defiant all of a sudden. And by that sign, I realized the Cardassian hadn't made a mistake after all.

My mind raced. If Red Abby's name *was* Brant, our expedition was not what I had been led to believe. Far from it, in fact.

Back on Milassos IV, I had concluded Red Abby was a shallow fortune hunter—a money-hungry adventurer who had gotten a whiff of Dujonian's Hoard. At the time, it was the only possibility that made sense.

Now, I saw the matter in a new light. If Red Abby was related to Brant, perhaps even his wife . . . she was no mere fortune hunter after all. She was a brave and determined woman risking her life for someone she loved.

The Hoard might still have played a part in it, I conceded. But more and more, it looked like the icing rather than the cake.

Not that it would matter to Gul Ecor why Abby had set out after Brant. It would only matter that she *had*—and that she might lead him to the glor'ya lost to Cardassia hundreds of years ago.

Finally, Red Abby spoke again. "How do you know who I am?" she demanded of the gul.

Ecor shrugged. "We have our sources in this sector. They told us who you were and what you were after."

Astellanax's eyes narrowed considerably. "So you've been tracking us since we left Milassos Four?"

The Cardassian nodded. "We remained patient for a long while, waiting for the proper moment to overtake you." He smiled a thin smile. "That moment came rather precipitously, I'm afraid. But once you conducted a long-range sensor sweep and discovered our presence, we could no longer be content to pursue you from afar."

There was a gleam of more than triumph in Ecor's eye. But then, he had a lot to be pleased about. He was on the verge of advancing his career by leaps and bounds.

For a Cardassian, the Hoard of Dujonian was the prize to end all prizes, its recovery the accomplishment to eclipse all accomplishments. Indeed, what could have brought more prestige, more glory to Ecor and his superiors, than the retrieval of the Hebitians' legendary glor'ya?

Clearly, Ecor would go to any length to get what he wanted. Almost certainly, he would resort to torture. In fact, the gul was probably savoring the prospect of it even as we confronted one another.

I knew from personal experience how masterful the Cardassians could be at that grisly art. I knew how easily they could destroy their victim's mind as well as his body.

Or, in this case, *her* body.

I gazed at Red Abby and feared what might happen to her. Not because she was weak, but because she was strong . . . because, if I was any judge of character at all, she would sacrifice herself rather than reveal the whereabouts of Richard Brant.

And then, just in case there was any doubt as to Ecor's intentions, he smiled at Red Abby. "I'm glad to have had this chance to meet you. You and I have much to talk about," he told her.

She met his gaze. But again, she fell silent.

For a moment, the gul seemed inclined to say more. Then he gestured and the Cardassians behind us prodded us with the barrels of their weapons. It appeared the show was over.

Madigoor

"HAH," SAID ROBINSON, grinning broadly in his beard. "So Red Abby wasn't at all what she seemed to be."

"Not at all," Picard confirmed.

"People seldom are," the Captain of the *Kalliope* observed.

"Not so," Bo'tex countered. "I am *exactly* what I seem to be."

"More's the pity," Dravvin said under his breath, eliciting a belly laugh from Hompaq.

Bo'tex looked at the Rythrian. "Excuse me?"

Dravvin dismissed the remark with a wave of his hand. "Nothing. Really." Then he turned to Picard. "I've had a couples of run-ins with the Cardassians myself. The second time, I nearly lost my life to them."

"And you'll regale us with that story in due time," said Robinson. "But right now, it's our friend Picard who's spinning the yarn."

The Rythrian regarded Robinson for a moment. Then he inclined his head slightly, causing his ears to flap.

"Of course," Dravvin said flatly. He turned to Picard. "My apologies. Spin away, Captain."

Picard leaned back in his chair and resumed his tale. "As I was saying, the show was over . . ."

The Tale

WE WERE HERDED BACK down the corridor under the careful eyes of our captors and returned to our cargo bay. The rest of Red Abby's crew awaited us there. Or rather, the portion that had survived.

At that point, our guards left, closed the doors behind them, and activated the forcefield. It didn't appear we would be going anywhere.

"What happened?" one of the crewmen wanted to know.

"Where did they take you?" asked Assad.

"They destroyed the *Daring*," Red Abby replied evenly.

The news of their ship's demise made the crewmen's eyes grow round with dread. After all, without a vessel in which to escape, what kind of future could they expect? A life of hard labor in some Cardassian prison camp, ended only by death?

"They wanted us to watch," Red Abby went on. "Me, in particular."

"What for?" someone wondered.

The captain shrugged. "Out of spite, I think, as much as anything else. They *are* Cardassians, remember."

Corbis glared at Red Abby. "I can see them showing *you*—you're the captain." He jerked his head to indicate me and Worf. "But why *him?* And this other one?"

"Because they were working the bridge," Astellanax explained. "At least, that's what our friend the gul told us." He frowned. "They identified us by the sensor readings they took of our bridge."

Corbis turned to me. If looks could have killed, I would have been stricken dead on the spot.

"It's your fault we're here," he snarled.

"My fault? And how do you come to that conclusion?" I asked.

The Pandrilite pointed a meaty blue finger at me. "You were at the helm when the Cardassians showed up, weren't you?" He glared at Worf. "And unless I'm mistaken, the Klingon was at tactical."

My lieutenant raised his chin. "What of it?"

I stepped in front of Worf, coming between him and Corbis. "We did our best," I said. "I can't help it if we were overmatched."

The Pandrilite grunted. "Couldn't you?" He looked around at the others. "I've never seen this Hill character before—and I've been on a lot of voyages to a lot of different places. How do we know he wasn't in the Cardies' pay? How do we know he didn't hand the ship to them on a platter?"

There was a rumble of assent—mostly from the Oord and the Thelurian. But a few others had been swayed by the Pandrilite's speech as well.

"You're insane," I said, refusing to yield an inch. "I was the one who discovered the Cardassians."

"Did you?" Corbis sneered. "Or did you just make it look that way—so you could go on spying for them?"

"I'm not a spy," I told him. "Not any more than you are."

The Pandrilite smiled a nasty smile. "And all we've got to go on is your word, eh? Well, I'll tell you what I think, human. I think it's *you* we've got to thank for where we are." He cast a glance at Worf. "You and your cowardly cur of a Klingon."

That settled it.

It was no small thing to question a Klingon's loyalty. But to question his courage? The accused had little choice but to take the remark as a challenge—and that is precisely the way Worf took it.

I tried to restrain him, but it was no use. Barreling past me, the lieutenant bared his teeth and went for Corbis.

What's more, the Pandrilite was ready for him. When Worf smashed him in the face, he staggered but didn't fall. The Klingon tried to connect with a second punch, but his adversary warded it off—then struck back with a hammerlike blow of his own.

I tried to get between Worf and Corbis, but the Thelurian leaped on me from behind and dragged me down. Digging my elbow into his midsection as hard as I could, I freed myself of his company and got to my feet.

However, my freedom was short-lived. Corbis's other friend, the Oord, bowled me over. By the time I stopped rolling, he was on me again, trapping me beneath his bulk.

I struck the Oord once and then again, but it didn't seem to faze him. If anything, it made him hold on to me that much tighter.

By then, much of the crew was cheering, though I wasn't sure whom they were cheering for. Perhaps they weren't sure, either.

Worf, meanwhile, was standing toe to toe with the Pandrilite, trading one devastating blow after the other. Both fighters were bloodied, but neither seemed likely to yield until he was knocked unconscious—or worse.

"That's enough!" cried Red Abby, her voice cutting through the emotion-laden atmosphere in the cargo bay.

She kicked the Oord in the side with the toe of her boot, doubling him up. With a hard shot to his jaw, I got him to roll off me.

Next, Red Abby tried to separate Corbis and Worf. After all, she was still their captain, still the one to whom they had given their allegiance. It was her job to maintain order.

She might as well have tried to stop a matter-antimatter explosion. The Pandrilite dealt her a backhanded smash to the shoulder, spinning her around so hard she reeled into the bulkhead.

It occurred to me that I might have stopped Worf, at least, with a direct order. However, our comrades didn't know I was his commanding officer and I sincerely wished to keep it that way.

Gritting my teeth, I resigned myself to the physical approach. Needless to say, I had little faith in it at the moment.

But before I could throw myself into the fray again, the door to the cargo bay opened—and a handful of armed Cardassians stepped inside. A hush fell over the prisoners.

Worf and Corbis didn't seem to notice. They kept pummeling each other, making the cargo bay resound with the crack of their blows. That is, until Gul Ecor walked in and gestured to his men.

I cried out a warning, but it was too late. The Cardassians hit my lieutenant and the Pandrilite with a couple of seething, white energy beams, sending them flying off their feet.

For a moment, I feared the beams might have been lethal. Then I saw Worf and Corbis stir, if only feebly, and I knew the Cardassians' weapons had been set merely to stun.

I went over to Worf and knelt beside him. He looked up at me, disgusted with the way the combat had ended, but remarkably lucid for a man who had taken the kind of punishment he had.

"Well," said Ecor, "it seems I've stumbled on a disagreement. I *do* hate to see a lack of harmony amongst my prisoners."

I wondered why he was there. Clearly, not just to break up the fight. He could have sent an underling to do that.

Ecor turned to Red Abby. "I just discovered something interesting," he told her. "At least, I found it so. As it turns out, we have quite a celebrity in our midst."

Red Abby and her men looked at each other. No one had the faintest idea what the Cardassian was talking about.

Suddenly, Ecor turned to me. "Isn't that so . . . Captain Jean-Luc Picard of the Federation *Starship Enterprise?*"

There was silence in the hold for a moment. Shocked silence—and *I* was perhaps more shocked than anyone. I felt all eyes upon me, reinterpreting my presence there, and Worf's as well.

Corbis cursed colorfully beneath his breath. "A damned spy, after all," he rumbled menacingly.

Red Abby's eyes narrowed. "I should have known."

"Well," the gul replied amiably, "you know now."

Briefly, I considered denying my identity—telling Ecor I didn't know what he was talking about. However, this was no wild guess he had made. He obviously knew whereof he spoke.

As I riffled through my options, seeking a way out of my narrowing straits, I realized how the Cardassians had made the identification. I didn't have to wait long before Ecor confirmed it for me.

"In case you were wondering," the gul explained, "every Cardassian warship carries a record of recent encounters with the Federation in its computer. When one of my bridge officers decided you looked familiar, he accessed those records—and came up with a positive match."

It was just as I had suspected. "How enterprising of him," I told Ecor. "No pun intended."

The gul chuckled, obviously savoring his confrontation with me. After all, I had had my share of run-ins with the Cardassians. It would have been a coup for Ecor to bring me back to Cardassia Prime with him.

But he still had a greater coup in mind—the same one Red Abby had set her sights on. For the time being, at least, a trip to Cardassia was hardly at the top of our agenda.

Ecor pressed his palms together. "I must admit," he said, "I believed this was a private expedition at first. A grab for treasure. I see now it was a Starfleet effort all along."

His conclusion couldn't have been further from the truth. However, I wasn't about to mention that. The less he knew, I thought, the better.

"Now, then," the gul declared, turning to Red Abby, "I would very much like to know the coordinates of the Hoard of Dujonian."

The woman remained silent. She didn't deny that she had what Ecor wanted. She just wasn't going to give it to him.

After all, Richard Brant's life hung in the balance. Whatever Red Abby's relationship to him might have been, she obviously didn't want to place the fellow in jeopardy.

Though the Cardassian continued to smile, his eyes took on a decidedly harder cast. "Come now, Captain Brant. I can save you a lot of pain if you divulge the information on your own. That is, without my having to . . . extract it from you."

Red Abby had to be scared out of her wits, but somehow she managed not to show it. "I have nothing to say," she replied, her voice remarkably unwavering under the circumstances.

The muscles rippled in Ecor's jaw. Clearly, he wasn't pleased with her response. As a result, he turned to *me* again.

"What about you, Captain Picard? Will you prove a bit wiser than your colleague and share the coordinates with me?"

"I don't know them," I answered truthfully. "Though if I did," I went on just as truthfully, "I don't know that I'd be inclined to share them."

Out of the corner of my eye, I saw Red Abby glance at me. She seemed surprised. And perhaps, I think, a bit more impressed with me—though it hadn't been my intention to impress her.

Having found a couple of strong links in the chain, Gul Ecor eyed the rest of the crew. He had to have known that Worf, a Klingon, wouldn't crack under his threats. But to his mind, no doubt, there were a great many others who might have.

The Cardassian scanned them, making the same kind of threats he had made to Red Abby and myself. Thadoc seemed unmoved. Astellanax muttered a curse and received a rifle butt in the ribs for it. But in the end, Gul Ecor found his weak link.

It was Sturgis, the navigator. "All right," he said, his complexion pale and waxy with fear. "I'll tell."

Red Abby glared at him and shook her head. "Don't do it," she said.

Sturgis looked at her apologetically. "I can't help it, Captain." He tried to smile and failed badly. "The prospect of torture has never held much appeal for me."

"And what *is* your destination?" Ecor asked him.

Sturgis hesitated for a moment, knowing there would be no turning back once he revealed the information— no returning to Red Abby's fold. He took the plunge anyway.

"Strange as it may seem," he told the gul, "the *Daring* was on its way to Hel's Gate."

At first, I thought I had misheard the man. Then I saw the astonished expressions on everyone's faces—except those of Red Abby and her officers, of course—and I realized I'd heard correctly after all.

No one was more astonished than Gul Ecor. "Hel's Gate?" he echoed. "But how can that be?"

It was a good question—one to which we all wanted to know the answer. Hel's Gate, after all, was a celestial anomaly of great turbulence, which was rumored to emit deadly radiation in powerful waves. No one in his right mind would have made such a place his destination.

And yet, Red Abby had done just that. Or so it appeared.

"To tell you the truth," Sturgis replied, "I don't *know* what the captain had in mind. She never told me that much. But it was the Gate we were heading for, as plain as the nose on my face."

The gul leaned into the man's face. "You're certain of this?"

Sturgis nodded. "Certain."

"No other possibility?"

"None," the navigator confirmed.

Ecor studied him a second longer. Then he gestured to one of his men. "Put him in a cell. And equip it for torture."

Sturgis's eyes opened wide. "What are you saying?" he piped, stricken with fear. "I *told* you what you wanted to know!"

The gul watched as two of his men grabbed the navigator by his arms. "Quite possibly," he told Sturgis, "you *have* been honest with me. If that's so, I'll know it."

"But by then—" the navigator protested.

"By then," Ecor interrupted, "it won't do you any good, I grant you. But it will benefit *me* immensely."

"No!" Sturgis shrieked, struggling against his captors to no avail. "No, dammit, no!"

But his cries fell on deaf ears. The gul pretended not to notice as his men dragged the human away. I exchanged glances with Worf, but we were hardly in a position to help the poor wretch.

"I told you the truth!" Sturgis wailed. "The truth!"

And then he was gone, though the echoes of his screams still remained. Finally, even those were gone.

The irony of Sturgis's plight had not been lost on me. The fellow had betrayed his captain and his crewmates to escape the torture chamber—yet he was to be tortured nonetheless.

A grisly prospect, I reflected. I did not envy him.

Ecor turned to Red Abby then. And to me.

"For the moment," he said, "you've been spared. After all, I can torture you only once—and our discussions will prove more fruitful after I've spent some time with your friend."

The gul's mouth twisted with anticipation. It was the first clear-cut sign of his sadism.

"You see, my friends, getting answers is largely a result of knowing which questions to ask. And before long, I expect, I will have a great many questions for you."

I didn't doubt it for a second. Ecor didn't appear to be the sort who gave up easily.

As I watched, he left the cargo bay, his guards trailing in his wake. Then they were gone and we were left alone to contemplate our fate.

Madigoor

"So your cover was blown," Flenarrh observed.

Picard nodded. "Thoroughly. I was revealed as a Starfleet captain—in the midst of those who had reason to hate and fear Starfleet. It was not a positive development, as you can imagine."

"But . . . were you *truly* headed for Hel's Gate?" Dravvin asked. He sounded more than a little skeptical.

"Yes," said Bo'tex. "Was that really what Red Abby had in mind? Or was it simply what she had told Sturgis?"

"A good question," Picard responded. "In fact, I found myself mulling the same one, as I sat there in the Cardassians' cargo bay. Why on Earth would anyone purposely chart a course for something like Hel's Gate? It seemed foolish, to say the least—perhaps even suicidal."

Robinson eyed him. "And yet?"

Picard shrugged. "I decided to put the question to the only person who would know for certain—Red Abby herself."

"Wasn't she wary of you?" asked Hompaq.

"Naturally," Picard said. "However, I pointed out that we were in the same boat, so to speak. Whatever we had been in the past, we were at that moment fellow prisoners."

"And she accepted the argument?" asked Dravvin.

"Apparently," Picard answered.

The Tale

"Is it true?" I asked.

Red Abby looked at me. "About Hel's Gate, you mean?" She nodded. "It's true all right."

I frowned. "But how *could* it be?"

She chuckled grimly. "I asked the same question. Hel's Gate is a maelstrom, I said. Why the devil would anyone want to go near the place?"

"And?" I prodded.

"And it's a maelstrom all right." Her eyes took on a faraway look. "But it's also a dimensional wormhole of some kind. And beyond it, on the other side, is Dujonian's Hoard."

"You've seen it?" I asked.

Red Abby shook her head. "No." She smiled bravely at me. "I mean not yet. But I will. Bet the farm on it."

I had to admire her courage if not her grasp of the trouble we were in. But she still hadn't satisfied my curiosity.

"If you've never been there yourself . . ." I began.

Red Abby spoke softly, so no one else would hear her. "My brother's been there."

"Your brother," I echoed just as softly. "You mean Richard."

She nodded, a lock of red hair falling across her forehead. "The one in trouble. And the one you're supposed to rescue, I imagine. Or is it strictly the Hoard you're interested in?"

I considered how much I ought to tell her. The part about Richard Brant had become obvious. There didn't seem to be any harm in confirming it.

"Your brother is part of it," I replied. "At least, to me he is. He was Starfleet, after all."

Red Abby smiled a grim smile. "But the Hoard is the bigger part. You don't want it falling into the hands of the Cardassians."

She had hit the nail on the head, of course. I shrugged noncommittally. "I suppose one could read that into it."

The woman laughed. It was a good laugh, an open laugh, not the kind I had heard from her before. "Always so circumspect, you Starfleet types."

"Are we?" I asked.

"Why not come out and say it? You're here to save my brother from a pack of mercenaries. But unlike me, you're not doing it out of any real concern for him. You've got your own agenda. There's no shame in that."

"It's not that simple," I told her.

She grunted. "No, it never is."

Certainly, the woman could be exasperating. "What I mean," I continued, "is that there is no lack of concern for your brother—either on my part or on Starfleet's. But I would be lying if I said it's our *only* concern."

Red Abby leaned back against the bulkhead. "Honesty," she said. "I'm impressed. Especially in light of all the lies you told me."

"Regrettable," I told her. "But necessary."

She looked at her hands, as if she'd suddenly found

something fascinating about them. "Not bad, actually. I really thought you were some kind of adventurer. When I learned you were a Starfleet officer . . . a captain, no less . . . as I say, not bad."

"People don't fool you very often," I observed.

Red Abby turned to me. "No," she agreed, "they don't, now that you mention it. You either, I'd guess."

"Not often," I conceded. "Though you did."

"Me?" she said. "How?"

"I thought you were motivated strictly by greed," I explained. "Now it seems you're out to save your brother from his abductors."

"I didn't make any claims one way or the other," she reminded me.

"That's true," I said. "But you fooled me nonetheless."

For a moment, we looked at each other—not as captain and crewman or as adversaries, but as two people might look at each other. And I found a great deal to like in Abby Brant.

Then she looked away. "What are our chances of getting help from that Starfleet of yours?"

I frowned. "Almost nil. My associate and I were out here very much on our own. Due to the delicate nature of our mission, you understand."

"I do," said Red Abby. "I guess his name's not Mitoc, then?"

I shook my head. "It's Worf."

She grunted softly. "You might as well have called him Worf. I wouldn't have known the difference."

"At the time," I said, "I had no way of knowing that."

Silence again. But this time, she didn't look at me. In fact, she seemed to be making a point of *not* looking at me.

"Have I said something to offend you?" I asked.

Finally, Red Abby looked up. "No," she told me. "You haven't offended me. But you *have* managed to—"

Just then, I heard the cargo bay's door iris open. A handful of Cardassian guards came in, their weapons at the ready. Finally, Gul Ecor entered and stood among them.

"Unfortunately," Ecor announced, "our friend Sturgis didn't survive his interrogation. It seems he wasn't as durable as he looked."

I could hear Abby curse under her breath. What's more, I understood her anger and her pain. In the end, Sturgis had fallen victim to his fear, it's true. But prior to that, he had been a loyal and efficient crewman—a man she had trusted and perhaps even liked.

I, of course, had another reason for mourning the man. As you'll recall, he and I had fought side by side against the Cardassians. For all I knew, Sturgis had saved my life.

"However," the gul went on, either ignorant of Abby's muttered curse or unimpressed by it, "the fellow swore with his dying breath that he hadn't lied to me—and that Hel's Gate was indeed the *Daring*'s destination."

He turned to Red Abby. "That presents me with a problem, Captain Brant. I know where you were headed—but not what you planned on doing when you got there, or how it was going to help you find the Hoard."

"And?" she said.

"And I don't intend to expose my ship and crew to a phenomenon like Hel's Gate until I have a better understanding of the situation."

"You won't get it from me," she told him.

Ecor smiled tautly. "I beg to differ with you." He gestured to his fellow Cardassians. "She's next."

As the soldiers reached for Red Abby, I determined I wouldn't stand by and allow them to take her. The fact that I had little or no chance of stopping them didn't enter into the equation. I simply couldn't let her be seized without a fight.

Apparently, Lieutenant Worf was of the same mind. But then, as I've noted, he is a Klingon.

Since there was a Cardassian standing behind me, I drove my elbow into his ribs. As he doubled over, I shoved him as hard as I could into the bulkhead behind him.

Worf attacked the nearest guard as well, with much the same results. His man lay on the deck, bloodied and gasping for air, before he or anyone else could prevent it.

But that was as far as either of us got. I felt something strike me in the side with the force of a sledgehammer— a directed energy beam, no doubt, fortuitously set on stun. As I lay on the deck, half-numb, I saw my lieutenant had suffered the same fate.

Gul Ecor came to stand over me. "Be patient, Captain Picard. If Captain Brant doesn't prove cooperative, you'll get your turn." He laughed. "In fact, you'll get your turn no matter what. I'm sure there's a good deal I can learn from the commanding officer of a starship."

As I mentioned earlier, I had already suffered at the hands of a Cardassian torture master. I had no desire to suffer that way again.

Still, as Abby was led away, I found I was more concerned for her than I was for myself.

Madigoor

"OUR HERO'S PROSPECTS are not good," the Captain of the *Kalliope* said slyly. "Nor, for that matter, are his friend Red Abby's."

"As is often the case," Dravvin noted, "in a tale of high adventure."

"Indeed," Flenarrh added, "why else would anyone listen to such a tale—except to see how the hero escapes his bad prospects?"

"Sometimes he *doesn't* escape," the Captain of the *Kalliope* said.

"True," Hompaq agreed. "Sometimes he has the good sense to perish. In fact, that is the hallmark of a good adventure story—a brave death in the face of terrible odds."

"I suppose that's good *sometimes,*" Bo'tex allowed.

Hompaq glanced pointedly at Picard and made a derisive sound deep in her throat. "Not sometimes, fat one. *All* the time. An honorable death is not an enemy, to be feared and avoided. It is a prize to be coveted, the ultimate reward for courage and devotion."

Flenarrh chuckled, enjoying the Klingon's remark. "I do believe our friend is baiting you, Captain Picard."

"Baiting him *again*," Dravvin noted.

Picard could see that Hompaq's annoyance with him wasn't going to go away. At least, not without some effort.

He smiled, the picture of tolerance. "As well she should," he replied. "After all, Hompaq makes a valid point—a particularly Klingon point. And like any Klingon, she's willing to stand up for it."

Hompaq's eyes narrowed. "Then you agree with me?"

Picard shook his head. "Not completely, no. I'm not quite so eager to embrace death as you are. But I respect your opinion nonetheless."

Hompaq considered him for what seemed like a long time. "Perhaps I spoke too soon," she conceded at last. "It seems you have an appreciation for the Klingon soul after all."

"A great appreciation," Picard assured her.

"That still doesn't tell us how you escaped your predicament," Bo'tex reminded him.

"Allow me to correct that deficiency," Picard said. "As you'll recall, Red Abby had just been taken away for interrogation. And I was recovering from the stun beam a Cardassian had inflicted on me . . ."

The Tale

AS SOON AS THE CARDASSIANS left us alone, Astellanax knelt by my side. "Are you all right?" he asked.

I nodded. The numbness in my arm and my side was already beginning to wear off, leaving a dull ache in its place.

"I'll live," I told him. I glanced at the door, which had closed in the Cardassians' wake. "But I'm not so sure about your captain. She'll die before she gives Ecor what he wants."

The first officer nodded. "Agreed."

"We can't just let them kill her," protested Thadoc, who was standing behind Astellanax. "We must do something."

"This is a Cardassian warship," Dunwoody reminded him, "full of trained soldiers. It won't be easy."

"No," said another voice. "It won't."

I turned and saw it belonged to Corbis. He looked around the cargo bay at his fellow prisoners, captivating them by virtue of his size.

"I don't know about the rest of you," he went on, "but

I signed on to find treasure—not to risk my skin for a captain I hardly know."

"She is not just our captain," Thadoc countered. "She is one of us."

"And if I don't do something to help her," said Astellanax, "what right have I got to expect help when they take *me* away?"

"Well said," I declared, getting to my feet—no easy task, I might add, but one I deemed necessary. "However, Mr. Dunwoody has a point. As I told Red Abby herself, there is no easy way out of here."

"Oh, no?" asked a broad, dark-haired Tellarite named Gob. His tiny eyes squinted at me expectantly.

Corbis grunted, picking up on the Tellarite's meaning. "Not even when we've got a high-and-mighty Starfleet captain among us?" He turned to Worf. "And his Klingon lapdog?"

I eyed my lieutenant, counseling patience with my glance. Somehow, he found the wherewithal to embrace it.

"Not even then," I told the Pandrilite reasonably. "Certainly, I have a working knowledge of Cardassian vessels and the technologies that drive them. But before I can use that knowledge to advantage, we've got to get out of this cargo bay."

"Then, let's do it," Astellanax said. He looked around. "There's got to be a way out of here. It's just a matter of finding it."

I frowned. The Orion was long on enthusiasm but short on suggestions. And as it happened, I'd been racking my brain for a way out since the Cardassians threw us in there.

Assad pointed to a narrow, raised section of ceiling running from one bulkhead to another. If you've ever seen the schematics for a Cardassian vessel, you know it contained power-distribution circuitry.

"If we could get up there," he said, "maybe we could

short out the ship's energy grid." He looked around at his fellow prisoners. "It's worth a try, isn't it?"

Worf scowled. "Even if there was a way for us to reach it, we would be risking an explosion that would rip this bay apart."

Astellanax started to suggest it might not be so bad a risk after all. I emphasize the word "started," because at that moment we heard the shrill complaint of a half-dozen klaxons.

Clearly, something had gone wrong on the warship. Something *serious,* I told myself, with a certainty that depended on instinct more than logic.

I looked at Worf, wondering what it could be. An accident in the engine room? Or perhaps the approach of an enemy?

Either way, it represented a danger to us—one we were helpless to do anything about. If something was amiss, the Cardassians would likely worry about themselves first and about us not at all.

Then something else happened. We felt a jolt, right through the deckplates. The lights went out at the same time, leaving us nothing to see by except the ghostly glow of blue-green emergency strips.

Corbis moved to the doors and pounded on them with the flat of his big, blue hand. "Let us out!" he cried.

I knew he'd get no satisfactory response. As it happened, he got no response at all.

But that was good—the best outcome we could have hoped for, in fact. It meant our guards had abandoned us to attend to an emergency elsewhere on the ship—and with the power that maintained the force field down, the only thing that stood between ourselves and our freedom was the doors themselves.

Standing beside the Pandrilite, I tried to dig my fingers into the tiny crevice between the rhodinium surfaces.

"What are you doing?" asked Thadoc.

"Trying to pry the doors open," I explained. "And if it's all the same to you, I could use some help."

Even before I spoke, Worf had come over to join me. As he and Thadoc dug their fingers into the opening, Corbis lent his efforts, as well.

"Heave!" I cried.

We heaved. The doors parted ever so slightly.

"Heave!" I cried again.

This time, with a little better grip, we made more progress. A space the width of two of my fingers opened between the doors.

"Heave!" I cried a third time.

We put our shoulders and our backs into it, tugging as hard as we could. I felt some unseen restraint give way and the doors slid back into their wall-pockets, clearing the way for our escape.

The corridor outside our cell was dark as well, only the lighting strips providing illumination. With a cheer, the other prisoners pushed us into it, unmindful of what we might find there. Fortunately, there wasn't a single Cardassian in sight—but that didn't mean it would stay that way.

Even if all other systems were down, internal sensors from other parts of the ship might pick up the movements of so many beings. It would only be a moment or two before the Cardassians realized what had happened, and less than a minute before they responded.

Two things were clear to me. First, we had to go on the offensive. Second, if we didn't recover Red Abby immediately, we might never get another chance to do so.

And there was only one place they would keep her.

"This way," I shouted over the tumult of voices, and started down the corridor toward the nearest lift.

"Where are you going?" asked Astellanax.

"The gul's quarters," I told him.

"Why there?" asked Thadoc.

117

"Because," I said, "that's where we'll find your captain, assuming she's still alive."

"Wait a minute!" someone bellowed.

The Oord—Corbis's friend from the melee in the mess hall—stepped forward with a belligerence characteristic of his species. He made an exaggerated gesture of dismissal with his arms.

"I don't give a *damn* about the captain," he rumbled. "I want to know where the escape craft are."

More than a dozen voices went up in support of the Oord's demand. With the casualties we had sustained on the *Daring* and the loss of Sturgis, that represented almost half our number.

But there was no time to argue. "Very well," I said, pointing past them. "They're over there. Two decks down."

The Oord looked at me with narrowed eyes, no doubt wondering if I had any reason to lie to him. Then he took off in the direction I'd indicated, with the green-splotched Thelurian and several others on his heels.

To my surprise, Corbis wasn't one of them. The Pandrilite watched his friends go for a second, then turned to me. He seemed ready to follow where I led—at least for the moment.

Suddenly, the deck rocked beneath our feet, forcing us to grab the bulkheads for support. I was no longer willing to accept the accident theory. More and more, it was becoming clear to me that the ship was under attack—though I couldn't divine by whom and for what reason.

"The captain!" Astellanax cried, even before we'd recovered.

Thrusting myself away from the bulkhead, I made my way toward the lift. Ideally, I'd have proceeded with the kind of caution we had employed on the *Daring,* but there simply wasn't time for that.

So when we came around a corner and met our first

squad of Cardassians, we were almost nose to nose with them before either party knew it.

As we were unarmed, the close quarters worked to our advantage. I drove an uppercut into the jaw of one Cardassian while Worf decked a second with an open backhand. Corbis lifted a third soldier and sent him flying into his comrades, just as Thadoc used a Romulan lightning jab to crush the windpipe of a fourth man.

The fighting was savage and unrestrained, but mercifully quick. And when the proverbial dust cleared, our side had emerged victorious. In fact, we hadn't lost a single combatant. Knowing how lucky we'd been, we grabbed whatever arms we could and surged down the corridor.

Reaching the lift, we jammed in and Worf programmed it for the main deck. I half-expected the compartment to halt in midtransit, interdicted by a command from the bridge. But it did nothing of the kind.

While we were in the lift, the ship lurched twice. The second time was the worst one yet. All the more reason to move quickly, I mused.

When the doors opened, I took a quick look around in the darkened corridor. Seeing no evidence of an ambush, I tightened my grasp on my Cardassian pistol and led the way to Gul Ecor's suite.

Our goal was almost in view, I told myself. There was a chance we would make it—an outcome on which I wouldn't have wagered a strip of latinum just a few minutes earlier.

We came to the end of the corridor, turned right and then right again. And there before us, not more than fifty meters away, was the entrance to the gul's quarters. Unguarded, no less.

It seemed too easy. And it was.

Someone cried out and we whirled. A moment later,

the Cardassians' energy beams exploded in the darkness. All but one of them missed.

In the eerie half-light of the emergency strips, Astellanax glanced just once at the blackened, oozing mess that had been his stomach. His eyes grew round and wide. Raising his weapon, he fired off a blast. Then he toppled forward, dead before he hit the ground.

The rest of us fired as well, sobered by the Orion's destruction. I regret to say he was not the only casualty we suffered in that encounter. One of the humans among us cried out and crumpled, followed by a Bajoran and a squat, light-haired Tellarite.

Still, we created equal havoc in the ranks of the Cardassians. Before long, we had forced them to retreat to the joining of corridors behind them.

"The gul's quarters!" I rasped, ducking another flash of deadly energy. "Move if you value your lives!"

I didn't dare check to see who had responded to my command. I was too busy laying down cover fire for them, with Lieutenant Worf on one side of me and Corbis on the other.

"Picard!" a voice said, crackling in the darkness. "Quickly!"

It was a woman who had called me—and not just any woman. The summons had come from the throat of Red Abby.

"Dammit, Picard, get in here!" she cried.

As if to emphasize the urgency of her summons, a whole new flood of Cardassians filled the corridor, stepping over the bodies of their fallen comrades. Worf and Corbis and I retreated as one, continuing to provide cover for the other prisoners.

Then we ducked into the gul's quarters, and the door irised closed in our wake. It cut off any possibility of our being hit by enemy fire—temporarily, at least.

In the muted blue-green glow of the emergency lighting, I turned to Red Abby. She was hefting a Cardassian energy rifle, scanning the ranks of those who had retreated into the room with me.

Abruptly, she turned to me. "Astellanax?" she asked, her brow creased deeply with concern.

I shook my head. "He didn't make it."

Madigoor

FLENARRH SIGHED and shook his head. "I was hoping," he
said, "that Astellanax would survive this adventure."

The Captain of the *Kalliope* nodded. "I was beginning
to like him."

"So was I," Picard replied. "He was loyal, depend-
able—all the things a first officer should be."

"He was a warrior," Hompaq said. "He died as one."

Picard decided Hompaq's epitaph was as good as any
he could have come up with. Satisfied, he went on with
his story.

The Tale

RED ABBY WAS SADDENED by the Orion's death—that much was clear. But she didn't let it incapacitate her.

"What about the others?" she inquired.

"Some chose to leave in a shuttle while they could. Those you see elected to stay and effect a rescue."

Red Abby spared them a glance. There was gratitude in it, spoken without words but sincere nonetheless.

Then she grabbed my arm. "We don't have much time," she said, and pulled me in the direction of the next room.

Through the open archway, I could see a shadowy pair of legs lying on the gray, carpeted floor. Unless I was mistaken, they belonged to Gul Ecor. Yet, the last I had seen of the gul, he was accompanied by a contingent of guards.

I turned to Red Abby. "What happened?"

"The lights," she said, "couldn't have gone out at a better time."

She didn't seem inclined to provide more of an

explanation than that. But then, she didn't have to. I had an imagination.

As I entered the room, I saw that Ecor wasn't the only one lying there. Two of his guards were sprawled on the floor as well. I didn't need a medical officer to tell me all three Cardassians were dead.

Red Abby led me across the room to the gul's workstation, which stood in the starlight cast by an oval-shaped observation port. The workstation would give me access to the warship's entire command network—assuming, of course, that the system was still operational.

Some of the others entered behind us and moved the corpses over to a bulkhead. Perhaps *pitched* them would be more accurate.

Again, the deck bucked beneath us. Reminded that time was of the essence, I sat down at the chair in front of the workstation, propped my energy rifle against the bulkhead beside me, and got to work. A minute or so later, I found the entry point I was looking for.

It gave me access to not only the ship's command logs, but its sensor logs as well. I took a moment to scan them, to assemble the pieces of the puzzle. What I learned caused me to exclaim in surprise.

"What is it?" asked Red Abby.

I looked at her. "We've been attacked all right—and not just by anyone. It seems our adversary is a Romulan warbird—C Class."

Dunwoody cursed. Worf scowled at the mention of the Romulans, for whom he had no great love. After all, they had killed his parents in the now-infamous Khitomer Massacre.

I turned back to the monitor. "The Romulan commander, an individual who identifies himself as Tacanus, claims the Cardassians were trespassing in Romulan space."

"A likely story," Red Abby commented.

"They're after the Hoard of Dujonian," Worf observed.

"Like everyone else," Assad noted.

"What do we do now?" asked Dunwoody.

Red Abby bit her lip. "This tub is no match for even a C Class warbird. It's a wonder it's held out this long."

Our ship shuddered, as if for emphasis. Not that any was required, mind you. We were acutely aware of our disadvantage.

"If the Romulans win," I said, "it won't help to try to escape in a shuttlecraft. They'll hunt us down like Gosalian hacklehawks descending on a field mouse."

"Agreed," said Red Abby. "Somehow, we've got to stand up to the Romulans and beat them." She looked around. "Any ideas?"

No one seemed to have one, at first. Then it hit me, like a phaser beam on a heavy stun setting.

"If Worf's right about the Romulans coveting the Hoard," I said, "they won't be content to just destroy the Cardassians. They'll want to interrogate them as the Cardassians interrogated us."

Corbis eyed me. "So?"

"What he's saying," Thadoc informed the Pandrilite, "is the Romulans will have to send boarding teams to take prisoners—or at least, beam some Cardassians onto their vessel."

"And they can't do either of those things," said Dunwoody, "unless they drop their shields for a moment."

I nodded. "Precisely. And that's when they'll be vulnerable."

Understanding dawned in Red Abby's eyes. "Very clever. But we'll need to get to a transporter room."

"We will indeed," I replied thoughtfully, weathering yet another quaking of the deckplates.

And yet, as far as we knew, there were still Cardassians

laying in wait for us outside the gul's suite. Clearly, we would have to get past them in order to reach our objective.

Once again, my knowledge of Cardassian ship design stood us in good stead. I pulled my chair halfway across the room until it stood directly beneath an oval-shaped vent in the ceiling.

"What is he doing?" Corbis wondered.

"Your guess is as good as mine," said Gob.

Stepping up onto the chair, I pried the vent cover loose and stuck my head into the opening. A rather ample passageway was revealed to me—much larger than the vent itself had suggested.

"Of course," said Thadoc, a note of admiration in his voice.

"A ventilation shaft," Red Abby noted, for those who still hadn't figured it out. "Where does it go, Picard?"

"Not very far," I told her. "The ventilation nexus for this section of the ship is only about fifty meters away. But it should be enough to get us past the Cardassians watching our door."

Dunwoody grunted. "They pulled the same trick on us back on the *Daring*. Crawling through the ventilation shafts, I mean."

I glanced at him, remembering all too vividly the vicious nature of that firefight. "That's correct," I said. "And I see no reason why we should not return the favor."

"Nor do I," said Red Abby.

"Then, follow me," I told her, and hoisted myself up into the shaft.

She followed. So did the others, including Lieutenant Worf. I led them along the length of the shaft, bypassing several vents until I came to the one I was looking for.

Peering through its slats, I checked to see if there were any Cardassians in the immediate vicinity. The corridor seemed empty in the glow of the emergency strips, though a bulkhead panel at the far end had exploded and was sparking savagely.

Satisfied that we wouldn't be dropping into a trap, I removed the vent cover and lowered myself to the floor. Phaser in hand, I looked around. There was still no sign of trouble.

I gestured for the others to descend, as well. They did this with the utmost dispatch, ghostly figures in a taut, blue twilight. Then I led the way down the corridor, Worf and Red Abby right behind me.

My comrades and I negotiated passageway after twisting passageway, enduring one vicious jolt after another as the warship absorbed the Romulans' attacks. After a while, we came to a corridor filled with smoking, sparking chaos, and a slew of Cardassian corpses.

We made our way through it slowly, carefully, unable to see more than a few inches in front of our faces. The smoke seared our throats and invaded our lungs, until we were coughing as much as breathing.

The skin on the back of my neck prickled. I felt as if, at any moment, I would be cut in half by a Cardassian disruptor beam.

Fortunately, it didn't happen. We came to the end of the corridor without either firing or being fired upon. As I wiped my watering eyes and proceeded through the thinning smoke, I saw what looked a great deal like the transparent doors of a Cardassian transporter facility.

It was a dozen meters ahead, perhaps less. What's more, it appeared to be unguarded—but as we had seen before with regard to the Cardassians, appearances could be lethally misleading.

As it happened, I was still in the lead at that point. With the utmost caution, I advanced on the transporter facility. When I got close enough, its door began to iris open.

Madigoor

PICARD PAUSED to take a sip of his wine. He was approaching the bottom of the glass.

"And?" said Bo'tex. "What did you find?"

"What do you think?" asked Hompaq. "The place was as empty as a poor man's feast hall."

"Empty?" said the Captain of the *Kalliope*. He stroked his beard. "Why would you say that?"

"Because they are Cardassians," the Klingon spat. "If they had the brains to safeguard a transporter facility, they would never have lost Dujonian's Hoard in the first place."

Robinson chuckled. "A good point."

"Perhaps it is, at that," said Flenarrh.

Dravvin turned to Picard. "And *was* it empty?"

Picard set his glass down. "Not exactly," he replied.

The Tale

THE PLACE WAS GUARDED BY a single Cardassian—one who had obviously been surprised by the opening of the door. As I spotted him, he was still drawing his disruptor pistol.

Leveling it, he fired at me. I fired as well.

Luck was on my side. I dispatched the fellow with my first shot.

Of course, we didn't yet know he was alone. We had to approach the facility carefully, looking and listening for evidence of other Cardassians. Finally, satisfied the place was secure, we swarmed inside.

Like every other place on that vessel, it was cast in a blue-green glow. Immediately, I located the room's control console and commandeered it. Presetting as many controls as possible, I obtained a lock on the Romulan ship and waited for its commander to do as I had predicted.

By then, the doors had closed behind us, fortifying us against unwanted interruptions. Corbis came up beside me.

"What now?" he asked.

"Now we exercise patience," I replied.

"Patience?" he said, as if it were a curse.

I nodded. "That's right."

As it turned out, we needed quite a bit of it. The minutes dragged by, unmindful of our anxiety. We looked at one another, searching for answers our comrades couldn't provide.

As captains of your own vessels, you know uncertainty is a terrible thing. It can gnaw at you until your very sanity gives way. We began to get a taste of that in the Cardassian transporter room.

After a while, we wondered if we had guessed wrong about the Romulans' plans. Perhaps they had already obtained the information they needed. Perhaps, in destroying our Cardassian captors, they were merely eliminating a competitor for the Hoard.

I had already begun to consider alternative schemes, none of which was particularly satisfactory, when the sensors showed me what I had been hoping so desperately to see. The Romulans had dropped their deflector shields. Almost at the same time, they began to conduct transporter activity on one of their middle decks.

Encouraged, I activated the Cardassian transporter system and darted across the room. The Cardassian version of a transporter pad wasn't very impressive-looking, but it was very nearly as efficient as the Federation model. Taking my place on it alongside Abby, Thadoc, Corbis, and three other men, I drew my phaser and waited.

In a heartbeat, we found ourselves on the Romulan bridge.

The commander of the warbird was sitting in a central chair with a rounded back. He was surrounded by seven or eight officers tending to various duties, their faces caught in the glow of bright green status screens on the bulkheads around them. Before they could register our presence or react to it, the place came alive with a host of diamond-blue energy beams.

Every one of the Romulans fell instantly—with one exception, and Thadoc took that one out with a blow to the back of the neck. Worf and the rest of our comrades materialized in the next second or two, but to their chagrin there was nothing for them to do. A bizarre stillness reigned as the magnitude of our victory sank in.

Through sheer audacity, we had taken over the bridge of a Romulan warbird—and as far as we knew, no one on the vessel except us had any inkling of it. Of course, that would change soon enough.

Advancing to the Romulan commander's seat, I moved his unconscious form aside. Then I turned to Thadoc.

"We need a security lockout," I said. "Can you give us one?"

I was only guessing that he'd had some experience serving on Romulan vessels. Being only half-Romulan, he might not have. It didn't occur to me that, even if he did have the expertise, he might not be willing to apply it on my behalf.

After all, we were no longer fighting for our lives in some corridor. We were on a bridge again, even if it wasn't that of the *Daring*. The situation cried out for a captain—and Thadoc turned to the one he had in mind for the position.

In other words, Red Abby.

It was no time for politics. Taking the woman by the arm, I pulled her off to the side, where we could speak one-on-one.

"Listen," I said, "I don't care who sits in the center seat once we have secured this vessel. But for now, I need the cooperation of everyone—you included."

She frowned, clearly reluctant to comply. But after a moment, she turned to Thadoc.

"Do whatever he says," she commanded.

Without a word, Thadoc opened the Romulan commander's control panel and gave me the lockout I had requested. "From this point on," he announced, "no one will be able to enter the bridge without our permission."

"Sounds good to me," Dunwoody remarked.

Thadoc turned to me. "What next?"

I didn't need much time to think about it. "Conduct an emergency override, deactivating all transporter facilities. Then check to see how many Romulans have already been sent to the Cardassian ship."

Again, Thadoc complied. After a second or so, he looked up. "Transporters are all locked down. As for how many have left the warbird . . ." He shook his head. "All boarding parties are still here."

"No one left?" I asked. "Are you sure?"

His expression told me he was *very* sure.

I frowned. "Some astute Romulan officer must have noticed our transport and called a halt to the boarding operation."

"Let's make sure the situation doesn't change," said Red Abby. She turned to Thadoc. "Raise the shields."

He nodded. "Done."

Red Abby looked at me, the epitome of cooperation. "What now?" she asked.

"Now," I told her, "I give them their walking papers. Mr. Thadoc, would you activate the ship's intercom?"

It took only a moment for him to do as I had requested. Choosing my words judiciously, I addressed the warbird's crew, trusting the system's translation protocols to make my announcement understandable to them.

"Attention," I said. "We have secured control of your vessel."

A chorus of cheers went up from the throats of Red Abby's men. Or most of them, anyway. Red Abby herself remained silent. If she harbored any resentment toward me, she didn't show it.

Not that I would have stepped aside in any case. I was clearly better prepared for this stage of the operation than she was.

"At this time," I continued, "we recommend you leave the ship by any means available to you."

Thadoc glanced at me, his brows raised in surprise.

"They are Romulans," he whispered, too softly to be heard over the intercom system. "That recommendation will *not* sit well with them."

"I'm aware of that," I whispered back. "But they are also painfully vulnerable under the circumstances. And though I have no desire to take advantage of their vulnerability, they have no way of knowing that."

In fact, the Romulans had no idea who I was or what I was capable of. What's more, I had no intention of enlightening them.

"It's all right," Red Abby told Thadoc. "Picard's got the ball." She looked at me. "Let's see if he can run with it."

If it was a vote of confidence, it was hardly a resounding one. Nonetheless, I went on.

"I will allow you to make use of all shuttles and life-pods," I told the crew. "If you decline to do so, I will cut off your life support and you will die slowly for a lost cause. The choice is yours."

At that point, I terminated the communication. Worf was standing in a corner from which he could keep an eye on the Romulans lying about the bridge. He nodded approvingly.

"Do you think they'll respond to your generosity?" Assad asked.

"I suspect they will," I told him. "But one never knows. There are Romulans and there are Romulans."

A moment later, an indicator lit up on the commander's board. Someone was boarding one of the life-pods.

"I've got at least one taker," I noted.

In the next several seconds, I saw five more indicators.

Three of them were life-pods, the others shuttles. Obviously, at least part of the crew had decided to take me up on my offer.

"It's working," Worf observed.

"So it is," Thadoc said. He looked at me. "But what do you propose to do if there are stragglers? Romulans who would rather die than renege on their oaths and abandon their ship?"

It was a fair question.

"I have a plan for them," I assured him. I jerked my head to indicate the Romulans we had knocked unconscious. "Just as I have a plan for our sleepy friends here."

"What about the Cardassians?" Corbis asked.

Another fair question. To be sure, something had to be done about them.

I turned to Thadoc again. "The Cardassians must be caught in some kind of tractor beam. See if you can release them."

As he got to work, I looked at the viewscreen. The Cardassian warship hung there in space, battered and blackened, its hull glowing a savage red in the places where it had taken the most damage.

After a few moments, the vessel began to drift away from us. With all it had gone through, its crew had no control over its movements.

"There," I said. "That should take care of the Cardassians."

The warship would hang in space like a broken toy until such time as its fellow Cardassians saw fit to look for it. It might take quite some time, of course. However, we were showing our captors more kindness than they had shown us.

Meanwhile, the Romulan evacuation was proceeding apace, shuttles and life-pods issuing from the warbird in several different places. But it seemed Thadoc had been right to ask about stragglers. Some of the escape vehicles were being ignored, even in what should have been the most populous sections of the ship.

Red Abby seemed to have noticed as well. "If you've really got a plan," she told me, "this would be a good time to implement it."

I checked the sensor readout on the commander's control panel. Three of the shuttles had left their bays, but two were still close to the ship. I turned to Thadoc and indicated the Romulans lying among us.

"Obtain a transporter lock on them," I said, "and beam them onto one of those shuttles. Then find another half-dozen Romulans and do the same, again and again—until we're alone on this vessel."

The helmsman regarded me for a full second, no doubt trying to find a flaw in my scheme. Apparently, he was unsuccessful, because he eventually bent to his task.

As he worked the warbird's transporter controls, the Romulan bridge crew began to shimmer. Almost instantly, it was gone. And in the next few minutes, the same thing took place all over the ship.

Thadoc seemed to be enjoying his work. But in time it ended, as all good things will.

Red Abby looked around and nodded. "Well," she observed, "I suppose that's one way to get rid of unwanted guests."

I found myself smiling—not so much at the quip itself as at the tone she had used. It was the first time I had heard the woman even come close to making a joke.

"So it is," I agreed.

Thadoc looked at Red Abby. "We should get out of here. There may be additional warbirds in the vicinity."

She looked at me. I nodded, telling her the captain's chair was hers again. I would keep my end of the bargain.

"You've got the helm," she told Thadoc. "Chart us a course for Hel's Gate."

Madigoor

"A BOLD MOVE," said Hompaq, "this transport onto the enemy's ship—even if *was* just a pack of Romulans."

Flenarrh looked at her from beneath his white tuft. "I wouldn't take the Romulans lightly if I were—"

The Klingon snarled at him.

"—me," he finished lamely.

"I'm impressed, too," said the Captain of the *Kalliope*. "I don't think I ever would have thought of that tactic myself."

Robinson chuckled. "Don't be so hard on yourself, lad. Where you come from, they don't *have* transporters."

The Captain of the *Kalliope* grunted good-naturedly. "That's true. Still, it was a clever maneuver."

Dravvin stroked his chin. "From what you've said, Picard, there couldn't have been more than thirteen or fourteen of you left to man the warbird—and to effect repairs where it was damaged in the battle."

"That's correct," said Picard.

136

"It doesn't seem any of you would have gotten much rest," the Rythrian noted.

"Not much at all," Picard agreed, "though it was sorely needed after all we had been through."

"I can't operate without rest," Bo'tex remarked. "No Caxtonian can. If we don't get our beauty sleeps, we're liable to run our ship into the nearest asteroid belt."

"I'm sure you're exaggerating," said Robinson.

"Not one iota," Bo'tex insisted. "Ever hear of Captain In'dro?"

Robinson shook his head. "I don't believe so, no."

"He and his crew were models of Caxtonian efficiency. Then they were kept up one night by engine noise. The next day, they fell asleep on their bridge and got caught in a subspace anomaly." Bo'tex paused for dramatic effect. "They were never heard from again."

"Enlightening," Dravvin said dryly. "But tell me this, Captain Bo'tex . . . if In'dro and his crew were never heard from again, how do you know exactly what happened to them?"

The Caxtonian stared at him for a moment. "I . . . er, that is . . ."

The Rythrian grunted. "As I thought."

The Captain of the *Kalliope* turned to Picard. "While our colleague Bo'tex is trying to answer Captain Dravvin's question, you may want to go on with your story."

Picard nodded. "Indeed. As I was saying, rest was certainly on all our minds. And repairs were needed as well. But before she addressed those concerns, Red Abby had something to say to us. To *all* of us."

The Tale

As you may have gathered, this wasn't a woman who liked to stand on ceremony. She spoke plainly and from the heart.

"When a captain picks her crew," she said, "there's no science to it. All she can do is listen to her instincts and hope they're right more often than they're wrong."

Red Abby paused. "Astellanax was one of the best choices my instincts ever made. He was smart and diligent and faithful, and that's pretty much what you want from a first officer. I'm grateful for all he did for me, not just on this voyage but also on those that preceded it."

Her gaze seemed to soften as she scanned the remnants of her crew, her disordered red hair catching light from the Romulan monitors. She was taking some care in selecting her words.

"I want to thank everyone on this bridge as well," she said. "Without you, I'd still be holed up in that gul's quarters, waiting for the Romulans to come and drag me out. As long as I live, I'll never forget your loyalty or your courage. And with luck, I'll still be able to reward you for what you've done . . . with Dujonian's treasure."

I was touched by Red Abby's words. Judging by the looks on their faces, I'd say my comrades were as well. At that moment, inspired by her gratitude, they would gladly have followed her into hell.

Or, at the least, through Hel's Gate.

Corbis, perhaps, was the lone exception to the rule. He stood in the corner, scowling. But if he was less than electrified by his captain's speech, he kept it to himself.

"Now, then," Red Abby went on in a more business-like tone, "we'll need to assess damage and make repairs. If we run into another hostile ship, Romulan or other-wise—and at this point, it wouldn't surprise me in the least—I don't want to get caught with our pants down."

"Nor do I," I replied. "On the other hand, we need some sleep. We've barely shut our eyes in the last two days."

"I agree," said Red Abby.

She set up a schedule of duty assignments. Thadoc and I would eventually take turns at the helm—though until I familiarized myself with the Romulan control panel, we would have to work together.

Worf and Dunwoody would switch off at tactical. The remainder of the crew would try to effect repairs as best they could, with at least two teams roaming the warbird at any given time.

Whoever wasn't on duty would find a place to sleep. Whoever *was* on duty would find something useful to do. There were no exceptions—not even Red Abby herself, apparently. To make that clear, she volunteered to begin the first shift by leading a repair squad.

I was pleasantly surprised by the woman's egalitarian-ism. After all, I had seen her reluctance to cede me the captain's chair even temporarily.

Then again, as I noted earlier, we were no longer on the *Daring*. We were ensconced aboard a Romulan vessel, with which Red Abby had little familiarity. It made sense for her to help however she could.

"If there's the least sign of trouble," she told Thadoc pointedly, "contact me immediately."

"I will," he assured her.

Then Red Abby departed with the repair teams, leaving Thadoc, myself, and Worf on the bridge alone. While my lieutenant busied himself running diagnostic routines at tactical, Thadoc taught me what he knew about the Romulan helm console.

As it turned out, it wasn't so different from the Klingon version, which I had come to know in my dealings with the Empire. Nor did the similarity come as a surprise to me.

As you may know, the Klingons and the Romulans were allies for a while, in the middle of the twenty-third century. During this period, they pooled their expertise in a great many areas of military technology, ship design being only one of them.

"It's quite simple, really," Thadoc told me.

I nodded. "Of course, I won't feel comfortable until I've performed some maneuvers myself."

He shrugged. "There's no time like the present. Perform some maneuvers now, if you like."

I took Thadoc up on his offer. Without diverging substantially from our course, I put the warbird through one rigor after another, testing the precision of her steering system and the responsiveness of her engines.

I was pleased with the results. While the Romulan helm *looked* like its Klingon counterpart, there was no comparison between the two systems in terms of performance. The Romulans had clearly outdistanced their former allies over the last hundred years.

"She turns on a dime," I said.

Thadoc looked at me quizzically.

"An old expression," I explained. "It means she handles well."

He grunted softly. "That, she does."

His eyes lost their focus for a moment. It seemed to me Thadoc was lost in some long-ago memory.

"You served on a warbird," I noted, guessing that that was what he was thinking about.

"I did," he confirmed. "For six years."

"As helmsman?" I asked.

"Eventually," Thadoc told me.

"But you left."

He nodded. "I did indeed."

"Didn't you like it anymore?" I asked.

Thadoc looked at me. "I was good at what I did, make no mistake. Still, I was not held in wide esteem. Perhaps it was the Bolian blood in me, I don't know. A few years ago, shortly after the Klingon Civil War, our warbird ran into a Federation vessel in unaligned space."

I thought for a moment. "The *Potemkin?*"

He seemed impressed with my knowledge of the incident. "Yes. In any case, we lost the encounter. My commander needed a scapegoat so he wouldn't have to take the blame himself."

I understood. "And he made you that scapegoat."

"I was accused of incompetence," said Thadoc, "and a failure to heed my commander's orders. All I could do was exercise my right of statement and deny the charges. In the end, it did me no good whatsoever."

"You were sentenced to death?" I asked.

He shook his hairless, blue head. "My commander knew I had done nothing wrong, and he was not entirely without conscience. He saw to it I was sent to a penal colony instead."

"Charitable of him," I commented.

"En route there," said Thadoc, "our transport vessel ran into a subspace anomaly. There was considerable damage to the ship—hull breaches and the like. Casualties ran heavy. As luck would have it, most of the survivors were prisoners like myself."

141

He stopped himself. After a moment, he frowned.

"No," he decided. "They were prisoners—but not like myself. The others were violent, desperate men, guilty of the crimes for which they were to be punished. I alone was innocent."

I asked him what happened then. Thadoc told me, dredging up memory after vivid memory.

"The prisoners took over the ship, but it was useless to them. The engines had been damaged irreparably by the anomaly. We couldn't go anywhere. Worse, we discovered a buildup of energies in the artificial singularity that powered the warp drive. You're the captain of a starship; I don't need to tell you what kind of threat that represented."

"You were in danger of being destroyed," I said.

"Precisely," he confirmed. "Fortunately, the buildup was a slow one. We sent out a distress call and hoped for the best. Days went by, with no response. We wondered if our communication equipment had been damaged as well, in some way we couldn't detect."

"Entirely possible," I remarked.

"Time passed painfully," said Thadoc, "with no improvement and none in sight. Tempers flared. There were arguments—and bloodshed, even among the prisoners. Every day, it seemed, someone was found dead in some corridor. The last of the guards was killed just for spite. And all the while, the singularity grew more and more unstable."

Hellish, I thought. But I didn't want to interrupt.

"There were several attempts on my life," he noted, "though I kept mostly to myself and offended no one. The first few times, I was able to ward off my assailants. In time, however, I was forced to kill them to keep them from killing me.

"Then the energies in our power source, which had been building slowly to that point, began to accelerate. If we were lucky, we realized, we had a few hours left. With no possibility of survival and no fear of punishment, my shipmates tore at each other like fiends, their hatreds fueled by the pettiest of slights.

"Except for me. I alone fought to defend myself, though I had no more reason to hope than they did. I sequestered myself on the bridge, which no one else seemed to care about any longer, and endured the sounds of the others slaughtering one another.

"It was fortunate that I was there," said Thadoc, "and not somewhere else, or I might have missed the communication that lit up the tactical console. Apparently, someone had received our distress call and responded. What's more, they were nearly in transporter range."

He looked at me. "It was the *Daring.*"

I nodded. No wonder the helmsman was so loyal. Red Abby had taken him off a doomed ship. She had saved his life, and perhaps his sanity as well.

"At great risk to herself and her vessel," he told me, "the captain transported me off, along with the others who still lived. There were shockingly few of them left.

"Once our injuries were treated, we were invited to tell Red Abby our stories. Mine was the only one she believed. She put off the others at the nearest port of call, giving them a chance to make of themselves what they could. I, on the other hand, was invited to join her crew.

"Unable to return to Romulus, faced with the possibility of having to sign on with someone less scrupulous, I took Red Abby up on her offer. Nor," said Thadoc, "have I ever had reason to regret it."

I smiled. "Not even now? With our numbers depleted and Hel's Gate looming on the horizon?"

He didn't hesitate to answer. "Not even now."

Madigoor

PICARD WAS ABOUT TO SAY MORE . . . when something long and green skittered across the table.

Suddenly, the intruder stopped and looked around with almost comical intensity. It was some kind of lizard, it seemed—a gecko, unless the captain was mistaken—and contrary to his earlier assessment, it wasn't entirely green after all. In fact, it wore a sprinkling of bright yellow spots.

Bo'tex pushed his chair back, his face twisted with loathing. "What *is* that?" he demanded.

"It's a gecko," said the Captain of the *Kalliope*.

Picard nodded. "That's what I thought."

"As I recall," said Robinson, "the little fellows are found in the tropics. And don't worry, Captain Bo'tex. As fearsome as they look, their diet is restricted to insects."

The Caxtonian scowled. "Very funny."

"Where did the thing come from?" asked Dravvin.

"Where indeed?" said Flenarrh. "In all the time I've

been patronizing this place, I've never seen anything like it."

"Could it be someone's pet?" asked the Captain of the *Kalliope*.

"I don't know how else it could've gotten in here," Bo'tex replied.

"That's true," said Robinson. "Unless it's a captain in its own right, and we simply haven't recognized the fact."

Hompaq chuckled. "Too bad it doesn't have a little more meat on its bones. It looks like it would make a tasty snack."

Bo'tex grimaced. "You want to *eat* it?"

The Klingon grinned. "I'd eat *you*, my plump friend, if I wasn't loathe to catch your stench."

The Caxtonian harrumphed. "I told you, dammit, it's *not* a stench—it's a mating scent. On my homeworld, other males envy me. They'd kill for a bouquet like mine."

"That may be true on your homeworld," said Hompaq. "Here, people are willing to kill to get *away* from you."

Bo'tex thrust out his chest. "If my smell is so offensive, why do you put up with me?"

The Klingon bared her teeth. "I have a cold," she told him.

By then, the gecko seemed to have made itself at home. It looked at Picard and blinked.

"It wants to hear the rest of your story," Robinson quipped.

Picard looked at him. "Far be it for me to disappoint a lizard," he said—and went on with his tale.

The Tale

I WAS STILL TESTING the operational parameters of the Romulan helm when I received a summons from Red Abby.

I looked up from my console. "Picard here."

"I'm in the commander's quarters," the woman told me. "I need you to take a look at something."

Returning the helm to Thadoc, I left the bridge and took a lift to the deck in question—a residental one, apparently. Then I made my way down the corridor to the commander's suite.

The doors opened at my approach, revealing a large room with tan and gray walls, in keeping with the ambiance that characterized the rest of the vessel. There was a triangular mirror set into one wall. On the wall facing, a winged predator clutched two globes, one green and one blue—a symbol of the Romulan Empire, which claimed the planets Romulus and Remus as home-worlds.

I didn't see Red Abby right away. It was only after I had looked around for a moment that I found her hunkered unceremoniously between a long Romulan divan and a opening in the wall. A bulkhead panel was lying on the deck beside her, along with the Romulan equivalent of a tricorder.

"You asked to see me?" I said.

She turned away from the cavity in the wall long enough to glance at me. "I'm glad you're here. Come take a look at this."

I knelt beside Red Abby, craned my neck, and glanced into the opening. There was something inside—a dark mechanism about the size of my fist lodged in a tangled nest of colored circuitry.

It bore a string of raised characters—distinctively Klingon characters, I noted—which was, I supposed, why the woman had summoned me to see it instead of Thadoc.

"Do you know what it is?" Red Abby asked.

I nodded. "Those characters form a Klingon phrase: Wa' DevwI' tu'lu. Translation: There is one leader."

I thought she might comment on the saying's applicability to our own situation. She refrained, however.

"That's nice," she said. "What does it mean?"

"It's a threat," I explained, "meant to intimidate potential mutineers. After all, one may often be tempted to destroy one's commanding officer—especially if one is a Klingon. However, the temptation diminishes dramatically when such an act ensures one's own destruction."

Red Abby's eyes narrowed. "One's . . . own destruction? Are you telling me this is a self-destruct mechanism?"

I confirmed that it was. "It's designed to initiate a sequence of events that will blow up a vessel from within. It became quite popular among Klingon captains several years ago—until a couple of ships exploded and the High Council was forced to outlaw it."

Picking up her tricorder, I took some readings. They allayed my concerns—at least for the time being.

My companion shook her head. "But what's it doing *here,* in a Romulan warbird?"

I could only speculate, of course. "Perhaps the commander of this vessel had reason to distrust his subordinates. Perhaps he was about to give them reason. Perhaps he was simply paranoid. In any case, he must have obtained the device on the black market and installed it himself, then announced its existence to his staff."

"So they would think twice about taking him down," Red Abby noted.

"That's my guess," I said. "On the other hand, he might not have mentioned it at all. His only motive might have been revenge."

"Sour grapes," she observed. "If I can't have command of this vessel, no one can."

"Exactly," I told her.

Red Abby leaned back against the divan. "Good thing the device isn't active."

"Actually," I pointed out, "it *is* active."

She eyed me. "It *is?*"

"Without question," I said.

"Then why do you look so damned calm?" she asked.

"There's no need to panic," I told her, putting the tricorder on the floor beside me. "The device is not set to go off for several hours."

"Good," said Red Abby. "Then I can panic later."

I shrugged. "If you like."

"I don't get it," she said. "We stunned that Romulan commander before he could move a muscle. Unless . . . someone else came in here and activated the mechanism. But that—"

"Doesn't make sense in light of my speculations?" I suggested.

Red Abby frowned. "Unless I'm missing something."

"It's rather simple," I told her. "Unlike the self-destruct mechanisms one finds on Starfleet vessels, this one is not *armed* by a sequence of commands—it's *dis*armed."

My companion looked at me, surprised. "So . . . this thing is set to go off all the time?"

"Exactly," I said. "Every twenty-six hours, the commander of this vessel was required to reset the mechanism—because if he failed to do so, his ship would be reduced to atoms."

Red Abby's nostrils flared. "That's very interesting. But as you may have noticed, the commander of this ship is no longer aboard. So we either have to disarm the mechanism permanently, figure out the reset code, or get the hell off the ship before she blows."

It was an accurate description of our options. "I vote for disarming the mechanism," I told her.

"That's fine," she said. "I take it you've done this before?"

"I have not," I confessed, turning my attention to the device again. "But faint heart and all that."

"Faint heart?" Red Abby echoed.

"Never won fair lady," I said, finishing the thought. I glanced at her. "Surely, you've heard the expression before?"

"Not until now," she told me.

"Well, then," I replied amicably, "this would appear to be a first for both of us."

"A first?" Red Abby seemed wary of me suddenly.

"Yes, I said, smiling. "For you, the first time you've heard the saying about faint hearts. And for me, the first time I've disarmed a Klingon self-destruct device."

She seemed to drop her defenses again. "Right."

I considered the mechanism. "You know," I said, "I hate to leave this sort of thing unattended."

"But?" Red Abby prompted.

"But I could use some tools. You'll find them in

whatever storage compartment you got the tricorder from."

"Any particular kind?" she asked.

"Whatever looks useful," I said.

"Consider it done," Red Abby muttered.

As I analyzed the connections between the self-destruct mechanism and the surrounding circuitry, she left the room. A couple of minutes later, she returned with an armful of Romulan tools.

"One of everything," Red Abby stated, laying the implements down in front of me.

I inspected them and chose what looked like a charge inverter. It was long and narrow, with a handle at one end and a tiny bulb at the other, much like the Federation version.

"You're sure that's the right thing?" she asked.

"I will be," I said, "once I scan it with your tricorder."

I proceeded to do just that. As luck would have it, I had chosen well. The tool was precisely what I needed.

"We're in good shape?" Red Abby inquired.

"For the moment," I told her.

By then, I had worked out exactly what I would have to do. As far as I could tell, the self-destruct mechanism interfaced with the circuitry in three separate places. I would need to deactivate all three interfaces without creating an energy imbalance in the circuitry—because that would trigger a self-destruct command as well.

It wasn't a complex job, but it was an exceedingly delicate one. It would require several minutes to complete, perhaps more.

"Let me know if you need anything else," Red Abby said.

I nodded. "I will."

Then I set to work.

Disabling the first connection took the most time and attention, largely because of my lack of familiarity with the Romulan charge inverter. Despite its appearance, the implement was significantly slower and less precise than its Starfleet counterpart.

Once I got past that hurdle, however, I felt comfortable enough to engage my companion in conversation. Nor, to be honest, was it merely a way of easing the tension. I was driven to know more about the woman who called herself Red Abby—and this was my first opportunity to speak with her in private.

"Were you especially close?" I asked her—rather abruptly, I'm afraid. "You and your brother, I mean?"

Red Abby looked at me, as if trying to decide whether to answer such a personal question. In the end, she decided in my favor.

"He was my brother," she said. "My only sibling. How could it have been any other way?"

I too had possessed but a single sibling—my brother, Robert, back on Earth. He had perished in a fire. I took his death rather badly. But for most of our lives together, we had failed to see eye to eye.

I said as much.

Red Abby shook her head. "It was never that way with Richard and myself."

"No?" I said.

"Not in the least. Growing up, we were always very much alike—rebellious and undisciplined, determined to blaze our own paths instead of following those of others." She paused. "Somehow, my brother managed to ignore those qualities in himself and wound up in Starfleet Academy."

"Where he did rather well," I noted.

The second interface was deactivated. Without pause, I went on to the third one—trying not to notice how alluring the smell of Red Abby's hair was. Like lilacs, I thought.

"Yes," she said. "Richard did *very* well."

Her tone of voice told me she meant to say more. "But?" I prodded gently, hoping to hear the rest.

"But he didn't have an easy time of it."

"I'm sorry to hear that," I said.

"The regimentation, the lip service he had to pay to his so-called superiors . . ." She shrugged. "He hated all that. But he managed to accept it because he wanted to explore the galaxy and Starfleet seemed like the best way to do that."

"He must have derived some satisfaction from the job," I suggested. "A person doesn't often rise to the rank of executive officer without a certain degree of commitment."

Red Abby nodded. "It satisfied him, all right—even more than Richard expected, I think. But only for a while. Then it got to him, little by little, just as I told him it would."

"He felt stifled?" I asked.

I glanced at her, suddenly aware of how close she was to me. Aware of her every feature. Her fiery red hair, flowing over one slender shoulder. Her eyes, with the mystical blue of a summer sky in them.

Her mouth, full and inviting.

"Claustrophobic," said Red Abby. "Restrained by one rule or another. But even then, he didn't give it up. Someone always seemed to be counting on him for something, depending on his skills and experience—and Richard never in his life let anyone down."

She lapsed into silence for a moment. Perhaps, I thought, she was renewing her resolve not to let *him* down.

"In any case," Red Abby went on, "his tour eventually ended and he took the opportunity to resign his commission. He'd had enough. He wanted to try something different. Something without so many rules."

The last of the three interfaces gave way, rendering the self-destruct mechanism harmless. Breathing a sigh of relief, I took hold of the device and withdrew it from the bulkhead cavity. Then I showed it to Abby.

"That's it?" she asked.

"That's it," I told her.

Red Abby nodded. "Good work."

Neither of us got up, however. That was fine with me. I still yearned to know more about her.

"And you've never had the urge to try Starfleet yourself?" I asked. "Never wondered what it was like?"

Red Abby laughed and leaned back against the Romulan divan again. "I know myself too well."

I gazed at her. "What does that mean?"

"I've grown even less patient than Richard, less tolerant of sprawling bureaucracies and red tape." Her tone grew more serious. "Frankly, Picard, there's only one thing in Starfleet I've ever coveted, and that's only a very recent development."

Her remark made my curiosity boil. "If I may ask," I said, "what *is* that one thing?"

She didn't answer right away. Then, unexpectedly, she swung her legs beneath her and leaned forward, and kept leaning until her face was right beside mine. I could feel the warmth of her breath in my ear as she answered with remarkable frankness.

"You."

Madigoor

PICARD PAUSED in his tale. But his companions at the Captain's Table wouldn't hear of it.

"Go on," Flenarrh spurred him.

"By all means," said Bo'tex, leaning forward in his chair. "We're just getting to the good part."

Picard looked at him. "The good part?"

The Caxtonian shrugged. "Yes, well . . . you know."

Picard looked at Bo'tex askance. "I believe you're reading something into my remarks that wasn't there. I've merely related what Red Abby told me, as faithfully as I can. I've described a conversation."

Flenarrh laughed suggestively. "But there was more than conversation, was there not?"

Picard hesitated.

"Well?" said Hompaq. "Flenarrh asked you a question."

Even the gecko seemed to want to know what had transpired.

Suddenly, a Bajoran youth seemed to appear out of

154

nowhere. He was carrying a tray full of drinks with practiced ease.

"Refills," he said.

Picard didn't recall ordering one. Still, he was glad to see it arrive, as it brought him a respite from the other captains' questions.

Dravvin frowned. "What timing," he said dryly.

"The worst," Bo'tex grumbled.

The Bajoran looked at them. "Should I come back later?"

The captains exchanged glances around the table.

"Er . . . perhaps not," said Robinson. "One never knows when one will suffer an awful thirst."

"That's true," Flenarrh confirmed.

"All right, then," said the youth. "Who had the bloodwine?"

"Here," Hompaq told him.

"And the Ferrin's Dark?"

"That would be me," said the Captain of the *Kalliope*.

"Romulan ale?"

"Mine," said Bo'tex.

The Bajoran picked up a long, thin glass and scrutinized it in the light. "Um . . . some kind of green stuff?"

Robinson grinned in his beard. "You can set that one down here, lad."

And so it went.

Before long, the youth's tray was empty of its cargo. Only then did he seem to catch sight of the gecko sitting on the table.

"Uh . . . where did *that* come from?" he asked.

"Beats me," said the Captain of the *Kalliope*.

"In case you were wondering," Robinson declared cheerfully, "it's a gecko."

"Tropical," said Dravvin.

"Eats insects," Hompaq noted.

"But, then," said Bo'tex, jerking a thumb at the Klingon, "so does *she*."

The Bajoran frowned. "Do you, uh . . . want me to get rid of it?"

Flenarrh shook his head. "Don't do so on my account. I've gotten accustomed to the little fellow."

"Me, too," said the Captain of the *Kalliope*.

The lad considered the lizard for a moment. "Then, I guess I'll just leave it here."

"I guess you will," said Dravvin.

The Bajoran started off through the crowd. But before he could get very far, Hompaq reached out and pinched the youth's buttocks.

Wincing with pain, he looked back over his shoulder at her—at which point she leered at him. The Bajoran scurried off as if the devil himself were after him—and perhaps she was.

The Klingon made a clucking sound with her tongue. "Too bad he's built so sparsely—even worse than the lizard there. I bet I'd enjoy making a warrior out of him."

Dravvin chuckled. "If you attempted it, you'd have to notify the poor lad's next of kin."

Everyone at the table took a sip of his or her drink—except Hompaq, who downed half of it at a single gulp. Then they turned to Picard.

"I hope," Flenarrh said, "you didn't think we had forgotten about you."

Hompaq laughed. "He's not off the point of the bat'leth yet."

"So," said Bo'tex, *"was* there more than conversation? Between you and Red Abby, that is?"

Picard regarded him. "Let us assume, for the moment, that there was—except it was you on whom Red Abby had bestowed her admiration. Would you recount it for us now, detail for detail?"

"Damned right I would," Hompaq interjected. She pounded her powerful fist on the table, making it and the beverages on it shudder with the impact. "What's a conquest without a hearty song to commemorate it?"

Ignoring her, Picard fixed Flenarrh with his gaze. "Would you?" he asked his fellow captain.

Flennarh thought about it for a moment. Then he smiled. "Perhaps not. I see your point, my friend."

Hompaq heaved a sound of disgust. She folded her arms across her ample chest and leaned back in her chair. "I should have stayed in the Empire," she rumbled sourly.

"Then we're to hear nothing of your dalliance?" Dravvin asked.

"I didn't say there *was* a dalliance," Picard reminded him.

The Rythrian sighed. "But surely, *something* followed."

Picard reflected on the comment, but declined to respond to it directly. Instead, he took a circuitous route.

"What ultimately came to pass," he said, "was this: An alarm sounded through the warbird, summoning us to the bridge."

"Another instance of poor timing," Bo'tex noted.

Picard ignored him. "Red Abby and I took a lift and arrived on the bridge in a matter of moments—only to find ourselves face-to-face with a viewscreen full of strange vessels."

The Tale

THEY WERE PIRATES, like the ones we had encountered before. At least, the diversity of ships in their fleet seemed to indicate as much.

But this time, there were twice as many of them.

"Jaiya again?" I wondered out loud.

"No," said Abby appraisingly. "This isn't Jaiya's bunch. Unless I'm sorely mistaken, this one's a damned sight more aggressive."

I nodded. "Lovely."

We were seriously outnumbered. If it came to a battle, we would find ourselves at a marked disadvantage.

Abby turned to me. "Stand off to the side. You don't want anyone to see you." She glanced at Worf. "You, too."

As it happened, Assad was on the bridge at the moment. Without waiting to be ordered, he took over at tactical. Thadoc simply remained where he was, at the helm.

As Worf and I moved to the periphery of the Romulan bridge, I considered the irony inherent in our situation.

Not so long ago, my lieutenant and I had had to conceal our desire to remain anonymous. Now, Abby was more concerned with our anonymity than we were.

But then, she didn't want to lose us. And if we were recognized by the pirates, she might well have done so. After all, as I noted before, a pair of Starfleet birds-in-the-hand were worth a great deal on the open market—perhaps even more than some fabled bird-in-the-bush.

Satisfied that we were out of sight, Abby turned to Assad. "Hail them," she said, referring to the pirates.

Assad complied. Less than a second later, the wrinkled, ratlike face of an Yridian filled the screen.

Abby seemed to know him. "Captain Dacrophus," she said, not bothering to conceal the antipathy in her voice.

The pirate captain seemed genuinely surprised at the sight of her. But then, when one hailed a Romulan vessel, one expected to find oneself conversing with a Romulan.

"It's good to see you," he said at last.

Abby frowned at Dacrophus. "I'd say that, too, if I were too stunned to think of anything else."

The Yridian shrugged. "Frankly, when I found the remains of your worthy ship, I thought you and your crew had been murdered. I'm glad to see my fears were groundless—especially since I'd rather deal with someone I know than some stranger." He paused to inspect our bridge. "Funny," he said. "You don't *look* Romulan."

"But I'm in charge of this warbird nonetheless," Abby told him. "What the hell do you and your people want from me now?"

Dacrophus smiled. "I know. It must appear that we're hounding your every step. But then, we have been—ever since we discovered what you were after." His smile deepened. "That is, the Hoard of Dujonian. As you can imagine, we'd like to unearth that treasure ourselves."

Abby muttered a curse. "Even if we assume I know where it is, why would I tell anyone—you especially?"

"Because if you don't," the Yridian warned her good-naturedly, "we'll blow you out of existence."

A compelling argument, I mused.

Dacrophus rubbed his hands together. "On the other hand," he said, "we pirates are not as greedy as people seem to think. If you're willing to be reasonable, we'd be perfectly happy with only half Dujonian's treasure. That way, no one has to go home empty-handed."

Abby frowned again. Dacrophus had cleverly given her an option she could live with—assuming, of course, she could trust him to honor it.

"All right," she said finally. "You can tag along if you like. But don't give me any reason to doubt your sincerity."

The Yridian chuckled. "I would never be so foolish," he told her. On that note, he cut off the communication, leaving us nothing to contemplate but a view of his fleet.

I moved to Abby's side. "I'm not sure that was wise," I said, in a low voice so no one else could hear it.

"Everything's under control," she assured me.

"I hope you're right."

Abby glanced at me sharply. "I *said* it's under control."

Something else occurred to me. "Tell me," I said, "how is it our friend the pirate seems to know you so well?"

"You sound suspicious," she replied.

"Merely curious," I told her.

Abby turned away from me and sighed. "All right. I suppose you have a right to know."

Know? I thought. What *else* had she concealed from me?

Abby's eyes seemed to glaze over as she stared at the Romulan viewscreen. "I was a pirate myself, once upon a time."

"You?" I asked, caught by surprise—though in retrospect, I probably should not have been.

"Me," she said. "Mind you, it wasn't for very long. I doubt anyone except Dacrophus remembers. But it was long enough to offend some of my fellow pirates. The most important ones, apparently."

"And that's why you're not with them anymore?" I asked.

"That's why," she confirmed. "Actually, they did me a favor kicking me out when they did."

"Why is that?" I asked.

"Had I stayed any longer, I would've known too much. They would've been forced to kill me."

"Thoughtful of them," I agreed a bit sarcastically.

It reminded me of the story I'd made up about myself and the Maquis, when I was still masquerading as Hill. I said so.

Abby nodded. "Now that you mention it, you're right."

She was silent for a moment.

"The funny thing," she went on abruptly, "is sometimes I can't help wishing I were still with them."

For a moment, I thought she was joking. Then I realized she was telling me the truth.

Abby shook her head. "There was a sense of camaraderie about them, a feeling of belongingness. And they weren't just privateers. Once in a while, they did something for someone who needed it."

I must have seemed skeptical, because her expression became more insistent. "At least," she said, "some of them did."

"If you say so," I remarked.

"In any case," Abby went on, "what's done is done. As you can see, my pirating days are behind me."

I couldn't resist. "Yes," I said, glancing pointedly at the viewscreen. *"Directly* behind you."

She didn't dignify the remark with a response. Under the circumstances, I couldn't blame her.

"Steady as she goes," she told Thadoc.

The helmsman nodded. "Aye, Captain."

For the next two days, we sped toward our legendary destination. And all the while, Dacrophus's pirate fleet remained close on our heels, a pack of jackals trailing a lioness in hopes of sharing her spoils.

On the other hand, we encountered no additional obstacles. That gave us ample time to effect repairs to our ship, though it turned out mercifully few were needed. It also gave us a chance to study the warbird's operating systems—an exercise that would soon prove useful.

For on the third day after our defeat of the Romulans, we came in sight of the phenomenon known as Hel's Gate.

Madigoor

"HEL'S GATE," FLENARRH REPEATED, savoring the notion like the bouquet of a fine wine.

The Captain of the *Kalliope* chuckled. "With a fleet of treasure-hungry pirates on your tail."

"And Brant's kidnappers somewhere up ahead," Bo'tex noted.

"No danger of being bored, at least," remarked Robinson.

Flenarrh leaned forward. "What was it like?" he asked, his eyes alight. "The Gate, I mean?"

Everyone waited to hear his answer—even the gecko, it seemed.

"Was it everything you expected?" Dravvin inquired.

Picard took a moment to answer. "Everything I expected," he said at last, "and more."

The Tale

HEL'S GATE LIVED UP to its reputation in every way. It was a dramatic, even spectacular phenomenon—and at the same time, a decidedly dangerous one.

The thing's core was a pure, blinding white, difficult to look at even with our screen's light dampers in operation. But the fields that played around it, changing size and shape before my eyes, were quite the opposite. So beautiful were they, so varied in the iridescent hues they presented, it was difficult not to be mesmerized by them.

As I watched, enthralled, a dark red light appeared in the core and discharged itself into space. It happened again a few seconds later, and yet again a few seconds after that, as if the phenomenon were shooting gouts of blood from a severed artery.

A grisly image, I'll admit. Nonetheless, it was the one that sprang readily to mind.

"There it is," said Abby, unable to keep a note of awe and amazement out of her voice.

I turned to her. "You sound surprised."

She shrugged. "Maybe I am. I don't know."

Then I realized how it had been with Abby. She had been so intent on getting her brother back, so focused on putting together a ship and an adequate crew for that purpose, she hadn't had time to fully consider what she was getting herself into.

And now that she was able to see it with her own eyes, now that it blazed before her with a wild and hideous intensity, it had taken on a reality for which she was unprepared.

But Abby was nothing if not resilient. She turned to Thadoc.

"Any sign of the mercenaries' ships?" she asked.

She was unconcerned about giving away any secrets. After all, there were only four of us on the bridge at the moment—myself, Worf, Thadoc, and Abby herself— and we were all aware of her search for her brother.

The helmsman consulted his monitors. "No, no sign."

To be sure, there were no mercenary vessels represented on the viewscreen either. But then, with the light display coming out of Hel's Gate, it would have been easy for a ship or two to conceal themselves.

"But they *were* here," Worf pointed out from the tactical station.

Abby looked back over her shoulder at him. "How do you know?"

My lieutenant frowned. "I've picked up traces of at least three ion trails and possibly more. The traces are faint but unmistakable. And they all lead into the phenomenon."

"Into it," Abby echoed pensively.

But not necessarily through it, I thought. What's more, I suspect I was not the only one completing her comment that way.

"Even if there *is* a dimensional entry in there," I said, regarding the savage brilliance of the thing's core, "I don't see how anyone could have lived to reach it."

"A point well taken," Thadoc grunted.

I had a sudden flash of insight. "That is," I noted, turning to Abby, "unless you've got something up your sleeve."

She returned my scrutiny without giving away a single emotion. "In fact," she admitted, "I *do*." She eyed the screen. "The approach typically taken by those who enter Hel's Gate is that they try to negotiate the phenomenon under full power."

"A mistake," I deduced.

"A big mistake," Abby explained, "since Hel's Gate tends to reflect energy back at its source. The key, according to my brother, is to enter the phenomenon under absolute minimum power."

"Without active propulsion," I noted.

Abby nodded. "Exactly. You just coast through it on momentum, at the lowest possible speed."

"Sounds nerve-wracking," I observed.

"And difficult," she agreed, "in that you've got to figure out what the lowest speed might be. But it's the only way through."

Indeed, I couldn't think of any other. I considered the phenomenon anew, weighing what Abby had told me.

"Let's try it, then," I said.

Of course, Abby would have done so with or without my encouragement. In any case, she had Thadoc plot a course and a speed.

"What about the pirates?" Worf asked.

Abby looked at him, a smile finally pulling at the corners of her mouth. "They'll have to figure it out on their own."

The Klingon didn't object to the strategy—and neither did I. After all, I had no great desire to remain in the company of Captain Dacrophus and his cronies. And if it took something like Hel's Gate to pry them away from us, so be it.

"Full impulse ahead," Abby ordered.

"Full impulse," Thadoc confirmed, and moved us forward.

"Captain Dacrophus is hailing us," Worf reported.

Abby hesitated a moment. "On screen," she said, obviously no longer concerned about concealing my identity.

A moment later, the Yridian's visage filled the viewscreen. "What are you doing?" he demanded.

"What does it look like?" Abby answered evenly and unflinchingly. "I'm entering the Gate."

Dacrophus's eyes narrowed. "Then I'm following. But don't try any tricks, my friend. You'll regret them."

Abby nodded. "No doubt." She cast a glance at Worf. "You may terminate the communication, Lieutenant."

The Klingon complied. The Yridian disappeared, replaced by the violent splendor of the phenomenon.

We proceeded for about thirty seconds on impulse power, Hel's Gate looming before us. Then, hoping for the best, we minimized energy usage on board, cut power to our engines, and entered the phenomenon on momentum alone.

"There," said Abby, leaning back in her captain's chair. "Now we'll see who regrets what."

Over the years I had served in space, I had developed a great respect for those oddities the universe had thrown in my path. And yet, there I was, arrogant enough to believe we could defy something as fierce and powerful as Hel's Gate and live to tell about it.

I felt like a particularly small and foolhardy minnow offering myself up to the leviathan of legend. And the closer we came to the heart of the phenomenon, the more apt the analogy seemed.

Running only on emergency power, we couldn't have provided Hel's Gate with much energy with which to batter us. Yet, batter us it did. The warbird lurched this way and that like a creature in torment, threatening to tear itself apart with its gyrations.

"I thought we would be safe if we cut power," Worf barked.

"There must have been some energy already trapped inside," I responded, grabbing the back of the captain's chair for support. "Perhaps from previous attempts to run the Gate."

"Thadoc," Abby cried out, hanging on to her captain's seat as best she could. "Report!"

"Shields down to seventy percent," the helmsman shouted back, fighting a jolt. "No—make that sixty percent. And falling."

The captain turned to Worf. "Can we reduce power any further?"

My officer shook his shaggy head as an unnerving shudder ran through the ship. "Not without losing helm and life support."

He'd barely finished when the captain's seat seemed to fly out of my grasp. I had time to recognize that as an illusion, to realize it was I who was flying away, head over heels, before I came up against something hard with bone-rattling force.

Tasting blood, I fought to remain in control of my senses. Raising my head, I looked around—and saw the bridge littered with bodies. No—not corpses, I told myself, unless corpses were capable of groans and curses. My comrades were still alive.

But no one was at his or her post. And most alarming of all, with Thadoc stretched out limply against a bulkhead, there was no one piloting the Romulan vessel. In a place like Hel's Gate, such a deficit could have proven devastating—the difference between survival and being torn into a hundred bloody fragments.

In Thadoc's absence, the helm was my post. My responsibility. Girding myself, I grabbed the bulkhead behind me and staggered to my feet. The deck jerked beneath me and I almost went sprawling again. But somehow, I stood my ground, and even took a few steps toward the piloting controls.

Another impact. Another few steps. Impact, steps. By then, I was close enough to hurl myself at the console.

My fingers closed on it just as the warbird whipped me backward again. But this time, I managed to hang on, my muscles screaming with the effort. With an immense application of will, I hauled myself into the helmsman's seat.

My monitors showed me we were still on course, more or less. Making whatever adjustments I could without applying thrusters and adding to our miseries, I rode out the next upheaval and the one after that.

By then, Worf had wrestled himself back into place behind the tactical station. He called to me in his deep, booming voice.

"Are you all right, Captain?"

"Well enough!" I replied, despite the numbness in my side and the ringing in my ears.

Mercifully—or so I thought—the tremors began to subside a little. One by one, Abby and Thadoc dragged themselves off the deck and came to stand beside me. Unfortunately, Thadoc was cradling one of his wrists. Judging by his wretched expression, he had broken it— perhaps in more places than one.

On the viewscreen, the nature of the phenomenon changed. After all, we were no longer attempting to peer into Hel's Gate, speculating on what it could possibly represent. Now, for better or worse, we were fully and irrevocably *inside* it.

What had earlier seemed like an flawless center of brilliance now showed us its true colors—more specifically, striations of midnight blue and neon green and rich umber, running lengthwise along the inside of a colorless cylinder. And it all seemed to tremble with uncertainty, as if it might take on another appearance at any second.

Despite a bruise on the side of her face, Abby smiled. It was a welcome sight, to say the least.

"We're in," she said, collapsing in the Romulan commander's chair.

"So we are," I added.

Our vessel had lost momentum, of course, in the process of entering the Gate. But as I checked my instruments, I realized we were no longer doing so. Clearly, this was a frictionless vacuum, though it was nothing like any vacuum I had ever seen.

Abby turned to Worf. "Status?"

The Klingon checked his monitors. "Shields down to fifteen percent," he reported. "Some of our internal sensor nodes are off-line, but otherwise the ship is functional."

The captain nodded. "Excellent."

"How much longer before we emerge on the other side?" I asked.

Abby shrugged. "My brother didn't say."

As it turned out, our stay in the cylinder lasted only another thirty seconds or so. Then we saw a bright light at its end, similar to the one we had seen at its beginning, and we began to experience turbulence again.

Considerable turbulence.

"Brace yourselves!" I shouted.

It didn't help.

As badly as we'd been tossed about on the way in, we were treated even worse on the way out. Clutching my console for dear life, I was wrenched this way and that, feeling like little more than a rag doll.

Finally, the deck bucked and dipped and spun me loose, sending me crashing into the base of someone else's console. Nor can I say what took place immediately after that, as I wasn't conscious to witness it.

Madigoor

"BUT YOU GOT THROUGH," said Flenarrh, "didn't you?"

"Of course he did," Bo'tex laughed derisively. "What kind of story would it be if he hadn't?"

"A rather pointless one," Dravvin agreed. "And I don't think our guest would tell a pointless story." He regarded Picard with a glint of irony in his eyes. "Would you, Captain?"

Picard smiled. "Not if I could help it, no."

The gecko tilted its head.

So did Robinson. "Then you *did* make it to the other side."

Picard nodded. "I did indeed."

"And what did you find there?" asked Flenarrh.

Picard recalled the moment of his awakening on the far side of the Gate. "I found another part of space," he replied. "Or perhaps another universe altogether. I can't tell you for certain. All I can say is that the constellations I saw were unfamiliar."

"And the Hoard?" Flenarrh prodded.

Dravvin rolled his protuberant eyes. "For the sake of Canarra, he'll get to it. Be patient, will you?"

Picard couldn't help but chuckle at Flenarrh's eagerness. "Indeed, at the moment when I woke from my battering, I wasn't thinking of the Hoard. I was thinking of Dacrophus and his pirates, who were rather conspicuous by their absence. We and our warbird were coasting through the void all alone."

"They hadn't followed you in?" Bo'tex asked.

"Or had they followed and been torn apart?" Robinson inquired.

Picard shook his head. "To this day, I don't know."

"But they were gone," the Captain of the *Kalliope* established.

"They were," Picard agreed.

"And good riddance," Bo'tex chimed in. "Lazy lungwarts. Why don't they go out and get themselves real jobs?"

"Mind you," said Picard, "I was not pleased at the prospect of the pirates having lost their lives. To my knowledge, they hadn't committed any serious crimes—and even if they had, I'm not certain anyone deserves to perish that way. In any case, they were no longer a problem for us."

"Again," Bo'tex exclaimed, "I say good riddance."

Picard smiled tolerantly.

The Tale

As I SUSPECTED, Thadoc's wrist had been broken. Dunwoody, who had had some medical training, confirmed that conclusion.

However, Thadoc insisted that he remain on the bridge—if not as helmsman, then at least as navigator. Abby agreed, and I was the first to applaud her decision. Though it fell to me to become full-time helmsman, Thadoc's expertise with a warbird was still far superior to my own.

There were other injuries as well, but none too severe. In effect, we were bloodied but unbowed.

Remarkably, when I ran a diagnostic check of our propulsion system, I found the engines hadn't been damaged in the least. I was pleased to report this—almost as pleased as Abby was to hear it.

"Tactical systems are also functional," Worf announced. "Shields at seventy-five percent and improving. They should be back to full strength in a matter of minutes."

"What about weapons?" Abby asked.

The Klingon paused. "One of our aft control centers is off-line. However, I can route commands through a backup center."

"Do so," Abby told him.

Worf arched an eyebrow.

"Please," she added.

The internal sensor network had suffered the greatest disruption, but that was of no immediate concern to us. All in all, we had been lucky.

"You see?" Abby asked me, looking satisfied with herself. "I told you I had everything under control."

I grunted sarcastically. "If you can call nearly costing us our lives being under control."

"Nearly doesn't count," she declared.

There was no winning that argument. I could see that with the utmost clarity. "If you say so," I replied.

Our viewscreen showed us a great many stars, but one was burning a lot more brightly than the others. Abby pointed to it.

"That's our destination," she said.

Thadoc worked his controls with his one good hand. "Long-range sensors indicate seventeen planets. Two of them are inhabitable."

Clearly, I thought, if we were to find the Hoard, it would be on one of those two worlds. Apparently, Abby saw it that way as well.

"Chart a course," she told Thadoc.

He did as he was asked. Moments later, I had the warbird clipping along at warp four, the solar system in question dead ahead.

But even at warp four, it would be several hours before we got there. Abby and Thadoc opted to get some rest in that time, leaving Worf and me on the bridge by ourselves.

"You are injured," the Klingon observed.

I glanced back over my shoulder at him. "You can tell that from all the way back there?"

Worf nodded. "You are bleeding. From a head wound."

My hand went to the back of my head. I found a sore spot. When I inspected my fingertips, there was blood on them, but not a lot. Idly, I wondered if it was a new wound or an old one that had reopened.

"A scratch," I concluded.

My lieutenant grunted with something like humor. "A Klingon would no doubt say so. Most humans would not."

I turned back to my console and smiled. "I hope you don't think I'm like most humans, Mr. Worf. After all the years we've served together, I should hope you know me better than that."

His response wasn't long in coming. "I do, sir."

A moment later, the lift doors opened and my old friend Corbis stepped out onto the bridge. He wasn't alone, either. The Tellarite known as Gob was at his side.

"Is something wrong?" I asked Corbis.

He eyed me with some of the hostility he had harbored toward me earlier. "That's between me and the captain, Starfleet."

It didn't seem he was speaking of any danger to the ship, so I refrained from forcing the issue. "Suit yourself," I told him.

"Where is she?" asked the Tellarite.

I glanced at him. "You mean the captain?"

"Yes," he said, "the captain."

"She's sleeping, as far as I know." I returned my attention to my instruments. "I'd advise you not to wake her. She'll need her wits when we get where we're going."

Gob snorted. "That's what we want to talk to her about—where we're going." I imagined his tiny eyes narrowing as he scrutinized me. "Has she located the Hoard of Dujonian?"

Again, I glanced over my shoulder at him. "I thought you wanted to discuss that with the captain."

"We do," said Corbis.

"You do," the Tellarite told him. "I just want an answer. I don't particularly care who gives it to me."

"The captain thinks she knows where the Hoard is," I responded. "But as I'm sure she told you from the beginning, there are no guarantees."

"We've gone through hell," Gob grumbled. "And we've lost a lot of men. I'd hate to think it was all for nothing."

I nodded. "So would I."

And that was the end of it. Corbis and his newfound companion left without another word.

But as soon as they were gone, Worf spoke up. "I will be watching Corbis even more closely than before, sir. And Gob as well. They will pose a problem for us before this is over."

Unfortunately, I found myself agreeing with him.

Madigoor

"I *TOLD* YOU Pandrilites were nasty," Dravvin reminded them.

Robinson nodded. "So you did."

"Tellarites are no picnic, either," said Flenarrh. He looked around to make sure there was no one of that species in earshot. "No one's quicker to anger, not even the Klingons."

Hompaq cleared her throat. "Present company excepted, of course."

Flenarrh inclined his tufted head. "Of course. By no means did I mean to imply your fuse was anything but short."

The Klingon eyed him, suspecting that she was being toyed with. But she found no evidence of it in Flenarrh's face, so she flashed her long, sharp teeth and let the matter pass.

"What happened then?" asked the Captain of the *Kalliope*. He indicated the gecko with a tilt of his head. "My friend and I want to know."

177

"Nothing," said Picard. "At least, not right away. In fact, my whole shift went by without anything remarkable happening."

The Tale

AT THE END OF IT, I turned to see Abby and Thadoc walk out onto the bridge. They appeared refreshed by their respective naps, and the helmsman looked a bit more comfortable with his arm in a sling.

I glanced at Abby. "You're in a good mood."

"A little sleep can work wonders," she said.

But I knew it wasn't sleep alone that had caused her spirits to rise. It was the prospect of finding her brother.

Abby cast a look at the viewscreen. "How are we doing?"

"As you can see," I told her, "we're approximately halfway to our destination. In fact—"

Worf interrupted me. "Three ships off the port bow, sir."

I turned my attention to my monitors. As the Klingon had indicated, our sensors had detected three small vessels on an intercept course. Not surprisingly, I had never seen their fluted design before.

"Shall I hail them?" asked Worf.

I looked to Abby, who was standing by the captain's seat. "I think it's a good idea," I told her.

True, I was unfamiliar with this milieu and its politics, and we might well have been trespassing in someone's territory. But if we had ruffled any feathers, it was all the more important to establish communications so we could smooth them.

And in all honesty, the explorer in me yearned to see what kind of beings we had encountered.

She considered it for a moment, then nodded to Worf. Dutifully, he carried out the order. A moment later, our viewscreen showed us the grim-looking individual in charge of the alien formation.

His skull was oblong and hairless and his skin was bone white, providing a striking contrast with the faceted, ruby red ovals of his eyes. Jagged, brown horns protruded from either temple, echoed by smaller versions at the sides of his long, narrow chin.

"Greetings," said Abby. "I'm—"

She never finished her sentence. The alien didn't give her an opportunity to do so.

"You have entered Abinarri space," he advised her in a gravely voice, "in blatant violation of seventy-seven separate Abinarri statutes."

"I assure you," said Abby, "it wasn't our intention to break any laws. We'll be gone before you—"

Again, the alien interrupted her. "Do not attempt to flee. Our tractor rays will take hold of your vessel momentarily."

She shot the Abinarri a disparaging look. "The *hell* they will. Terminate communication, Mr. Worf."

The image on the viewscreen changed. Once more, we found ourselves gazing at the alien formation.

Abby turned to me. "Get us out of here, Picard—and I mean now."

I did the last thing the Abinarri would have expected. I shot right through the center of their formation. By the time they wheeled in response, we were making good on our escape.

"Maximum warp," said Abby.

"Maximum warp," I confirmed.

As we accelerated, I could feel a subtle pull on my face and body. After all, inertial dampers are not as high a priority in warbirds as they are in Federation vessels.

But then, Romulans are by all measures stronger and more durable than most Federation races. It would have come as no surprise if their tolerance for G-forces was higher, as well.

In any case, after a few moments I expected to have given the Abinarri the slip. As I discovered, I was quite wrong. Not only had they not been left behind, they were actually *gaining* on us.

Thadoc deposited himself behind the navigation console. "Quick little vessels, aren't they?"

"Yes, they are," I replied.

I could have made the warbird go faster, as well, but I didn't think I could maintain such a rate of speed for long. Could the Abinarri maintain it? At the time, I had no idea.

"Rear view," said Abby.

Worf manipulated his controls. Abruptly, the image on the viewscreen changed, showing us the Abinarri vessels in hot pursuit.

"They are powering up their weapons banks," the Klingon reported.

"Let's do the same," said Abby, staring at the viewscreen.

Worf worked for a moment. "It is done," he announced.

Abby tapped a stud on the armrest of the commander's chair. "This is Captain Brant. We're about to go into battle again. If I were you, I'd find someplace cozy and brace myself."

It occurred to me that Corbis and Gob would be displeased. Of course, this was hardly my greatest concern at the moment.

"Target and fire!" Abby barked.

Worf unleashed a barrage of disruptor beams, striking the lead ship in the Abinarri formation. According to my monitors, the aliens' deflectors were all but obliterated.

Thadoc glanced over his shoulder at Worf. "Good shooting."

The Klingon didn't respond to the compliment. He was too busy targeting the lead ship again.

"Fire!" Abby told him.

Worf looked at me, knowing his next volley would destroy the Abinarri if he wished it. I didn't want that.

"Target their propulsion systems," I said.

"Aye, sir," he responded.

Abby shot me a dirty look but didn't say anything. It was an awkward command situation, especially in the middle of a battle. Still, we were both resolved to make the best of it.

"Fire!" Abby cried again.

Worf fired.

This time, our disruptors tore into the alien's hind-quarters, disabling their warp drive or whatever equivalent means of propulsion they employed. Instantly, the craft dropped out of warp.

That left only two Abinarri on our tail, though they were getting closer with each passing second. If they hadn't fired yet, it was no doubt because we were outside the range of their weapons.

A moment later, that no longer seemed to be a problem for them. Our viewscreen lit up with a greenish burst of light. It jolted us.

Another burst, another jolt.

"Damage?" asked Abby.

"Nothing serious," said Thadoc, his features cast in

the orange glow of his Romulan controls. "Shields are down only fifteen percent."

Apparently, the Abinarri's bark was worse than their bite. Not that I was complaining, mind you.

"Fire at will!" Abby commanded.

Having already received my approval, Worf did as he was told. A second Abinarri vessel saw its shields shredded by our disruptor beams. Then the Klingon disabled it as he had disabled its sister ship.

This one, too, dropped below the speed of light. That left only a single adversary with which we had to concern ourselves.

But the Abinarri hadn't had their fill of us yet.

Even closer than before, they fired again—and at short range, their beams packed more of a wallop. I felt the impact through the deckplates—once, twice, and a third time.

"Shields down thirty-six percent," Thadoc noted.

When Worf returned fire, our greater proximity to the Abinarri worked in our favor as well. His first barrage ripped through their shields and breached their hull. The next one destroyed not only their propulsion system, but also half their weapons banks.

Like the other Abinarri, the vessel dropped back as if it had reached the end of its tether—while the warbird continued to knife through the void at maximum warp. The alien was millions of kilometers behind us before we could draw another breath.

Abby nodded approvingly. "Well done," she said, watching the stars fall away in our wake.

Worf inclined his head—his way of saying thank you.

Abby looked at me. "You too, Picard."

"What did *I* do?" I asked her.

"You had the sense to dart right through their formation," she observed. "If you hadn't, they might have caught us in a cross fire. Then our encounter might have had a different ending."

I shrugged. "Perhaps."

After all, I wasn't looking for accolades. My only objective was to bring my mission to a satisfactory conclusion. At least, that was what I kept telling myself as I used my controls to return to warp four.

There was, of course, the matter of myself and Abby Brant. Not Red Abby the captain, not the tough-as-nails transport commander, but the woman with whom I had forged something of a bond.

A bond of mutual respect, one might say. Of camaraderie—and maybe a bit more than that.

Such were my thoughts. No doubt, they ended up commanding more of my attention than they should have.

"Picard," said Thadoc.

I looked at him. "Yes?"

"If you like," he told me, "I could take over the helm for a while. It's time for the change of shifts, and one hand should be enough as long as there's no trouble."

I nodded. "Of course."

Standing, I turned the helm over to him. At the same time, the lift doors opened and Dunwoody emerged onto the bridge—at which point Worf moved aside and let the other fellow man the tactical station.

But the Klingon didn't leave the bridge. Instead, he moved to one of the aft stations.

I looked at him. "What are you doing?" I asked.

He looked back. "Going over the data I obtained."

"The data . . . ?" Red Abby repeated. Obviously, the woman had no idea what Worf was talking about.

But then, I was only beginning to understand myself.

"While the Abinarri ships were unshielded," I ventured, "Mr. Worf must have taken the liberty of establishing a datalink with their computer."

"A subspace datalink," the Klingon explained. "Though it was in existence for only a few seconds in each case, I was able to upload a significant amount of information."

If I had ever underestimated my tactical officer, I promised myself never to do so again.

Abby too looked at the Klingon with new respect. "Of course. In case we happen to run into the Abinarri a second time."

"Either the Abinarri," I granted her, "or any of the other species described in their database. One never knows what sort of knowledge will prove useful in uncharted waters."

"Very impressive," said Abby.

Worf shrugged. "It seemed like a good idea at the time."

Then he turned his attention to the data coming up on his screen. His brow beetled in response.

"Captain," he said, "take a look at this."

I followed his gesture to a list of Abinarri statutes—which their commander had cited as reasons for detaining us. It turned out there were rather a lot of them. Thousands, in fact.

"Quite the busy little legislators," I said, "aren't they?"

My companion grunted. "And it seems they impose their laws on a great many other species."

The data on the monitor screen bore that out. The Abinarri had subjected no less than thirty other species to their peculiar brand of justice, and they were currently attempting to add two more.

I frowned. It was one thing to follow one's own cultural imperatives. To force others to follow them was another matter entirely.

"I don't understand," said Thadoc, who had apparently overheard our conversation. "How can they lord it over so many other worlds when their vessels are so unimpressive?"

"Unimpressive to us, perhaps," Abby pointed out. "In comparison to all the other civilizations here, they probably boast the height of technology."

Dunwoody smiled. "For our sake, let's hope so."

Silently, I added my hope to his own. Then I turned back to the monitor, eager to learn all I could about the tyrannical Abinarri.

Madigoor

"AND WHAT DID YOU LEARN?" asked the Captain of the *Kalliope*.

"Yes," said Flenarrh, "what?"

"A great deal," Picard said. "It seems the Abinarri were originally a rather wild and iconoclastic people."

"A nation of hermits," Dravvin observed.

"More or less," Picard confirmed. "Time and again, their primitive attempts at civilization were brought down by anarchy and lawlessness."

"Not unlike my own people," Hompaq grumbled.

"Actually," said Picard, "the ancient Abinarri make early Klingons look polite and reserved."

Hompaq's eyes narrowed. "You lie."

"I do not," Picard assured her. "They were utterly savage, capable of the most heinous acts one can imagine. It was not unusual for an early Abinarri to kill his mate or his children over a shortage of food. Cannibalism not only ran rampant, it was the preferred diet in some places."

"Lovely," said Robinson.

Picard glanced at him. "Indeed. It was only after long years of chaos and unrestrained brutality that a strange, new caste emerged among the Abinarri. The data we had didn't tell us how or why, but it did say these people were known as the Lawmakers."

"Apt," said Bo'tex.

Dravvin rolled his eyes. "If rather obvious."

Picard continued. "The Lawmakers decided that their people were incorrigible. Unless an elaborate system of laws was instituted, the Abinarri would simply destroy one another."

"And how were these laws to be enforced?" asked Flenarrh.

"At the point of a spear," Picard told him. "At least, at first. But after a while, the laws simply became the laws, and people obeyed them. Again, our information was incomplete on this point. But two things were clear to us: Chaos gave way to order, and civilization thrived."

"By all accounts," Bo'tex remarked, "a good thing."

The gecko blinked. No doubt, he thought so, too.

"In any case," Picard said, "the Abinarri came to understand the world around them as never before. They produced superior scientists and philosophers, painters and musicians . . ."

"And writers?" the Captain of the *Kalliope* suggested.

"Those as well," said Picard. "But the Lawmakers— who had eliminated the earliest obstacles to civilization and were therefore still venerated—were needed less and less as time went on."

Robinson grunted. "No doubt, a difficult pill to swallow."

"So difficult," Picard noted, "that the Lawmakers refused to recognize the fact. Instead, in the grand tradition of self-perpetuating institutions, they went on creating law after superfluous law. Before long, they had rendered the Abinarri system of justice nearly impossible to understand—and even more impossible to apply."

The Captain of the *Kalliope* frowned. "I can only imagine what this did to personal freedoms."

"As you suggest," said Picard, "it trampled them. It ground them down, spit them out, and made people forget they ever existed. Finally, the time came when there were no Abinarri behaviors left to be prescribed, no Abinarri freedoms left to curtail or regulate."

"And?" Flenarrh asked, apparently sensing there was more.

"And," said Picard, "that was the day the Lawmakers looked up and gazed greedily at the heavens."

Robinson sighed. "It's an old story, I'm afraid. When you're finished oppressing your own people, you set your sights on oppressing others. On my world, we called it colonization."

"A good analogy," Picard mused.

Dravvin eyed him. "I take it the Abinarri had begun to explore space by that time?"

"Yes," said Picard, "though they had yet to make contact with other self-aware species. Under sudden pressure from the Lawmakers, their stellar expansion program was drastically accelerated. All Abinarri resources and technologies came to be focused on the noble effort to find sentient beings on distant worlds."

Robinson chuckled mirthlessly in his great, white beard. "So they could impart the beneficial Rule of Law to the infidel."

Picard nodded. "And that is what they did. They found any number of civilizations, conquered them, and imposed their statutes on them. Where Abinarri statutes didn't seem to apply, the Lawmakers were only too happy to make up new ones."

"How interesting," said Flenarrh.

"Yes," Dravvin replied sardonically. "Especially for

all those species the Abinarri were generous enough to subjugate. Those people must have found the situation *extremely* interesting."

Picard looked at the Rythrian. It was only natural that he should make such a comment. His people had labored under an off-world tyrant for nearly a decade in the early part of the twenty-fourth century.

"At any rate," said Picard, "that is the way matters had proceeded in that universe for well over two hundred years. The Abinarri had taken control of world after world, star system after star system, all for the purpose of spreading their gospel of Law. And no one had had the wherewithal to stand against them."

"Until you came along," said Bo'tex.

Picard shook his head. "We only succeeded in winning a skirmish. The Abinarri barely felt our passage."

Suddenly, Hompaq made their table shudder with a thunderous blow. Everyone looked at her.

"I have heard enough about these Abinarri," she said. "If they are inferior warriors, as your account suggests, they are beneath my notice." She leaned forward, her lips pulling back ferociously from her teeth. "Tell me instead about the Hoard of Dujonian."

Picard smiled. "Rest assured, Captain Hompaq, the Hoard was still very much on our minds—and even more so on the minds of our crew."

"But did you *find* it?" the Caxtonian asked.

"A fair question," Dravvin judged.

"You'll learn that soon enough," Picard told him. "After all, we're coming to the most important part of the story."

The Tale

WORF AND I COULD HAVE continued to study the Abinarri all day. However, our rest period was over before we knew it. I replaced Thadoc at the helm and Worf took back the tactical station from Dunwoody.

As I got myself settled, I found the stars sailing by me as they did when I was on the bridge of the *Enterprise*. I found myself thinking about my Starfleet crew, wondering how things were going for them.

I had no doubt they were doing fine without me. My executive officer was more than capable of running a starship on his own, and the rest of my staff was seasoned as well.

Still, I dwelled on each one of them. I couldn't help it. I was, after all, their captain.

One of them in particular kept turning up in my thoughts. His name was Data and he was my second officer. He was also an android—that is, an artificial being created in the mold of a man—who was discovered by Starfleet on a world called Omicron Theta in the year 2338.

Data was the superior of any human in almost every way one could name. For one thing, he was eminently more durable than any man or woman. For another, he could survive indefinitely without food or air.

Data could exercise superhuman strength and incredible quickness when the need arose. His mind could race at computer-like speeds. But since the day I met him, he had aspired to only one thing—the single aspect of the human condition denied to him.

In short, he wished to experience emotions. *Human* emotions.

For a long time, it seemed such an experience was beyond Data's reach. Then it came to light that his creator, Dr. Noonien Soong, had manufactured a positronic chip that would grant the android his fondest wish.

By inserting the chip into his brain, the android could know love, rage, happiness, jealousy—the gamut of human feelings. However, as great opportunities often do, this one came with a terribly steep price.

As you can imagine, a human overcome by emotion might injure his or her companion. But an android overcome in such a way would almost certainly kill that companion. And so it would be with Data.

All too aware of this danger, he chose not to insert the emotion chip—his legacy and only route to real happiness. Instead, he placed it in a safe place in his quarters on the *Enterprise-D*.

Perhaps one day, Data would incorporate the chip into his positronic matrix and discover what it was like to be a human being—the joys and the sorrows, the delights and the disappointments, the pride and the pain. But for the time being, he took his responsibilities to others more seriously than his hopes and dreams.

It was a brave decision. I believed that at the time Data made it, and I believed it still as I sat there on the bridge of the warbird with Abby Brant at my side.

I hoped that, under similar circumstances, I would have the courage and the wisdom to make the right choice—as it seemed to me Data had.

Putting the android aside for the moment, I checked my Romulan instrument panel. I found we were on the brink of the system we had made our destination. Its outermost planets were almost in our grasp.

Abby had noticed, too. "Slow to warp factor one," she told me.

"Aye," I replied, and did as she said.

She then asked Thadoc to set a course for the sixth planet from the sun. It was one of the two spheres we had noticed earlier that appeared capable of supporting life.

At warp one, which was equivalent to the speed of light, it would take us another couple of hours to reach the sixth planet. Still, it was prudent not to go in any faster.

One never knew what sorts of complex gravitic relationships one might find in an uncharted solar system, especially one with seventeen planets whirling around it. And as comfortable as I now felt at the helm of the warbird, it was still an alien vessel, with eccentricities that might manifest themselves at the most inopportune times.

As it happened, the time passed quickly—for me, at least. The deeper we delved into the system, the more I was able to learn about the various bodies that comprised it.

For instance, the smallest worlds were either the closest to their sun or the farthest away from it—a common configuration. However, what was far from common was the size of the planets in the middle distance.

In most cases, the largest world in a system is no more than thirty times the size of its smallest sister planet. As captains of spacegoing vessels, you are no doubt aware of this.

In this system, two worlds—both of them gas giants—drastically exceeded the traditional proportion. The ninth planet from the sun was almost two hundred times the mass of the first planet—and the tenth planet was an incredible seven times as massive as the ninth.

I couldn't help speculating. After all, when gas giants of that size collide, as the proximity of these two suggested they might someday, the greater one has a chance to grow heavy enough to begin fusion.

If that happened, it would be reborn—not as a planet, but as a star, blazing within the formerly ordered bounds of an existing solar system. The term for it was super-Jovian planet ignition. Its result? Cataclysmic, in the case of systems with populated worlds.

First, the clash of the two gas giants would create new gravitic relationships. Other planets would be realigned, perhaps crash into each other or be drawn into their new sun. And those events, of course, would give rise to still further changes.

Second, whatever life may have existed on planets proximate to the new sun would be destroyed. Either they would be baked to death or perish from an excess of ultraviolet radiation.

This gave me yet another reason to glance over my shoulder at Worf every so often, it being his job to conduct long-range scans of the solar system. I wished to know if there were sentient life forms on the planets we had made our destinations—and to estimate their chances of survival in the event of a super-Jovian planet ignition.

Not because I thought we would be able to help them. That would be an impossibility, since the ignition would take place eons hence if at all. I simply had a need to know.

It was the same impulse that had compelled me to explore space in the first place. I longed to know things about distant places. No doubt, you have all felt the same way at one time or another.

It is, after all, why we are what we are.

Finally, Worf looked up from his console—but not to report on the planet to which we were headed. "I have located a vessel," he said.

Abby looked at him. "A vessel?"

The Klingon nodded his shaggy head. "It is of Orion manufacture."

I could see the excitement in Abby's face. And the urgency. More than likely, this was the vessel of the mercenaries who had abducted her brother.

"Where is it?" she asked.

"In orbit," he replied, checking his instruments again. "Around the fourth planet from the sun."

She didn't hesitate. "Set a new course, Mr. Thadoc."

"Aye, Captain," came the reply.

Abby turned to me. "Take her in, Picard. Full impulse."

"Full impulse," I acknowledged.

We found ourselves approaching the fourth planet in the system. It was small, mountainous, and mostly barren, with but a single small ocean. Still, it was what we in Starfleet would have called a Class M world—one that possessed an oxygen-nitrogen atmosphere not unlike Earth's and was generally suitable for human habitation.

Soon, Worf was able to tell us something new. "Sensors show humanoid life forms aboard the vessel. Twenty-two of them in all. However . . ." He looked up—first at me, and then at Abby. "None of them resemble any species known to the Federation."

Abby frowned, no doubt wondering what to make of the information. Unfortunately, I was unable to help her.

Up to that point, we believed Richard Brant had been

kidnapped by mercenaries from our universe. Nor could we rule that out, given the presence here of an Orion spacecraft.

Now it seemed possible that Brant's abductors had been denizens of *this* universe—either working on their own or in concert with the mercenaries we suspected earlier. The plot was thickening.

Abruptly, Worf spoke up again. "Captain Brant, I am receiving a message for you. Eyes only."

Abby's eyes narrowed. "For *me?* From the *ship?*"

The Klingon shook his head from side to side. "From the fourth planet. Do you wish to view it in private?"

She considered her options for a moment. "No," she said at last, "I'll take it at the captain's chair."

"Acknowledged," Worf replied. He did what he had to in order to send the message along.

Abby took the captain's seat and turned to one of the monitors in her armrests. For a moment or two, her expression remained wary and uncertain. Then it began to change.

Abby's mouth quirked at one corner. Then, slowly and subtly, a smile began to spread across her face. It was a beautiful smile, too—all the more so for its rarity.

"What is it?" I asked from my position at the helm.

She didn't answer my question.

"Captain?" said Thadoc.

Finally, Abby looked up. "We're beaming down," she said evenly.

"Who is?" asked her helmsman.

She thought about it—but only for a moment. "I am," she replied. Abby turned to me, still beaming. "Picard, too."

"I *am?"* I said.

I wished I knew what she had in mind. But then, I hadn't seen her monitor or the message on it.

"Come on," Abby taunted me. "Where's your sense of adventure, Picard?"

Obviously, she knew how to get to me.

"All right," I responded, getting to my feet. "I'll beam down with you—if only to satisfy my curiosity."

Abby turned to Thadoc. "Take the helm," she said, "and establish a synchronous orbit. We may be gone a few hours. And don't worry about the Orion. It won't give us any trouble."

"Aye," Thadoc replied. If he was the least bit skeptical, he managed not to show it.

Worf was another story. He was scowling as only a Klingon could scowl, not at all thrilled with the idea of exposing me to the unknown.

"I will go as well," he resolved.

"That won't be necessary," Abby responded. She was looking at me as she said it, requesting a favor with her eyes.

I decided to trust her. "Remain here, Lieutenant. I'll contact you if I need you."

Worf made a sound of disgust. "As you wish, sir."

Madigoor

"BUT WHAT WAS IT Abby saw on her monitor?" Bo'tex
wanted to know. "And who was it from?"

Flenarrh grunted. *"Now* who's the impatient one?"

The Caxtonian looked at him indignantly. "I'm just
asking, is all."

"Just as I said," Flenarrh countered, "you're being
impatient."

"It never hurts to ask a question," Robinson conceded, pacifying Bo'tex before he could emit an odor the
others would come to regret. "However, I sense our
friend Picard was about to *answer* your question—and
perhaps a number of others in the bargain."

The gecko turned to Picard as if it knew what was
going on.

The captain smiled. "True enough," he said.

The Tale

ABBY AND I EXITED the Romulans' bridge and repaired to their transporter room. Once there, we took our places on a hexagonal transporter grid, under the Romulan symbol of the birdlike predator with the globes in its claws. Assad did us the favor of beaming us down.

We materialized in a sunny, ochre-colored valley beneath a vast, blue-green sky. But we weren't alone. Not by a long shot.

There were several white, domelike enclosures scattered about. Among them stood a wide variety of humanoids, none of whom looked the least bit familiar to me. What's more, every one of them was armed——and at least half had leveled their weapons at us.

"I hope you know what you're doing," I told Abby, eyeing our hosts.

"So do I," she said.

Abby didn't make a move to go anywhere, so neither did I. The two of us just stood there, waiting for something to happen. I dearly wished I knew what it was.

Suddenly, someone else emerged from one of the domes. He was wearing a worn, brown coat made of some leatherlike material. And though he appeared somewhat scruffier than his Starfleet file image, it didn't take me long to determine his identity.

It was Richard Brant.

Abby, it seemed, had recognized him a moment before I did. She was making her way to him through the alien crowd, ignoring the weapons trained on her as if they presented no danger at all . . . looking to her brother with mingled joy and relief.

Richard was pushing his way toward her, as well, just as eager to embrace his sister as she was to embrace him. And a moment later, both of them got their wish.

"Richard," she said, hugging him as hard as she could.

"Abby," he replied. He rested his head against hers.

Though I'd missed it before, I began to see the resemblance between them. The eyes, the nose, the light sprinkling of freckles . . . there was no doubt in my mind they were brother and sister.

"I was afraid you were dead," Abby told him.

"But I'm not," Brant chuckled. "As you can see, I'm very much alive." He held her away from him so he could look at her. "You look pretty hearty yourself for a women who's gone through Hel's Gate."

"It wasn't as bad as you made it out to be," she said.

He laughed. "Only you would say that."

Abby turned to me. "Picard, I want you to meet my brother. Richard, this is Jean-Luc Picard. He's—"

"The captain of the *Enterprise*," Brant finished. "I recognize the name." He extended his hand. "Good to meet you, Captain."

He seemed untroubled by my presence there. But then, he must have suspected that Starfleet would take an interest in his disappearance.

"Likewise," I said, grasping the fellow's hand. "I'm glad to see you're in one piece, Mr. Brant. For a while there, we weren't so certain that would be the case."

"For a while there," Brant echoed, "neither was I."

I had some questions for him. I said so.

"About my friends here?" he asked.

With a sweep of his arm, Brant indicated the aliens assembled around us. Of course, they had put away their weapons by then, though a few of them still eyed me warily.

I shrugged. "If that's where you would like to start."

Brant dug his hands into the pockets of his coat. "Several months ago," he said, "I was on a one-man science vessel running medical supplies to the Badlands when I found myself pursued by a Federation starship. As I recall, it was the *Trieste* . . ."

"Hold on a second," I said. "You were smuggling for the Maquis?"

"Just medical supplies." Despite his admission, he seemed very much at ease with himself. "Does that shock you?"

"Yes," I said, "it does. On the other hand, you wouldn't be the first officer of my acquaintance to be drawn into the Maquis web."

Brant smiled tightly. "I wasn't drawn into anything, Captain. I was simply trying to make a living—and the exotic expedition business wasn't as lucrative as I had hoped."

"You could have returned to Starfleet," I pointed out.

He shook his head. "Trust me, it was no longer an option."

I remembered what Abby had told me on that count. "Go on."

"The *Trieste* was about to overtake me," he said. "I was in the vicinity of Hel's Gate and I couldn't think of any other way to elude pursuit, so I ducked inside the phenomenon. As I had hoped, the *Trieste* embraced the better part of valor and decided not to follow."

Abby looked at her brother askance. "You went into the Gate with your engines active?"

"I did," he told her. "But before the Gate could really work me over, my engines went off-line—warp as well as impulse. That saved me. It forced me to coast on momentum."

"And that was how you learned to make it through," I deduced.

Brant nodded. "When I emerged, my ship was damaged—but not as badly as it could have been. Unfortunately, I didn't know where the hell I was. None of the stars around me looked the least bit familiar."

"Tell me about it," said Abby.

Her brother continued. "With no other course of action open to me, I began to effect repairs. At some point, my ship turned up on someone's sensors. That someone came by to have a look at me."

I looked about. "One of *these* people?"

"She *was*," Brant explained soberly. "She's dead now, but that's another story. The important thing is she brought me to a planet very much like this one and introduced me to her comrades."

"Comrades . . . in what?" I wondered.

Brant glanced at them with an air of pride. "These people are rebels," he told me. "Not unlike the Maquis, though the analogy may not appeal to you. And that planet—like this one—was their base of operations, where they fought the good fight against an oppressive interstellar regime."

"An oppressive regime," I echoed, making a connection in my mind. "It wouldn't, by any chance, refer to itself as the Abinarri?"

His eyes hardened. "You've met them, then."

"We've sampled their hospitality," I replied.

"And taken down three of their ships," Abby added.

Brant seemed impressed. "I'm glad to hear it. In any case, they told me about their cause—and before I knew it, I was hooked. Their rebellion stirred something in me in a way I can't explain."

Still, he searched for words to describe it. Not for my sake, I'm certain, but for his sister's.

"It seemed to me," he said, "that this was what I'd been looking for all my life—something so right, so pure and untainted, I could put my entire being into it and never look back."

Abby didn't say anything. She just nodded.

"But," I said, "at some point you came *back* to our universe. What were you doing there if your fight was here?"

"Good question," said Brant. "One I would have expected from a Starfleet captain, in uniform or out."

"It's my duty to inquire," I told him stiffly.

"So it is," Brant agreed. "And believe me, Captain, I've got nothing to hide in that regard. I was just doing some recruiting on my old turf. That is, trying to gather people to our banner."

"People?" I asked.

"Yes," he said. "Adventurous sorts who might be attracted to a good cause, even if it was in unfamiliar territory." He scowled. "Unfortunately, it seems my efforts backfired."

"In what way?" asked Abby.

Her brother looked at her. "The mercenaries? The ones who kidnapped me, hoping I'd lead them to the Hoard of Dujonian?"

"Yes?" she said.

"That's how they got wind of me," Brant explained. "Through someone I tried to recruit for the rebellion. The next time I saw that person, it was a trap. The mercenaries showed up in their Orion ship and spirited me off—forced me to show them the way through Hel's Gate."

"But they didn't know what they were getting into," I ventured.

"That's correct," said Brant. "My comrades didn't take long to realize a ship had come through the gate— or that I was on it. In short order, they got me back and gave the mercenaries what they deserved."

I absorbed all the man had said—which was quite a lot. Then I asked the Question of Questions.

"And what about the Hoard?"

Brant looked at me uneasily. "Ah yes. The Hoard."

I pressed on. "Did you unearth it somewhere in this universe, as the mercenaries seemed to believe? Or was it, say, an enticement you dangled as part of your recruitment drive?"

Abby regarded him. "Is it here, Richard?"

Her brother smiled. "It is indeed. Just a couple of star systems from where old Dujonian left it two hundred years ago." He turned to me. "You'd like to see it, I suppose?"

I confess I felt a thrill of anticipation. "I would," I told him.

Abby's brother pulled a small device from its place beneath his tunic. Then he spoke into it.

"This is Brant. I need you to transport our visitors and myself into the vault."

There was a pause. "As you wish," came the response.

Brant eyed his sister, then me. "Brace yourself," he told us.

A moment later, I found myself in another place entirely—a large but low-ceilinged cavern full of stalagmites and stalactites, illuminated by blue lamps set up on tripods. Abby and her brother were there, as well, and by the ghostly light of the lamps, we laid eyes on the splendor of Dujonian's Hoard.

It stretched luxuriously into the farthest recesses of the

cave, an alien terrain of glor'ya-bearing goblets and armbands, necklaces and serving platters, statuettes and tiaras.

It was breathtaking, to say the least—and not only for the regal brilliance with which its every artifact flashed and glimmered, exhibiting the deep, rich colors of the spectrum.

To me, it was also a window into the minds and sensibilities of the ancient Hebitians, of whom not even their Cardassian ancestors had accurate records. On that count, it was priceless beyond any mercantile measure.

"Incredible," said Abby, the light reflected in the Hoard reflected a second time in her eyes.

She approached the mounds and valleys of casually strewn treasure with an almost religious awe. Then, kneeling in the midst of it, she picked up a long, glor'ya-encrusted necklace and let it spill like a river from one hand to the other.

"I never thought . . ." she began.

"What?" asked her brother, kneeling beside her. "That you would ever see it? Or that it would be so beautiful?"

Abby shrugged. "Both, I suppose."

I too knelt to inspect the stolen treasure. Picking up a goblet, I turned it in my hand, watching its glor'ya catch the light one by one. But before I was done, I noticed that two of the stones were missing.

"A pity," I said out loud.

Brant looked at me. "You mean the missing gems."

I nodded. "Yes."

"If you look closely," he said, "you'll find that's the case with the majority of these artifacts. But I assure you, it's not out of carelessness."

"Out of what, then?" I asked.

Brant picked up a tiara and ran his fingers over the glor'ya embedded in it. "My rebel friends discovered the Hoard a good many years ago, or so they tell me. Like the Cardassians, they understood these gems were useful as well as beautiful."

I began to see what he was saying. "They used the glor'ya to power their ships."

He nodded. "Of course, they could have used the gems all at once, and made their vessels juggernauts of destruction—just as the Cardassians might have. But they realized that their fight would be a long one, so they opted to use the glor'ya sparingly."

"Which is why most of them are still here," Abby concluded.

"Where they will stay," Brant said pointedly, putting the tiara down again. "At least, until we see the need to establish a new headquarters for ourselves. Without these little jewels, there would be no rebellion—so we've learned to guard them jealously."

He stood and gestured to indicate the limits of the cavern. "This place is several meters below a rather nondescript stretch of ground, and there's no way in or out of it except by transporter."

"So your enemies won't find it," Abby noted.

"Enemies," her brother replied with a smile, "and friends alike." He took out his communications device again. "This is Brant," he said. "We're ready to leave now."

"Wait," I told him.

He looked at me. "Stand by," he ordered his transporter operator.

"I'd like to take a gem with me," I told Brant. "Just one. So Federation scientists can replicate it and study it."

He considered the request for several seconds. "All right," he replied grudgingly. "Just one."

I took a closer look at the goblet in my hand. It was quite beautiful. Had it not already been deprived of some of its beauty, my task would have been a great deal more unpleasant.

Finding the glor'ya that seemed the loosest, I grasped it between thumb and forefinger and gradually worked it back and forth. Finally, it came out of its setting.

Showing it to Brant, I deposited it in a pocket of my jacket. Then I put the goblet down and got to my feet.

Abby rose as well, shaking her head at what we were leaving behind. Then she looked at her brother.

He spoke into his device. "Transport," he said.

I took a last look at the lost majesty of Dujonian's Hoard. Then I found myself back on the planet's surface, standing among Brant's fellow rebels as before.

He looked at his sister. "Disappointed?"

"About the Hoard?" asked Abby. She shook her head.

"Are you sure?" her brother asked.

"I'm sure," she replied honestly. "Oh, I'll admit it was exciting to think we might take home a legendary treasure. But to tell you the truth, Richard, it never mattered that much to me. I was much more interested in finding my brother."

Brant blushed and glanced at me. "I'm afraid Abby's always been this way, Captain. I may have been born first, but my sister has never stopped looking out for me."

I nodded. "As it should be," I said, wishing I had looked after my older brother a little better.

"And you need not worry about whom I recruited," Brant said knowingly.

I smiled. "My concern was that obvious?"

"It was written all over your face," the man told me. "I only approached a couple of my Starfleet colleagues about joining the rebellion, and neither of them was tempted to join me. In fact, my efforts didn't meet with much success in general."

"Much?" one of his comrades echoed.

The fellow was tall and thin, with orange scales in place of skin and distinctive, black markings under his eyes. He seemed to take exception to Brant's choice of adjectives.

Abby's brother heaved a sigh. "All right, Ch'wowtan. Make that *none.*" He took on a rueful expression. "Apparently, there aren't nearly as many adventurous souls out there as I'd imagined."

Madigoor

"I RESENT THAT," said Dravvin.

Hompaq bared her teeth. "I wish the p'tak were sitting at this table. I'd give him an adventure he would never forget."

"If he managed to survive it," Bo'tex suggested.

The Klingon grunted her assent.

"Obviously," said Picard, "Brant's luck would have been better if he had done his recruiting here."

"Absolutely right," Bo'tex agreed.

"But, of course, he *couldn't* have done his recruiting here," Flenarrh was quick to point out.

Picard smiled. "Ah, yes. Captains only."

"Indeed," Robinson commented slyly. "Keeps out the riffraff."

"Enough of that," said the Captain of the *Kalliope*. "Where were we? Or should I say, where was our friend Captain Picard?"

Dravvin harrumphed. "As I recall, Mr. Brant had told him there were no adventurous souls to be found."

"Damn his nostrils," Bo'tex spat.

"And no Hoard to be taken home," Flenarrh added wistfully.

"Damn his ears and his eyes as well," the Caxtonian hissed.

Robinson regarded them. "Listen to the two of you. It's not as if the Hoard would have been yours, in any case."

"True," said Flenarrh. "But I can dream, can't I?"

Hompaq made a sound of disgust. "We have discussed the treasure at length, have we not? Now, for the sake of Kahless, let us move on."

"A spendid idea," Dravvin said, in effect seconding the motion.

Bo'tex harrumphed. "Spoilsports."

"Indeed," said Flenarrh.

Making a point of ignoring them, Robinson stroked his ample, white beard. "As I recall, the erstwhile Mr. Brant was complaining about his inability to attract recruits."

"That's right," said Picard, glad the man had set them back on track. "However, our conversation took a different turn after that."

"In what way?" asked the Captain of the *Kalliope*.

Picard turned to him. "Once again, an alarm went off."

The Tale

BY THAT, I MEAN a high-pitched whooping that came from a dozen speakers around the rebel camp, stopping everyone in his or her tracks. At the same time, there was a beeping sound in our immediate vicinity.

Responding to it, Brant pulled out his communications device. His features were taut with urgency as he flipped the thing open again and spoke into it.

"What is it?" he asked.

The voice on the other end was deep and gruff. "A fleet of Abinarri ships, not more than a few minutes away."

Brant cursed. "How did they find us?"

"Does it matter?" asked the voice on the other end.

"I suppose not," Brant answered. He looked at Abby, then me. "Looks like they know this is our headquarters."

"Could our appearance have led them here?" Abby wondered.

Her brother shook his head. "Not likely—unless they

had a pretty good idea of our whereabouts to begin with."

"The question," said the tall fellow with the orange scales, "is what we're to do now. All of our vessels except the mercenary are off tormenting the Abinarri elsewhere."

Brant frowned. "And the mercenary can't stand up to a fleet all by herself." He bit his lip. "She can't outrun it, either. And even if she could, we couldn't all board her in time."

"Planetary defense systems?" I suggested.

"Good idea," Brant told me. "That is, if you're planning on staying in one place for a while. We can't afford to do that." He tilted his head to indicate the sky. "For this very reason."

The muscles fluttered in Abby's temples. "There's another possibility," she pointed out.

Her brother's eyes lit up with newfound hope. "Of course," he breathed. "The warbird!"

It was true—the Romulan vessel would make a difference in the battle. She was a powerful ship, as fit as she had ever been, and in the last few days Abby's men had begun to get the hang of her.

Abby looked at me with fire in her eyes. "I need your help, Picard. With Thadoc hurt, you're the only one capable of taking the helm."

I couldn't argue with the accuracy of her declaration. However, I wasn't a rebel like Richard Brant. I wasn't a treasure hunter. I was a Starfleet officer, who had vowed to serve one master and one master only—and that master was the Federation.

But I knew who the Abinarri were now. I understood how they operated and what they could do to a subject society. And though I hadn't seen their tyranny with my own eyes, I didn't have to.

Because I wasn't just a Starfleet officer. In the final analysis, I was also a man.

Abby's features went taut. "Don't think for a minute you're getting out of this," she told me.

"I wouldn't dream of it," I said, unable to keep my mouth from pulling up at the corners. "You've got yourself a helmsman."

Tapping my communicator, which I still wore under my tunic, I called up to the warbird. "Mr. Worf?"

"Aye, sir?" came the reply.

"Two to beam up."

A couple of seconds later, I found myself on the Romulan bridge again, Abby alongside me. Without a word, she swung into the center seat.

In our absence, Corbis, Gob, and a couple of others had come up to the bridge. All four of them were standing by the aft stations, staring suspiciously at Abby and myself.

I was not thrilled about their presence there. But for the time being, there were more important matters on the agenda.

Worf looked at me. I could tell from his expression that he had already detected the Abinarri on his sensor grid.

I joined him at tactical for a moment. "Brant's down there," I said sotto voce. "He's joined a group of interplanetary rebels. Those ships you see are bent on destroying them."

The Klingon wanted to know only one more thing. "Will we be fighting on the side of the underdog?"

I nodded. "We will indeed."

Worf smiled a grim smile. "I was hoping you would say that."

Just then, Corbis spoke up. "What's going on?" he demanded.

"We're engaging an enemy," Abby told him.

"Who is it?" asked Gob.

She whirled in her seat, her eyes spitting fire. "I told

you—it's an enemy. That's all you have to know."

"That's what *you* think," Corbis snarled. He pointed a long, thick finger at Abby. "I'm done fighting, done putting my life on the line. I want to see that treasure I've been waiting for!"

"Get off my bridge," Abby told him sternly.

The Pandrilite advanced on her. "Like hell I will."

She stood up and faced him. "I told you to leave the bridge, Mr. Corbis. If I were you—"

Before she could complete her warning, the Pandrilite belted her across the face. Unprepared for that kind of force, Abby flipped backward over her center seat and landed on the floor.

Then, before anyone could get to her, Corbis drew his weapon and put it to her head. I exchanged glances with Worf and Thadoc, but there was little any of us could do at the moment.

"Don't you see?" Corbis snarled at his comrades. "There's something going on here they don't want us to know about!" He turned to me, his eyes red-rimmed with fury. "Isn't that right, Starfleet scum?"

I swallowed. "You don't know what you're doing, Corbis. We've got to act quickly or we'll be destroyed."

It was no more than the truth. The Abinarri would likely take us for an enemy whether we entered the fray or not. We had to undertake evasive maneuvers or we would be ripped open.

Corbis's eyes narrowed dangerously. "We'll act quickly all right. We'll get the hell out of here." He glared at Thadoc, who had risen halfway out of his seat. "And we'll do it now, won't we—or I'll vaporize your precious little captain!"

"Don't listen to him," Abby said, wiping blood from her mouth. "Let him kill me. Just don't abandon those people down there."

The Pandrilite made a sound deep in his throat. "So there are people down there. Is that what this is about?"

Abby didn't say anything. No doubt, she regretted having opened her mouth at all.

"Is that why you came through Hel's Gate, dragging the rest of us along?" asked Corbis. "Is that why you risked the life of everyone aboard this ship? What happened to the Hoard, Captain? What happened to riches beyond our wildest dreams?"

"Yes," said Gob, his grotesque nostrils flaring wildly as he took a step toward Abby. "What *about* those promises you made us?"

"I made no promises," Abby told him. "I—"

Corbis silenced her with a jab from the barrel of his weapon. "Shut up," he said. "I've had my fill of your lies."

"I've got an idea," said Gob, grinning greedily. "We'll take the warbird and make a run for it. Then, when we're on the other side of the Gate, we can sell her to the highest bidder."

"That's what you think," I countered. "Once the Romulans find out you have their ship, you won't live long enough to find a buyer. They'll reduce you to atoms first."

"He's right," Abby groaned, despite the weapon held to her head. "Your only chance is to stay here and—"

The Pandrilite jabbed her again in the temple. "I thought I told you to keep your mouth shut."

It was all I could do to keep from charging at him.

Madigoor

"YOU SEE?" said Dravvin.

"YOU SEE?" said Dravvin.

Flennarh nodded. "You called it, all right. You *said* Pandrilites were trouble, and here's the proof of it."

The gecko looked appropriately astonished.

"Enough of that," Bo'tex declared. "I want to hear how Picard here got out of his spot."

"So do I," said the Captain of the *Kalliope*.

"What did you do?" asked the Caxtonian.

"Weren't you listening?" Hompaq snarled. "He said there was nothing he *could* do."

"Actually," Robinson explained, "that's a figure of speech. At the time, it *seems* there's nothing one can do. But inevitably, one finds some way to prove oneself wrong."

"And *do* something," Dravvin interpreted.

"Exactly," said Robinson.

"True," Picard noted. "At least, *most* of the time. In this case, however, there was literally nothing we could do. Nothing at all, if we valued Red Abby's life."

Robinson looked at him. "Nothing? *Literally?*"

216

"Nothing," Picard confirmed.

"Then how was she saved?" Flenarrh asked.

"Perhaps she wasn't," Hompaq pointed out. "Perhaps she died at the hands of the Pandrilite."

Dravvin snorted. "That would suit you, wouldn't it?"

"It would indeed," said the Klingon.

"It's not a matter of what would *suit* us," Robinson reminded them. "It's a matter of what *was*. Either Red Abby died on that warbird or she didn't—there's no middle ground."

Everyone at the table looked to Picard—the gecko included.

"As I was saying," he continued, "I restrained myself from making a run at Corbis. As for the possibility of the Romulans taking their ship back, Gob seemed thoroughly unimpressed."

The Tale

THE TELLARITE LIFTED his chin at me and snorted. "The Romulans," he said, his beady eyes gleaming, "are a risk we'll be glad to assume. At least we'll know who we're fighting—and why."

Corbis pointed to Thadoc with his free hand. "Get us out of here *now,* half-breed—or your captain's a dead woman!"

But before Thadoc could respond, the bridge jerked savagely beneath us. Corbis lost his footing like everyone else and grabbed a bulkhead for support. Seeing my chance and knowing I might never get another one, I threw myself across the space between us.

The Pandrilite fired at me. Somehow, his bloodred beam missed and vaporized a section of bulkhead instead. I grabbed for his phaser, and my momentum slammed us into a console. Then the deck jerked again and we went down in a tangle of arms and legs.

As we hit the floor, I tried to roll on top of him, but he snapped my head back with a blow to the jaw. Gritting my teeth, I got hold of Corbis's wrist and slammed his weapon-hand against the metal surface beneath us.

Once. Twice. And again.

The third time proved to be the charm. Crying out, Corbis relinquished the weapon, bellowing as it fell from his battered hand.

Quickly, I kicked it away. It skittered across the floor. Of course, by that time, the Pandrilite's weapon wasn't the only one I had to worry about. There were phasers discharging all around me, their beams crisscrossing wildly in the close quarters of the bridge.

As I tried to gather myself, I felt a cluster of powerful fingers close on my throat from behind. I tried to claw them loose, but Corbis was too strong for me. I could feel my windpipe closing, my air supply shutting down.

Little by little, I felt myself lifted into the air. Before I knew it, my feet were dangling inches above the deck.

I kicked backward while I still could, felt my heel hit the Pandrilite in the shin. It made him drop me to the deck, but it didn't loosen his grip one iota. If anything, it tightened it.

I could feel the blood pounding ferociously in my temples, see the darkness closing in at the edges of my vision. My hands and feet were beginning to lose all sense of feeling.

Then I remembered something I had learned not so long ago. Something I had seen a young woman do in the gym on the *Enterprise-D,* under the tutelage of her Klingon instructor.

I could only hope it worked as well for me as it had for her.

Groping for one of Corbis's wrists, I found it and took hold of it as Worf had demonstrated. Then I turned it and twisted as well as I could, considering I could already feel my eyes popping out of my skull.

The Pandrilite cried out and went spinning over my

hip, just as if he had been propelled by a phaser blast. I made a mental note to thank Worf if and when I had a chance to speak with him again.

Taking the deepest breath I could, I put some oxygen back in my bloodstream. Then I advanced on Corbis, hoping to capitalize on the surprise I had dealt him.

Unfortunately, it was he who dealt the surprise. As he came up, he had a phaser pistol in his hand—either the one he had lost earlier or someone else's. The Pandrilite's eyes were feral with hatred as he raised the weapon and pointed it at me.

But before he could press the trigger, a bright red beam knocked him off his feet and slammed him into a bulkhead. I heard a crack and saw Corbis slump to the deck, his neck bent at an impossible angle.

Impossible, that is, for someone still alive.

Turning, I saw where the beam had come from. Abby was on her knees behind me, a phaser pistol locked in both her hands. When she realized Corbis was no longer a threat, she lowered it.

I looked around in the unnatural quiet. Gob was lying on the other side of the bridge, the side of his face blackened beyond recognition. Corbis's two other companions were dead as well.

Thadoc stood up from behind his helm console, which featured a smoking hole the size of a phaser beam. He seemed whole, though—or at least, no worse off than before.

Worf hadn't been quite so lucky. His tunic was charred and ripped open in the vicinity of his rib cage—and blood had begun to soak into what was left of the material.

"Are you all right?" I asked him.

He nodded. "Fine."

That didn't tell me anything. He would have said he was fine if he was writhing in agony on his deathbed.

Suddenly, the warbird lurched under the heaviest

barrage yet. A plasma conduit broke, unleashing a stream of white-hot vapor. The viewscreen sputtered and went dead for a second; when it came back on, it was plagued by wave after wave of static.

Through them, I could make out more than a dozen triangular ships. They were coming at us from different directions, waiting until they got closer before they opened fire again.

And why not? We had yet to protect ourselves or get a shot off. It must have seemed to them that we were dead in the water—which would be true enough if we didn't act soon.

I flung myself into the helmsman's seat. At the same time, Worf took charge of the tactical panel. Cradling his wrist again, Thadoc deposited himself beside me at navigation.

"Report!" cried Abby.

"Damage to decks seven and eight," Thadoc grated. "One dead. Dunwoody's team is making repairs."

"All weapon arrays are still functional," Worf growled. "Shields down forty-two percent."

"The helm's responsive," I noted. That was the good news. "But the warp coils seem to have taken a beating. We could be limited to impulse power at any moment."

Abby frowned, her cheek bruised where Corbis struck her. "We'll worry about that if and when it happens. Evasive maneuvers, Picard. Let's see what you can do with *these* Abinarri."

If she had hoped to inspire me with a challenge, it was unnecessary. My desire to keep us alive was inspiration enough.

"Hang on," I said grimly. As I noted before, Romulan vessels weren't known for the effectiveness of their inertial dampers.

I engaged the impulse engines and executed a turn that took us out of the Abinarri's midst. However, they were on us again in a matter of moments, stinging us repeatedly with their energy weapons like a swarm of bees on an intrusive bear.

"Fire at will!" cried Abby.

It wasn't necessary. Worf was already attending to it.

On the viewscreen, two of the Abinarri vessels glowed with the force of our disruptor barrage. A second later, another Abinarri was dealt a glancing blow. But if they were damaged, if didn't stop them from harrying us.

The enemy seemed to prefer working at close quarters. That didn't surprise me in the least. As I'd noted in our last encounter, their weapons were significantly more effective that way.

But beyond any practical considerations, I got the feeling that was simply the way these people liked to hunt. Very likely, it was the way their ancestors had done it—by surrounding their prey and bringing it down through sheer weight of numbers.

I was determined that *this* prey wouldn't go down so easily. Working furiously at my controls, I negotiated the maze of enemy vessels and emerged from it a second time.

But a second time, the pack caught up with me.

Worf did his best to hammer at the Abinarri, managing to score several more hits. One ship even exploded in a paroxysm of blue fury. But as before, the Klingon's efforts didn't seem to faze the survivors.

"Shake them!" cried Abby.

"I'm trying!" I bellowed back.

I looked for the mercenary vessel, hoping it could offer us some relief. But my monitor told me our ally had troubles of her own. Like us, she was besieged on all sides.

On the other hand, the mercenary's attackers were fewer in number. They must have understood that she was the weaker of us and focused their efforts on the warbird.

Suddenly, one of the aft stations sparked savagely and

222

began to flame. Someone grabbed an extinguisher and began to put the fire out, but the station next to it ignited as well. Smoke began to fill the bridge, searing our throats and making our eyes sting.

"Shields at twenty-eight percent!" Worf reported over the din. "Starboard phaser banks partially disabled!"

On the viewscreen, a half-dozen Abinarri slid toward us. One by one, their weapons spat red fire at us. I was able to dodge some of the blasts, but not all of them.

The bridge was wrenched this way and that, sending us sprawling over our control panels. I thrust myself back and regained my chair, only to be flung to the deck by another energy assault.

A console exploded, sending pieces of hot metal spinning across the bridge. As black smoke twisted up from the thing, I saw one of our men slump against Abby. It was Assad.

He was dead, his throat a gaping wound.

With a stricken look, Abby lowered him to the deck. Then she took in the carnage all around her.

"Mr. Worf?" she said, her voice thick with emotion.

"Shields at thirteen percent," he told her, reading the information off his monitors. "The starboard phaser array is down."

Thadoc chimed in with more grim news. "Damage to decks four and five as well now."

I took us through a twisting turn, eluding one volley after another. It worked better than the other maneuvers I had attempted, buying us some time. But not enough, I told myself.

At this rate, we wouldn't last another ten minutes. Nor, I thought, would the mercenary vessel. The Abinarri were simply too good at this game, and we didn't have the resources to change the rules.

Then it came to me—perhaps we had the resources after all. Perhaps we had just what we needed.

Madigoor

"AND WHAT WAS THAT?" asked Bo'tex, unable to contain himself.

Robinson laid a hand on Picard's shoulder. "Don't get our friend the Caxtonian too excited," he advised. "He's capable of smells you wouldn't wish on your worst enemy."

"I'll keep my pheromones to myself," Bo'tex promised. "I only want to know what came next."

"Obviously," Dravvin concluded, "our friend came up with a scheme. He's all but said so."

"Yes," said Bo'tex, "but *what* scheme? Did he transport a tiny bit of antimatter onto each of the enemy's ships? Did he use his tractor beams to send one Abinarri crashing into the other?"

Picard shook his head. "We did neither of those things. For one thing, we were on a Romulan vessel, and they don't carry antimatter."

"That's right," said Flenarrh. "As Picard told us, they get their power from an artificial singularity."

"What's more," Picard noted, "transporting anti-

224

matter is a ticklish business. A *very* ticklish business. I've yet to see the containment field that would allow antimatter to pass through the pattern buffer."

"But what about using your tractor beams?" asked Bo'tex. "That would've been a good idea."

"It *might* have been," Picard replied, "except for two things. First, the Abinarri were moving too quickly for us to get a lock on them. Second, our tractor capabilities had been disabled by that time."

The Caxtonian nodded judiciously. "I see."

Hompaq grunted disdainfully. "It's clear what he did. He deployed his escape pods and smashed them into the enemy's vessels. By the time he was done, the odds were more in his favor."

"Not a bad notion," Picard conceded. "That is, if we had still had any escape pods to deploy. When we took over the warbird and forced the Romulans to evacuate, they took anything and everything in the way of auxiliary vehicles. All they left us was a single shuttle, and it wasn't quick enough to catch up with an Abinarri assault ship."

Robinson looked around the table. "Any other guesses?"

No one seemed inclined to venture one—not even the gecko, apparently.

The Captain of the *Kalliope* smiled. "So . . . what *did* you do?"

Picard smiled, as well.

The Tale

As I SAID, a plan had begun to form in my mind. I turned
to Abby and described it to her as briefly as I could.

She looked back at me, her pale blue eyes red with
smoke. "Let's do it," she replied.

"Mr. Worf," I said, "establish control over the ship's
transporters. Then contact the mercenary and tell our
friends we'll be beaming over."

The Klingon had overheard our discussion. Under the
circumstances, he could hardly question the wisdom
of it.

"Aye, sir," he responded crisply.

I looked at Thadoc, apologizing in advance for what I
was asking of him. "It'll be for only a minute," I said.

He glanced at me, knowing how long a minute could
be in the heat of battle. "Take your time," he told me.

Turning the helm over to him, I got up and headed for
the lift. Abby was a step ahead of me. We got in, punched
out a destination code, and watched the doors close
behind us.

As the compartment began to move, I drew a breath of

226

untainted air through my burning, smoke-ravaged throat. Letting it out, I drew in another.

Abby had slumped against the wall and closed her eyes for a moment. Half her face was black-and-blue, and the shoulder of her tunic was ripped open, exposing a patch of burned skin.

"It won't be much longer now," I told her.

She opened her eyes to look at me. "Either way, eh?"

I grasped her firmly by her shoulders. "Listen to me," I said. "We're getting out of here. We can't allow ourselves to think any other way."

Abby smiled a sad and weary smile. "Whatever you say, Picard. But just in case we don't—"

The doors to the lift opened then, revealing the residential corridor where the Romulan commander had had his quarters. The place was almost shockingly pristine, untouched by the chaos that had scarred most of the warbird.

Abby and I exchanged glances. There was no time for her to finish what she'd begun to say. But then, she didn't have to.

Together, we raced down the winding corridor and slid to a stop in front of the commander's door. It opened for us without hesitation and we scrambled inside—only to find the place filled with smoke.

As it billowed out at us, encompassing us, I cursed and used my hands to clear a path for myself. Little by little, cough by throat-searing cough, I made it across the room to the spot where Abby had discovered the Klingon self-destruct device.

The mechanism was still lying on the floor where we left it, amid the selection of engineering implements Abby had gathered for me. Dropping to my knees, I picked the thing up and inspected it.

"Is it intact?" Abby asked, hunkering down beside me.

"It seems to be," I replied.

As I had told her on the bridge, it would be a lot easier

to resurrect the thing than it had been to kill it. Still, it would take some time—and at the moment, time was in short supply.

The warbird shuddered terribly under the impact of another volley, forcing us to grab what we could to secure ourselves. A second or two later, the ship shuddered again.

"The Abinarri are closing in," Abby observed ruefully. "Thadoc can't elude them."

It came as no surprise to either of us. The fellow had the use of only one hand, after all, and I hadn't done much better with two of them.

Concentrating on the task before me, I began searching for my trusty charge inverter. The smoke made the job difficult, to say the least.

"Do you see it?" I asked.

Abby knew just what I meant. "No," she said after a moment. "Maybe it rolled away."

Eyes smarting, I groped about for it. Finally, I located the inverter near a leg of the commander's divan.

"Got it," I told her.

"Then get to work," she said.

My plan was a simple one, really. We would reactivate the self-destruct mechanism, set it, then beam off the Romulan vessel with the rest of the crew. Since the Abinarri had demonstrated an affinity for working at close quarters, we would allow them to do just that . . .

. . . until the moment the warbird's power source exploded in a frenzy of natural forces. Then if all went according to plan, the oppressor's ships would be caught in the blast.

As I said, a simple plan. But for it to work, I had to blow up the warbird before the Abinarri could.

Trying to see through the haze of smoke, I picked out one of the circuits that had fed the self-destruct device and began reactivating it. Unlike the last time, I worked in silence.

Abby and I could converse later, I thought. That is, if both of us managed to *survive*.

With some trouble owing to the stinging sensation in my eyes, I managed to restore the first connection. No sooner was I done than the warbird jerked again, sending me sprawling against the divan.

I bit my lip. Had the shock come a second earlier, I might have sent an unwanted charge through the circuit and blown up the ship prematurely. It was not a cheery thought, as you can imagine.

Abby helped me right myself. "Are you okay?" she asked.

"Right as rain," I assured her.

Spurred to a new sense of urgency, I went after the second connection. Again, we staggered under the force of the enemy's barrage—but this time I was prepared for it. Grinding my teeth together, I revived the energy flow and wiped sweat from my brow.

"Is it my imagination," I asked, "or is it getting hotter in here?"

"Hotter," Abby confirmed. "The damned Abinarri must have knocked out our life-supports."

I chuckled grimly to myself. The enemy seemed determined not to make this easy for us. Rude of them, I mused, as I turned my attention to the third and final connection.

It was trickier than the others. Apparently, I had done too good a job rendering it ineffective. The ship bucked and shook all around me, reminding me how little time I had to accomplish my task.

Sweat trickled into my eyes, making them smart even worse than before. The smoke was making me cough rather violently, which didn't help matters, and I was beginning to feel light-headed from a lack of oxygen.

Still, I plugged away with the Romulan charge inverter. And in time, I restored the deadly connection.

All that was left was to set the timer. I gave us three

minutes to reach the transporter room and pulled Abby to her feet.

"Done?" she asked.

"Done," I said.

"Will it work?" she wondered, as I tugged her across the room in the direction of the exit.

"It had better," I replied. "Otherwise—"

I never finished my sentence. Indeed, my entire reality seemed to turn inside out in a single, blinding moment.

The next thing I knew, I was stretched out on the deck—ears ringing, pain awakening with spectacular results in the whole right side of my body. Abby was lying beside me, inches away, her face turned away from my own.

I tried to speak her name, to no avail. I tried to extend my hand, to reach for her, but I couldn't do that either. In fact, I could barely roll my head to assess our situation.

Yet when I tried it, something strange and miraculous and thoroughly horrifying greeted my eyes through a break in the smoke. I found myself staring at the spattering of distant suns outside the ship—and not through the protective medium of an observation port. The stars were standing there before me, big and fierce and naked in the void.

How was that possible? I asked myself. How could the stars have invaded the sanctity of our vessel?

Then I saw a flicker of blue-white current and, deep in the folds of myself where my mind still functioned, I understood. The hull had been breached, I realized—but the warbird's structural integrity field was still holding our atmosphere inside.

And us as well.

But that could change at any moment. Another well-aimed blast and the integrity field would shatter as well, allowing us to be sucked out into the vacuum. And I was too dazed, too battered to do anything about it.

Worse, we had less than three minutes before the warbird destroyed itself. Perhaps by then we had only two minutes, or one—or a matter of mere seconds. I had no way of knowing.

Abruptly, out of the corner of my eye, I saw movement. Not Abby, but something else. Some*one* else, I realized. A powerful-looking figure, making its way toward us through the roiling fumes.

He loomed closer and I recognized him. It was *Worf.*

Kneeling, he gathered me up and slung me over his shoulder. Then he slung Abby over the other. Finally, rising under the weight of his double burden, he turned and headed for the exit with some urgency.

I was upside down, bouncing helplessly with each step, but I had an inkling of where we were going. We entered a lift, exited again, then negotiated corridor after spark-filled corridor.

After what seemed like a long time, too long for the warbird to still have been in existence, we arrived in the ship's transporter room. Worf set Abby and I down on the transport grid, crossed the room to work the controls, then joined us a second later.

I must have blacked out at that point. When I came to, I was on the bridge of the Orion ship, lying in a corner where soft, purplish lighting bathed me in violet shadows. Worf was hunkered down next to me, watching the bridge officers apply themselves to their various tasks.

On the vessel's diamond-shaped viewscreen, I could see two Abinarri ships. As I looked on, one of them was stabbed by a bolt of disruptor fire. A moment later, the vessel shivered and exploded in a flare of pure, white light.

"Got him!" exclaimed the weapons officer, an awkward-looking fellow with four arms and jet black skin.

"We've still got one more!" roared the being in charge—a ponderous female with wrinkled, gray flesh

231

and eyes like tiny, glittering diamonds. "Target and fire, Mastrokk!"

With an effort, I sat up. Every part of me felt bruised to the bone, but the ringing in my ears seemed to have stopped for the most part.

My lieutenant turned to me. "Captain . . .?"

Weakly, I held up a hand. "I'm all right," I assured him, though it came out little more than a whisper.

Then I remembered, and my throat constricted.

"Where's Abby?" I asked him.

Worf jerked his shaggy head.

Following the gesture, I saw her. Abby was lying in another corner of the bridge, surrounded by Thadoc, Dunwoody, and three of her other crewmen. Even in the eerie, purple lighting, she looked paler than the living had a right to be.

My god, I thought.

I remembered what Abby and I had said in the turbolift just a little while earlier. *"We're getting out of here,"* I had told her. *"We can't allow ourselves to think any other way."* And she had replied, *"Whatever you say, Picard. But just in case we don't . . ."*

I got up on shaky knees and started across the bridge. The Klingon grabbed my arm as gently as he could, hoping to restrain me—but I shrugged him off and kept going.

It can't be, I told myself. Not after we've come so far.

Thadoc and the others looked up at me as I approached. Their faces were grim, their eyesockets dark and hollow-looking—though not half as hollow-looking as Abby's.

Sinking to my knees in front of them, I reached out and touched her cheek with the back of my hand. It felt cold, waxy to the touch.

"Abby," I said.

Suddenly, her eyelids fluttered. A moment later, she opened them and took in the sight of me.

It took me a second or two to come to grips with my surprise. "You're not dead," I observed wonderingly.

Abby's mouth pulled up at the corners. "No," she agreed weakly. "But I think you may be." She shook her head. "You look awful, Picard."

I grinned, though my skin was so bruised, it hurt mightily to do so. "As matter of fact," I told her, "I *feel* awful."

Just then, someone yelled "Fire!" It turned out to be the female in charge of the vessel.

Before our eyes, the last of our attackers spasmed and blew herself to atoms in a moment of terrible splendor. Abby frowned.

"The last of them?" she asked. Apparently, she hadn't had her eyes closed the whole time.

I nodded. "The last of them."

Madigoor

"THEN IT WORKED?" asked the Captain of the *Kalliope*.

Hompaq grinned at the thought. "The warbird blew up and took your enemies with it?"

"So it would seem," said Picard.

The Klingon pounded the table with her fist. "Well done!" she rasped. "A feat worthy of a warrior!"

The captain nodded. "Thank you, Hompaq. Of course, I would rather have settled our differences with the Abinarri another way . . ." He shrugged. "But as I noted, they didn't leave us a great many options."

"But why did your lieutenant have to come and get you?" asked Flenarrh. He leaned forward in his chair. "What prevented him from simply beaming you out of the commander's quarters?"

"A good question," said Picard. "Apparently, by that time, site-to-site transports had been made impossible by the release of plasma gas all over the ship. Worf had no choice but to fetch us personally."

"It's a good thing it was the Klingon," Dravvin noted, "and not someone less powerful."

"Or less determined," Robinson added. "The warbird might have destroyed itself at any moment. Yet your man ignored that fact, risking his life to save your own."

Flenarrh grunted. "A brave man, that Worf."

"A warrior," Hompaq pointed out.

The Captain of the *Kalliope* chuckled. "Your first officer certainly knew what he was talking about."

Bo'tex looked at him. "His first officer?"

The Captain of the *Kalliope* nodded. "Early on in Picard's story, the man said Worf was worth several ordinary officers. The facts seemed to have proved him right."

"To be sure," Picard agreed.

"But surely," said Robinson, "you're not finished, Picard? What became of the fair Lady Abby? And her stalwarts?"

"And Brant?" the Captain of the *Kalliope* added. "What happened to him and his rebels?"

"And their Hoard?" Flenarrh wondered.

The gecko perked his head up. It seemed he had some questions of his own, if he could only voice them.

"You're right," Picard told them all. "There's more of my story to be told . . . if only a little."

The Tale

WE NEVER BEAMED back down to Brant's world. Rather, Brant and his fellow rebels beamed up to the mercenary vessel, along with all the equipment and supplies we had seen on the planet's surface.

And the Hoard as well.

Then we left the vicinity. Apparently, the rebels were well prepared, having decided in advance where they would rendezvous if they were ever attacked while their fleet was away.

Fortunately, the mercenary vessel had sustained little damage at the hands of the Abinarri. Cruising at warp eight, we would reach the rebellion's new headquarters world in a little less than two days.

In the meantime, we were treated for our injuries and given a chance to convalesce. Even Worf allowed his wounds to be dressed and subjected to a healing device of some kind. However, he refused to remain in the rebels' too bright, makeshift sickbay, preferring to prowl the purple-shadowed precincts of the ship.

I didn't have the strength to prowl with him, nor did I

pretend to. I remained in sickbay, Abby's bed just a few feet from my own. I remember lying there as weariness and my medications conspired to overwhelm me, glad to see her color starting to come back a little.

After all, I had begun to care about her. To care *deeply*.

Finally, I succumbed to sleep—a wonderful sleep, peaceful and without dreams. When I woke, I was surprised to learn I had been out for eighteen hours straight—and that Abby was gone.

I searched for her throughout the ship. A few of the rebels said they had seen her, speaking here and there with the survivors of her crew. Then one of them directed me to the observation lounge.

That's where I found her. She was standing with her brother, gazing at the streaking stars through a large, diamond-shaped port. They were cast in a purple light, like almost everything else on that ship.

If our vessel had still been operated by its original owners, the Orions, the place would have boasted a wide variety of gambling paraphernalia. As it was, it contained just a few tables and chairs. I made my way through them to join the Brants.

Abby turned and smiled at the sight of me. She looked a lot better than when I had glimpsed her last. Her pallor was gone and her eyes were as bright as before.

"Picard," she said.

I nodded. "Or anyway, what's left of me." I turned to Brant. "I take it our journey has been without incident thus far."

"It has," he confirmed. "With any luck, it'll stay that way."

"We need to talk," Abby told me.

"I guess that's my cue," said Brant. "Glad to see you're up and about again, Picard." Then he made his way out of the lounge, leaving his sister and me alone.

Abby was silent for a moment, strangely pensive. Then she said, "I've spoken to my men."

"How are they?" I asked.

"They're fine," she replied. "I . . . told them I was sorry."

"For what?" I asked.

Abby shrugged. "For letting them think there was a pot of gold at the end of the rainbow. One they could keep, I mean."

"You didn't know there wasn't," I reminded her.

"But even if I had," she insisted, "I would still have led them on. I would have done whatever it took to put a crew together."

"Only because your brother's life was at stake. At least, that's what you thought at the time."

"Still," said Abby, "there's no way I could have carried off this gambit without them—no way I could've made it to Hel's Gate, much less gotten through to this universe and helped turn away the Abinarri."

She had a point. Had her crew been any less capable or courageous, Abby would never have survived her encounters with the Cardassians and the Romulans—not to mention the pirates we kept running into.

"So they risked their lives over and over," Abby said, "and for what? In the end, they had nothing to show for it—except my unending gratitude and affection, as if that were worth anything on the open market."

"What did they say?" I asked.

"What do you think? Thadoc told me there was no need for an apology. He was glad to have followed me anywhere, for any reason." She grinned. "Dunwoody told me I'd have to make it up to him—say, with another voyage. After all, he said, Dujonian's Hoard isn't the only treasure in the universe."

I smiled. "That sounds like him."

Abby's smile faded. "I thanked him for the sentiment, of course. But I said that it wouldn't be possible for us to make another voyage. He would have to find someone else with whom to seek out those treasures."

"And why is that?" I inquired.

She glanced at me meaningfully. "Because I have decided to stay here with the rebels."

Somewhere deep inside, I believe I had known she would say that. Still, it knocked the stuffing out of me. As I noted earlier, I had grown rather fond of Abby Brant.

"I see," I said.

Perceiving that I was less than ecstatic about her announcement, she took my hand. "Try to understand," she told me. "This is a second chance for me. A chance to do some good for people, to fight the good fight the way some of those privateers fought it—whether you believe that or not."

"Abby . . ." I said softly.

"And this time," she finished, "I don't intend to screw it up."

The observation lounge echoed with the force of her words. Blushing, she looked away from me, as if she had suddenly taken an interest in the stars outside our ship.

"Thadoc said one word," she went on. "It was 'no.' I asked him not to make my decision any harder than it had to be. 'Who's making it harder?' he asked. 'Your brother needs all the help he can get.' "

"Then Thadoc's staying, as well?" I asked.

Abby nodded, her eyes sparkling with reflected light. "Dunwoody, too. He said he could use a change of scenery—if I'd have him."

"And you told him you would, of course."

She chuckled. "In a minute."

Abby had asked the other survivors as well, all three of them—but they hadn't been quite so eager as Thadoc and Dunwoody. They wanted to go home to their own universe.

She turned back to me, her eyes seeking mine. "It'll feel good to have a couple of familiar faces around while I'm chipping at the Abinarri."

"No doubt," I said hollowly.

Abby's brow creased. "It'd be even better to have one more around. Say, for instance . . . *yours.*"

I didn't respond.

"You and I," she said, "we've been through a lot in the short time we've known each other. We've proven we make one hell of a team, haven't we? Why not make it . . . a permanent one?"

I searched Abby Brant's features—her wise, pale blue eyes, her fine, freckled nose, her full and inviting lips. There was a great deal to keep me there, I mused.

And if I left, I would likely never see her again. After all, Brant's rebels would have to establish one new base after another. Even if I managed to reach this reality a second time, I would have no way to find them.

No way to find *her.*

To be honest, I was tempted by Abby's offer. There were worse ways to live than to fight every day for a cause. The problem was, I already had one. It was called the Federation.

Telling myself that didn't make my decision any easier. But it made me see it was the only decision I could make.

"We do make a hell of a team," I told Abby, "and part of me wants very much to remain. But like you, I've made a commitment—to others and to myself—and I cannot help but see it through."

For a moment, she looked as if she would argue with me, try to talk me into staying. Then it seemed she thought better of it.

"I understand," Abby told me, her voice wavering only slightly.

"I knew you would," I replied.

And that was that.

We spent the next night on the surface of another barren planet, helping the rebels set up their camp—while a select few of them used the Orion's transporter to bury their Hoard. I met people from races I had never seen before and would probably never see again. And I spent a few precious hours with Abby Brant.

The next morning, Worf and I—along with the three other men who had decided not to join the rebels—gathered in the center of the camp. We said good-bye to the friends we had made. Then Richard Brant called the mercenary vessel and told her captain to beam us up.

I gazed for the last time at Abby, doing my best to memorize everything I could about her—her eyes, her manner, her bearing. Then I found myself on an Orion transporter pad, alongside Worf and the others.

The transporter technician was slight and angular, with black, staring eyes, a bluish white topknot, and skin the color of bronze. He looked up at us after a moment.

"You're sure you want to go back?" he asked.

I nodded. "Yes."

"Too bad," he said, making no effort to hide his disappointment. "The Gate gives me indigestion."

"I'm sorry to hear that," I told him, but my mind was elsewhere.

Exiting the transporter chamber, I made my way out into the corridor and located a diamond-shaped observation port with a view of the world below us. As I stood there, we began to break orbit.

"Captain?" said a deep voice.

I turned and saw Worf standing behind me.

"Do you mind if I join you?" he asked.

I found I was glad for the company. "No," I told the lieutenant. "I don't mind at all."

Together, we watched the rebels' new home dwindle beneath us, until it was the size of a ball and then a coin and then barely visible at all. At last, I lost sight of it.

And, regrettably, Abby with it.

Nonetheless, I found I was happy for her. Happy beyond words.

After all, she had found a treasure far more precious

than anything she might have hoped for . . . an opportunity to start her life anew.

But if Abby Brant had found a treasure, Jean-Luc Picard had lost one. And no matter how far I traveled, no matter how many exotic star systems I explored, I knew I might never see its like again.

Madigoor

As THE STORY ENDED, there was silence around the table. Picard's companions looked at one another. Then they nodded.

"A good story," Bo'tex decided.

"A *very* good story," Dravvin insisted.

"Just very good?" Robinson responded.

"Masterful," said the Captain of the *Kalliope*. "I won't even attempt to tell one of my own."

Hompaq grumbled in agreement. "Why waste it when the contest has already been won?"

Flenarrh smiled at Picard. "I'm glad Lafitte didn't run you through before you could tell it."

"As a matter of fact," the captain replied, "so am I."

Just then, the gecko roused itself and skittered to the edge of our table. With a last look around, it leaped off and lost itself in the crowd.

"Talk about your fair-weather friends," commented the Captain of the *Kalliope*. "Show's over and he's *gone.*"

Smiling in his beard, Robinson leaned closer to his fellow human. "Answer a question for me, Picard."

The captain of the *Enterprise* shrugged. "Ask away."

"If your story's true," Robinson inquired, "why have I never heard of Hel's Gate before? As long as I've frequented the Captain's Table, and that's long indeed, why has no one ever mentioned such a phenomenon?"

"I was wondering that myself," said Bo'tex.

"Though perhaps you were too embarrassed to admit it," Dravvin suggested. He drew disapproving looks from around the table. "Perhaps . . . almost as embarrassed as *I* was," he confessed grudgingly.

Flenarrh looked relieved. "Thank Trannis. I thought I was just *me.*"

Hompaq nodded ruefully. "You shamed us all into silence, Picard. I don't know whether to slap you on the back or spill your blood."

"Well?" said Robinson, his eyes narrowing mischievously as he regarded Picard. "Is it possible you've woven a yarn for us—and a wonderful yarn it was—with no basis in fact?"

Picard looked around the table—and smiled. "That," he said, "is something that must remain between myself and my conscience."

"That's all you'll tell us?" Hompaq rasped.

"That's all," the human confirmed.

"It's an outrage!" the Klingon bellowed, attracting the attention of other captains in the vicinity.

"No," Robinson told her. "It's an enhancement."

Again, those assembled at the table looked at one another, considering the proposition. And again, they nodded slowly in agreement.

"It makes the story that much more exciting," the Captain of the *Kalliope* observed. "Never to know if it's fact or fiction, spun from personal experience or the imagination."

"Never to know if Hel's Gate really exists," Dravvin added. "Or for that matter, the dimension beyond it."

"Or the lovely Red Abby," Robinson noted.

Hompaq grunted, the lone dissenter at the table. "And never to sleep again for wondering."

Flenarrh quirked a smile. "I salute you, Picard."

"And I as well," Bo'tex told him.

Robinson clapped Picard on the shoulder. "Well done, my friend."

"Jean Luc!" came a voice.

Turning in his seat, Picard saw Neil Gleason making his way toward them. And he had a female on his arm.

"Gleason," Picard declared, unable to conceal his exasperation. "Where the devil have you been?"

His fellow captain gestured to the female. "This is Captain Prrghh," he said. "An old friend. We've been . . . er, catching up on old times." He smiled at Prrghh. "Isn't that right, my love?"

Prrghh smiled back at him with her vaguely feline features. "Yes," she purred. "Catching up."

It didn't quite explain the suddenness of Gleason's disappearance. However, it did seem to explain why it had taken him so long to turn up again.

"Pleased to meet you," Picard told Prrghh.

"Likewise," the female responded. She nodded to the other captains at the table, then turned to Gleason. "I suppose you have to go now."

He sighed. "Duty calls. We've got an early-morning meeting we don't dare miss on pain of death."

Prrghh laughed. "Until next time, then." And she kissed Gleason softly on the cheek.

Gleason reddened. "Till next time," he echoed.

By then, Picard's tablemates had begun some new discussion, which had nothing to do with either Hel's

Gate or Prrghh. Picard took advantage of the fact to stand and approach his friend.

"You abandoned me," he told Gleason.

His friend glanced at the table where Picard's companions still sat. "No one stays abandoned in this place for long," he said. He looked at Picard. "And can you say you didn't have a good time?"

Picard considered his surroundings and frowned. "Perhaps *abandoned* is too strong a word. Nonetheless, you could have warned me you were going to disappear. I was concerned that something might have happened to you."

Gleason chuckled. "Something *did*. But it was a most pleasant something, I assure you." He gestured. "Shall we?"

Following the gesture, Picard saw the door by which he'd entered the place.

He felt a tug on his sleeve. It was Robinson, reaching over from where he sat. "Don't tell me you're leaving us," the bearded man said.

"I'm afraid so," Picard told him. "Perhaps we'll meet again."

Robinson shrugged. "I'll be here."

Picard was about to say how unlikely it was he'd return to Madigoor IV. After all, if not for the conference, he might never have come here in the first place.

But that didn't mean he wouldn't return to the Captain's Table. In fact, he would make a *point* of returning.

Bo'tex waved good-bye. "Take care of yourself," he told Picard.

"Good voyaging," Dravvin chimed in.

"Fair ports," Flenarrh wished him.

Hompaq lifted her chin. "Qapla."

Picard smiled. "The same to you." He glanced at the

Captain of the *Kalliope*, who smiled back at him. "To all of you." Then he nodded to Gleason, and they headed for the door.

Before they could quite reach it, however, someone shouted to them. Turning, Picard saw it was the fellow behind the bar.

"I'm sorry," he told the bartender. "I didn't hear you."

The man cupped his hands and called out again. "Give my regards to Guinan, won't you?"

It took Picard by surprise—not that the fellow knew Guinan, since she had been to any number of places in the course of her long life. But how had he known that *Picard* knew Guinan?

Then he remembered. He had identified himself to his tablemates as the captain of the *Enterprise*. Obviously, someone else had overheard and mentioned it to the bartender.

Yes, he thought, that was it. It *had* to be.

"Of course," he finally shouted back. "I'll be happy to."

The bartender waved his thanks and went back to his duties. And Picard, even more intrigued with the place than before, nonetheless resumed his progress toward the exit.

He took one last look at the Captain's Table—at the people, the place . . . the eerie, uncertain, and yet insistently familiar landscape. And then he followed his friend Gleason into the night and the fog.

For a while, they walked in silence. And when Picard looked back, he couldn't find the sign anymore that identified the Captain's Table. But somehow, he knew, if he searched long and hard enough, it would be right there before his eyes.

Reaching into the pocket of his jacket, he found and

extracted the good-luck charm he had taken to carrying with him—a diamondlike jewel the size of a uniform pip.

"What's that?" asked his friend.

Picard shrugged. "A souvenir."

Of course, had Gleason been more of an archaeologist, he might have suspected the stone was a genuine glor'ya. But it was only a replica, given to Picard by one of the Federation scientists who had analyzed the real thing.

The captain had been tempted to show the gem to his comrades in the Captain's Table. However, as Robinson had noted, that would have detracted from the mystery surrounding his tale.

"Well?" asked Gleason. "Was the place everything I said it would be?"

Picard looked at him. "It was pleasant, all right."

"Just pleasant?" his friend probed.

The captain of the *Enterprise* took a deep draft of night air. "You mean, do I have as much on my mind as I did before?"

"Uh-huh. And do you?"

Picard shrugged. "Perhaps not. Or if I do, at least it isn't weighing quite as heavily." He smiled wistfully. "But then, a little fencing match always did put things into perspective for me."

The cool metal handle on the massive wooden door fit into Captain Benjamin Sisko's hand as if it were made for him. The feeling so startled him that he paused and glanced down, opening his hand without taking his fingers off the metal.

The handle's design was Bajoran, shaped almost like

another hand reaching out, yet without the delineation of a hand or fingers. It was clearly very old and very well made. The surface was worn smooth, polished by use. Sisko couldn't see anything that attached the handle to the door, almost as if the handle grew from the dark wood.

Above Sisko's head was a carved wooden sign that read simply "The Captain's Table." The sign was an extension of the door frame, and the letters on the sign were dried and cracked, obviously from the heat of the Bajoran summers. Yet the sign, along with the door and the griplike handle, seemed to reach out to Sisko and pull him in, welcoming him as if he were coming back to a childhood home.

A few weeks before, a captain of a Jibetian freighter had pulled Sisko aside on the Promenade and asked if he knew where a bar called the Captain's Table might be. Sisko had said he'd never heard of the place. Instead, he recommended Quark's.

The Jibetian had simply laughed and said, "If you ever get the chance, have a drink in the Captain's Table. There is no other bar."

Sisko had put the man's suggestion out of his mind until this morning. He was on Bajor because Dr. Bashir had threatened to have Sisko relieved of command if he did not rest. It was impossible to rest in the middle of a war, Sisko had argued, but Bashir was adamant. A Starfleet doctor did have the power to relieve someone of command, and rather than go through that fight, Sisko had agreed to two days on Bajor, two days without meetings, without Starfleet protocol, without decisions.

If he had stayed on the station, he wouldn't have been able to relax. Somehow the staff seemed to believe that Sisko had to decide which replicators remained on-line,

26 HRS = 1 BAJORAN DAY

which messages should be forwarded through the war zone, which ships would be allowed to dock. He had a competent crew; it was time, Bashir had said, to trust them with the details, and to sleep.

Bashir had wanted Sisko on Bajor for a week. Sisko wanted to stay overnight and return in less than twenty-four hours. They had compromised on two days.

"Two *full* days," Bashir had said. "If I hear of you on this station before forty-eight hours are up, I will order you to sickbay for the remainder of your holiday."

"I'll keep that in mind," Sisko had said, deciding that he'd rather remain on Bajor than subject himself to sickbay for even one hour. Bashir had smiled, knowing that he'd won.

Sisko spent his first day on Bajor in his rented cabin, sitting outside and wondering what the planet would be like when he retired there. If he got a chance to retire there.

By that afternoon, he was restless—despite Bashir's worry, Sisko had too much energy to relax. His concerns for the Federation, for the entire Quadrant, would not allow him to rest. Not completely. And no matter how much he loved Bajor, it didn't take his mind off the problems he would face when he returned.

He wandered the streets of the nearby village and had passed this very door more than once. On his third pass, the sign caught his attention and the Jibetian captain's words had come back to him. Sisko had his fingers wrapped around the handle before he'd even realized that he'd made a decision.

The door was so massive-looking that Sisko expected it to feel heavy as he pulled it open. Instead it moved easily, almost as if it had no weight at all.

Inside the coolness and darkness gripped him, pulling him out of the heat of the Bajoran day. Instantly he could feel the sweat on his forehead where moments before the dryness of the afternoon air had pulled it instantly away. He let the door swing shut slowly behind him, seemingly plunging him into complete darkness. His eyes struggled to adjust from the bright sunlight to the dim light. The coolness now wrapped completely around him like a welcome hand. While on Bajor he always drank regularly, but now, in the cool air, he was suddenly even more thirsty than normal.

Part of his thirst came from the smell. The interior had a soft scent, like the smell of fresh baked bread long after it had been eaten. Or the scent of coffee just percolating in the morning. Familiar smells. Welcoming smells. Smells that made him think of comfort and of home.

He stood still, with his back to the door, as dim shapes appeared, as his eyes adjusted.

Walls.

Pictures on the walls.

Soon he could tell he was in a short hallway fashioned out of smooth wood and decorated with images of old water-sailing ships. Only a single indirect light above the ceiling illuminated the small passage. Deeper inside he could hear talking and an occasional laugh. He stepped forward and around a corner.

In front of him was a large, yet comfortable-feeling room. The ceiling was low and a stone fireplace filled part of the wall to his left, a small fire doing nothing to take the comfortable coolness from the room. Most of the right wall of the room was filled with a long wooden bar fronted by a dozen or more stools. The surface of the bar looked worn and well used. A tall, thick man stood behind the bar and at least a dozen patrons from different races sat around some of the tables in small groups.

Sisko stopped in the entrance, giving his eyes time to finish adjusting to the dim light. It was then that he noticed the grand-style piano in the corner to his left.

It seemed old and very well used, its surface marred by what looked like hundreds of glass and bottle imprints.

Beside the piano a humanoid sat. He was from no race that Sisko recognized. The humanoid had slits for eyes, lizardlike skin, and four long talons on each hand. Sisko felt no fear or revulsion, but merely a sense of curiosity and a feeling of comfort coming from the creature.

"Welcome, Captain," the large man behind the bar said, smiling and motioning Sisko forward. With one more glance at the unmoving humanoid, Sisko turned and stepped toward the bar.

The bartender wore a white apron with an open-necked gray shirt under it. He had unruly white hair and a smile that seemed to take the dimness out of the air. Sisko liked the man instantly, not exactly knowing why, and not willing to explore why. Sisko was on vacation. It was time he relaxed. He usually knew better than to be lulled into a feeling of safety, and yet here he was. He was conscious of his back, conscious of the people around him, but he wasn't really wary. Not yet. And he wouldn't be unless something made him feel that way.

Sisko stepped between two of the bar stools. To his surprise, he had to look up to meet the gaze of the man behind the bar.

"They call me Cap," the bartender said in a deep, rich voice that seemed to have a touch of laughter floating through it. "Welcome to the Captain's Table. What's your drink of choice?" He wiped his hands on a bar rag, and then waited.

Sisko glanced down the long back bar filled with glasses of all shapes and sizes. Above the glasses were what seemed like hundreds of different bottles of liquor. He couldn't spot a replicator. He had a thousand choices, but at the moment he wanted something to take away the last of the Bajoran heat and dryness.

"Do you have Jibetian ale?"

Cap laughed and nodded. "You'll have to go a great deal further than that to stump this place. We have just about everything. Would you like your ale warm, cold, or lightly salted?"

Sisko had never liked the Jibetian habit of salting their ale. "Cold," he said. "No salt."

Betraying a lightness on his feet that didn't seem natural to a man his size, Cap spun and opened up a cooler under the back bar. A moment later he slid a cold, damp bottle of Jibetian ale into Sisko's hand.

"Thanks," Sisko said, tilting the bottle toward Cap in a small, appreciative salute.

Jibetian ale was the perfect drink for Sisko's mood. It was hard to come by, almost impossible since the start of the war with the Dominion. Quark claimed to have one bottle left in his stock, and the price he placed on it made it seem as if it were the last bottle anywhere in the universe. Sisko had thought he would have to forgo Jibetian ale until the Federation defeated the Dominion.

Almost as if he read Sisko's mind, Cap said, "I think I got a few more where that came from."

"Excellent," Sisko said. "I wish I had time for more than one."

Cap just smiled as if what Sisko had said had amused him. Then the bartender turned back to cleaning glasses.

Sisko watched him for a moment, then took a drink. The rich, golden taste of the ale relaxed him, draining some of the problems he carried, almost as if they didn't exist. He downed half the bottle before finally forcing himself to stop for a breath. He very seldom drank, so going too fast wasn't the best idea, no matter how good it tasted. And this was real ale, not synthehol. Its effects would be real as well.

Cap was still washing glasses, so Sisko turned and studied the bar. He had half-expected, in the middle of the afternoon, to be the only one inside. But that clearly wasn't the case. Five of the ten tables had groups at them, the sounds of their talk filling the low-ceiling bar with a full background sound. If Sisko focused, he could hear individual conversations, but overall the noise level was not too loud.

The patrons of this bar were an odd mix. A number of humans, a young, childlike man from a race Sisko couldn't identify, and a half-dozen other races he had seen on the station. He would have thought this mix normal at Quark's, which had the entire Quadrant to draw on. Here, in a small out-of-the-way bar on Bajor, the mix was odd indeed, especially since there were no Bajorans present.

A huge Caxtonian sat at the opposite end of the bar, nursing a drink. The Caxtonian looked as if he never left that stool, which struck Sisko. He had never heard of a Caxtonian ever visiting Bajor. There were a number of strange things about this place, and yet, he didn't feel uncomfortable. Perhaps that was the strangest of all. He had been on alert ever since the threat to the Alpha Quadrant began; he'd thought he wouldn't relax until the situation was resolved.

Perhaps Bashir was right. Perhaps Sisko had needed this.

He had finished off another quarter of the bottle and was about to ask Cap about some of the customers when behind him a loud, grating voice boomed over the background talking.

"Sisko! You are a long way from your precious station."

As Sisko turned, the mostly empty ale bottle in his hand, he noticed that Cap wasn't smiling quite as much as he had a moment before.

"I could say the same for you, Sotugh," Sisko said,

turning to face the Klingon who stood near a table on the far side of the room. Sisko hadn't seen him a moment before, yet he knew that voice without even seeing its owner. And now he was even more surprised at the patrons of this bar.

Sotugh, head of the house of DachoH, commanded a large percentage of the Klingon fleet under Gowron. He was loyal to the Empire almost to a fault, and made clear his disgust of the current alliance between the Federation and the Klingon Empire against the Dominion. Yet he had fought many brilliant battles in the course of the war. The last time Sisko had heard, Sotugh and his ships were patrolling a sector of the Cardassian border.

"Bah," Sotugh said, waving his hand in disgust at Sisko's comment. He was a large man, even for a Klingon. His graying hair flowed over his clothing, which, surprisingly, was not his uniform. Sisko wasn't sure if he'd ever seen Sotugh out of uniform before.

"Gentlemen," Cap said, his voice stopping Sotugh from continuing. "Instead of yelling across the bar, I suggest you sit down together and continue this conversation."

"Sit with Sisko?" Sotugh said, laughing at the suggestion of the bartender. "I will fight with him against the Dominion, but nothing more."

Sisko leaned over his ale. "Still mad at me for the Mist incident, I see."

Sotugh's hand went to his knife. "The Mist would have been members of the Empire if not for your action. Their weapons would help us fight the Cardassian and Dominion scum."

Sisko smiled. "As usual," he said deliberately, "your opinions blind you, Sotugh."

Sotugh stepped forward, his hand gripping his knife.

"Sotugh!" Cap said, his voice stopping the Klingon warrior in midstep. "Only a coward draws on an unarmed man. You are not known as a coward."

Sisko place the bottle on the bar and opened both his hands to show Sotugh that they were empty. The bartender clearly knew how to handle Klingons. Around the bar a few other patrons laughed softly.

Sotugh looked angry, but his hand left his knife.

"It seems," Cap said, "that since the Mist are considered nothing but legend, that there is a story behind this. Am I right, Captain?"

Sisko picked up his bottle and finished the last of the ale. "There is a story," he said. He grinned at Sotugh, who only sneered in return. Every patron in the bar now had his attention riveted on the two.

While the tension held the bar in silence, Cap opened another bottle of Jibetian ale and slid it down the bar, stopping it just beside Sisko's hand. Then he quickly poured what looked like a mug of bloodwine. "Arthur, hand this to Sotugh."

The young-looking alien, the one who looked like a slender child, grabbed the mug from the bar. He moved easily across the floor, his robes flowing around him, and handed the mug to Sotugh as if the glowering Klingon were nothing more a happy patron.

"I would be very interested in hearing a story about the Mist," Cap said. "Would anyone else?"

It seemed that from the yeses and applause, everyone agreed. Sisko only shook his head in amusement at Sotugh's expression of disgust. It had been a number of years since the meeting with Sotugh over the race called the Mist. There was nothing secret about the incident. But it hadn't become widely known, since shortly after it happened the Klingons invaded Cardassia. Now the story would only add to the legend of the Mist.

"Pull a couple of those tables together," Cap said, pointing at a few tables in the center of the room. "Does anyone need refills before the story starts?"

The young Arthur took Sotugh's bloodwine before the

Klingon had a chance to drink, and set the mug on an empty table. To Sisko's surprise, Sotugh did not seem to mind. He went to the nearest chair, chased away a yellow and green gecko, grabbed his mug, and took a long drink, slopping some of the liquid down the side. Miraculously, Arthur managed to avoid getting drops on his robe.

Two patrons quickly pulled another table over to Sotugh's. Sisko nodded to Cap and moved over to the group table, sitting across from the Klingon. After a moment everyone in the bar except for the Caxtonian at the bar and the strange lizard man near the door had gathered at the large table with drinks in their hands.

"Sotugh," Sisko said, smiling at his old adversary. "Would you like to start? Klingons are legendary for their ability to tell a story."

Sotugh simply waved his hand in disgust. "Klingons tell stories of honor. But this story has no honor for anyone. You tell it. I will correct your errors."

Sisko took a quick sip from the bottle of cold ale, then nodded at Cap, who stood near the bar.

"In my years in Starfleet, I have seen many strange things," Sisko said. "But few as strange as the Mist."

"Now, that," Sotugh said, "is something I agree with."

Sisko smiled at Sotugh. He had known it would be impossible for the Klingon to keep silent during this story.

Cap laughed. "Sotugh, you have given the story over to Captain Sisko. Please let him tell it."

Sotugh sat back in disgust, the mug of bloodwine clutched in his hands.

"Go ahead, Captain," Cap said.

"As you may have gathered, most of this story will be hard to believe. But I'm sure Sotugh will correct anything I may get wrong."

Sotugh only grunted.

"I first heard the legend of the Mist," Sisko said, "when I was a cadet in Starfleet Academy, but I didn't encounter them for many years. By then I had almost forgotten who and what they were. . . ."

*To be continued in Book Three of
Star Trek: Deep Space Nine
The Captain's Table:*

The Mist

Captain Jean-Luc Picard

by
Michael Jan Friedman

His Early Life

Jean-Luc Picard was born on Earth in 2305 to Maurice and Yvette Gessard Picard, and raised on a family farm in LaBarre, France, along with his older brother, Robert. Maurice Picard was a tradition-bound French vintner who didn't approve of advanced technology and encouraged both his sons to follow in his footsteps.

However, from a very young age, Jean-Luc had his eyes on the stars. As a boy, he enjoyed building ships in bottles, the pride of his collection being a legendary Promellian battle cruiser—a vessel he would one day discover in his voyages aboard the *Enterprise-D*.

These toy ships served as a springboard for the future captain's imagination. In his daydreams, he was in command of the vessels after which the toys had been modeled, a true heir to the legendary starship commanders who had gone before him.

Against his father's wishes, Picard applied for entrance into Starfleet Academy in 2322, at the age of seventeen. Unfortunately, he fell short in this effort.

Undaunted, the young Frenchman tried again and was admitted to the Academy a year later.

As a first-year cadet, in 2323, he ran the grueling Starfleet Academy marathon on Danula II. By passing four upperclassmen on the last hill of the forty-kilometer run, he became the only freshman ever to win the event. Picard won top academic honors at the Academy as well, scoring high enough to be named class valedictorian.

Still, his record at the Academy was not flawless. He committed a serious offense that was never made public. Years later, Picard credited Academy groundskeeper Boothby with helping him to rectify his error, thereby making it possible for him to remain a cadet in good standing.

Shortly after graduation with the class of 2327, Picard was on leave with several classmates at Starbase Earhart, where he picked a fight with three Nausicaans at the Bonestell Recreation Facility. One of the Nausicaans stabbed Picard through the heart, necessitating a cardiac replacement procedure and leaving Picard with an artificial heart.

Years later, as a young lieutenant, Picard met the legendary Sarek of Vulcan at the wedding of the ambassador's son. Picard was awed by Sarek, whose negotiations had helped to shape the Federation. On another occasion, Picard distinguished himself by leading an away team to Milika III to save an endangered Federation ambassador.

In 2333, Picard was a staff officer on the *U.S.S. Stargazer* when the ship's captain was killed. The twenty-eight-year-old Picard took charge of the bridge and for his coolheadedness in the emergency was offered command of the *Stargazer*—thereby becoming one of the youngest Starfleet officers ever to captain a starship.

Sometime later, Picard became fast friends with Jack Crusher, one of the officers reporting to him on the *Stargazer*. In 2344, Crusher introduced Picard to his fiancée, a medical student named Beverly Howard, to whom Picard was strongly attracted. However, as Crusher was a close friend, Picard never mentioned the attraction, either to Crusher or to Beverly.

Jack Crusher married Beverly Howard in 2348. The couple had a child, Wesley, a year later. When Jack was killed in the line of duty in 2354, it was Picard's sad task to inform Beverly Crusher of her husband's death. Picard still declined to reveal his love for Beverly at the time, because he felt to do so would be to betray his friend.

Picard commanded the *Stargazer* until 2355, when the ship was nearly destroyed by an unprovoked sneak attack near the Maxia Zeta star system. The assailant in the incident was unknown at the time but was later found to be a Ferengi spacecraft.

The captain would later recall that an unidentified vessel suddenly appeared and fired twice at point-blank range, disabling the *Stargazer*'s shields. Picard saved the lives of his crew by employing a tactic to be known as the "Picard maneuver."

However, the *Stargazer* was too badly damaged to repair. Picard abandoned the vessel, albeit reluctantly. The surviving crew, including the captain himself, drifted for several long weeks in lifeboats and shuttle-craft before being rescued.

Following the loss of the *Stargazer*, Picard was court-martialed, as required by standard Starfleet procedure. In the end, he was exonerated. The prosecutor in the case was Phillipa Louvois, with whom Picard had had a love affair.

Picard would see the *Stargazer* again, some years later, in an encounter with a revenge-seeking Ferengi. However, the vessel would be destroyed before the captain could salvage it.

While captain of the *Stargazer*, Picard had also been romantically involved with a woman named Jenice.

Although Picard and Jenice were strongly attracted to one another, the captain feared commitment and eventually broke off the relationship. It was a move he would come to regret.

Picard and Jenice would be reunited in 2364. At that time, the crew of the *Enterprise-D* would save the life of Jenice's husband, Dr. Paul Manheim, following a serious laboratory accident on planet Vandor IX.

The Enterprise-D

Picard was appointed captain of the *Enterprise-D,* the fifth starship to bear the name *Enterprise,* in 2363, shortly after the vessel was commissioned. It was in this capacity that he carried out his greatest accomplishments and achieved his greatest glory.

Still, Picard had served on the *Enterprise* for less than a year when he was offered a promotion to the admiralty by Admiral Gregory Quinn, who was attempting to consolidate his power base against a supposed alien conspiracy within Starfleet Command. Picard declined the offer, citing his belief that he could better serve the Federation as a starship commander.

Later on, however, the captain found that the conspiracy was real. A number of Starfleet officials had been taken over by a species of intelligent parasites, whose presence was marked only by a quill-like protrusion from the host's neck. With the help of his officers, Picard foiled the parasites' plans to take control of the fleet.

Picard's most frequent nemesis was the seemingly omnipotent, extradimensional being known as Q. Actually, Q was a single component of an entire continuum that called itself by the same name. Despite his amazing powers and long life, Q displayed a childlike petulance and sense of playfulness.

The captain's first encounter with Q took place during his first mission on the *Enterprise-D,* in 2364. Q detained the ship and made Picard the defendant in a twenty-first-century courtroom drama, in which Q accused captain and crew of being "grievously savage."

On his second visit to the *Enterprise-D*, Q offered First Officer William Riker a gift of Q-like supernatural powers. On his third visit, Q transported the *Enterprise-D* some seven thousand light-years beyond Federation space to System J-25, where Picard and his crew first encountered the powerful and dangerous race known as the Borg.

In 2367, Q cast Picard and his officers into an elaborate romantic fantasy based on the old Earth legends of Robin Hood. Two years later, Q presented Picard with what he claimed was the afterlife, allowing the captain to see what his life would have been like had he not made some of the rash choices of his youth. However, Picard discovered that it was partly the brashness of his youth that had made him the man he was.

In 2370, the Q Continuum decided to test Picard again, devising a paradox whereby he would be responsible for the destruction of mankind by creating an antitime phenomenon. Q himself added the wrinkle of having Picard shift among three time periods, with awareness of what was happening in each.

After Picard succeeded in solving the paradox, Q informed him that the experience had been a test. The Q Continuum had wanted to see if Picard could expand his mind and explore the unknown possibilities of existence—abilities he had demonstrated to the Continuum's satisfaction.

One of Picard's senior officers on the *Enterprise-D* was Beverly Crusher. As the vessel was designed to accommodate family life, Crusher was accompanied by her young son, Wesley. Another of his officers was Data, an android created by the legendary cyberneticist, Noonien Soong.

In 2365, an energy vortex near the Endicor system

created a duplicate of Picard that had originated at a point in the time line six hours in the future. Although the "future" Picard was identical to the "present" Picard, the captain had difficulty accepting the existence of his twin—largely because he believed his duplicate might have been responsible for the destruction of his ship. To Picard, this was a deeply repugnant idea.

Picard's artificial heart required routine replacement. This happened most recently in 2365, when complications in the cardiac replacement procedure performed at Starbase 515 necessitated emergency assistance by Dr. Katherine Pulaski. Pulaski had joined the crew of the *Enterprise* just a few months earlier, temporarily replacing Beverly Crusher.

In 2366, in an inadvertent violation of the Prime Directive, Picard was mistaken for a god by the Vulcanoid natives of Mintaka III. While he couldn't erase their knowledge of him, he was able to convince them to nonetheless follow a "rational" path in their development.

The captain met Sarek of Vulcan again in 2366, when the Vulcan ambassador's final mission was jeopardized by Bendii Syndrome. The disease caused Sarek to lose control of his emotions, a source of great embarrassment to a Vulcan. Picard mind-melded with Sarek to lend the ambassador the emotional stability he needed to conclude a historic treaty with the Legarans.

In 2368, Picard visited Sarek's deathbed to investigate rumors that Sarek's son, Spock, had defected to the Romulan Empire. Sarek told the captain that Spock perhaps was only attempting to reunite the Vulcan and Romulan peoples. Disguising themselves as Romulans, Picard and Data ventured to Romulus to discover the truth—and aided Spock when he was double-crossed by his Romulan allies.

The captain of the *Enterprise-D* enjoyed a great many friendships. One of his warmest and most unique associations was with a being called Guinan, who came to serve on the *Enterprise* as the bartender in its Ten-Forward lounge in 2365.

Guinan was a member of the El-Aurian race, which was nearly wiped out by the Borg in the late twenty-third century. While fleeing from the Borg 2293, she was briefly swept into an alternate reality known as the nexus—along with James T. Kirk and a number of other El-Aurians.

Like all her people, Guinan was long-lived. Born sometime in the nineteenth century, she was about five hundred years old when she served aboard the *Enterprise-D.* Guinan and Q were acquaintances, having met each other in the twenty-second century, but their relationship was a hostile one.

Guinan possessed an unusual sense that extended beyond linear space-time. She alone was intuitively aware of the damage to the "normal" flow of time when the *Enterprise-C* was swept some twenty-two years into its future, creating an alternate time line. Guinan warned Picard that history had been altered, persuading him to return the *Enterprise-C* to 2344 to repair the time line.

Picard also maintained a close rapport with Data. In 2365, the captain served as the android's attorney when a hearing tested Data's status as an enfranchised being. With Phillipa Louvois hearing the case, Picard argued successfully that all beings are created but not owned by their creator. Louvois's decision made it clear that Data was no one's property.

Picard formed a brief friendship with a Tamarian captain named Dathon in 2368. Dathon perished saving Picard's life, but managed to facilitate peaceful contact between the Tamarians and the Federation in the process.

Later that year, Picard accepted Ensign Ro Laren, a Bajoran with a checkered past, as a member of his crew.

Two years later, Ro disappointed him by aligning herself with the rebel Maquis and exposing a Starfleet ambush Picard had set for them. Reportedly, her greatest regret was betraying her captain, who had placed so much faith in her.

One of Picard's greatest sorrows as captain of the *Enterprise* was that he could not save the life of Tasha Yar, his first chief of security on the ship. Yar was destroyed by a creature called Armus in an attempt to rescue *Enterprise* personnel trapped on Armus's world.

In 2366, on the pleasure planet Risa, Picard met and fell for a beautiful and roguish woman named Vash. A year later, he played Robin Hood to her maid Marian in a fantasy environment created by Q.

The Borg

Picard was abducted by the Borg in late 2366 as part of a Borg assault on the Federation. Helpless in the hands of the invaders, Picard was surgically mutilated and transformed into a Borg entity called Locutus. As Locutus, Picard was forced to cooperate in the devastating battle of Wolf 359, in which he helped destroy thirty-nine Federation starships and the majority of their crews.

The captain was finally rescued by an *Enterprise-D* away team, then surgically restored to his human form by Dr. Crusher. However, he carried the emotional scars of his experience for quite some time.

Following his return from Borg captivity, Picard spent several weeks recovering from the terrible physical and psychological trauma. While the *Enterprise-D* was undergoing repairs at Earth Station McKinley in 2367, Picard took the opportunity to visit his hometown of LaBarre for the first time in almost twenty years.

In LaBarre, he stayed with his brother, Robert—and met Robert's wife, Marie, and his son, Rene, for the first time. Fiercely old-fashioned, Picard's brother had remained on the family vineyard to continue his father's work after Jean-Luc left to join Starfleet.

Robert was resentful of his brother's stellar achievements, though Robert's son seemed inclined to follow his uncle Jean-Luc to the stars. Once Robert's resentment was out in the open, the Picard brothers came somewhat to terms with one another. Jean-Luc even briefly toyed with the idea of leaving Starfleet to accept directorship of the Atlantis Project, but he eventually realized his place was still on the *Enterprise-D*.

In 2368, Picard encountered the Borg again, when the *Enterprise* recovered a lone Borg survivor of a spaceship crash. Scarred by his experience as Locutus, the captain fought his impulse to allow the Borg to die.

Cut off from his race's collective consciousness, the Borg became an individual referred to as "Hugh," not a threat as Picard had expected. When he was returned to the collective, Hugh's individualism figured to act as a virus, disabling a portion of the Borg collective as no weapon could have.

On two occasions, Picard had to save his ship singlehanded. In 2369, he was forced to outwit a pack of thieves who had snuck aboard while the *Enterprise-D* was shut down for maintenance work. In 2370, when a bizarre virus transformed the crew into their various evolutionary forebears, the captain had to work his way through the ship to stun a devolved Worf and facilitate a cure devised by Commander Data.

Picard also had to fight the *Enterprise-D* itself when it developed a network of nodes reminiscent of a neural web and began acting of its own volition. Eventually, the captain realized that the ship was indeed fostering its own embryonic intelligence. When that intelligence departed in the form of a fully mature entity, the *Enterprise-D* returned to normal.

Picard assumed an unprecedented role in Klingon politics when he served as Arbiter of Succession following the death of Klingon leader K'mpec in 2367. K'mpec took the highly unusual step of appointing an outsider as arbiter so as to ensure that the choice of K'mpec's successor would not plunge the Empire into civil war. Under Picard's arbitration, council member Gowron emerged as the sole challenger for leadership of the High Council.

A Man of Parts

The captain of the *Enterprise-D* was known as something of a Renaissance man, whose areas of interest ranged from drama to astrophysics. In particular, he was an accomplished fencer and wine connoisseur. His favorite beverage was "tea . . . Earl Grey . . . hot."

Picard was also an avid amateur archaeologist who was intrigued by the legendary ancient Iconians while still at Starfleet Academy. He occasionally published scientific papers on archaeology, and even addressed the Federation Archaeology Council in 2367.

Early in his career, at the urging of his teacher, noted archaeologist Richard Galen, Picard had seriously considered pursuing archaeology on a professional level. Picard's path later crossed Galen's again just before Galen's death in 2369, when Picard helped complete Galen's greatest discovery—the reconstruction of an ancient message from a humanoid species that had lived some four billion years earlier.

The captain actually had the opportunity to visit the mythical planet Iconia in 2365. However, an Iconian computer virus endangered the *Enterprise* and prevented him from exploring the place.

In 2370, Picard's expertise as an archaeologist stood him in good stead. Captured by pirates bent on finding a psionic superweapon developed by the ancient Vulcans, the captain was able to survive by posing as a renegade archaeologist.

Picard was also an accomplished equestrian. One of his favorite holodeck programs was a woodland setting in which he enjoyed riding a computer-simulated Arabian mare.

The captain played the piano when he was young, at the urging of his mother, but his deep love of music may have stemmed from an incident in 2268 when his mind received a lifetime of memories from the now-dead planet Kataan. At that time, he experienced the life of a man named Kamin, who had died a thousand years earlier. Kamin had played a Ressikan flute; Picard treasured the instrument because he shared Kamin's memories.

Picard's affinity for music led him to become romantically involved with Neela Daren, an *Enterprise-D* crew member, in 2369. When Daren was nearly killed on an away assignment, she and Picard realized they couldn't remain lovers while working as commander and subordinate, and she requested a transfer off the ship.

In 2369, Picard—like several members of his crew— was turned into a twelve-year-old child after passing through an energy field. With the help of Dr. Crusher and *Enterprise-D* engineer Miles O'Brien, they were restored to their original ages.

Picard suffered profound emotional abuse that same year when he was captured by Gul Madred, a high-ranking Cardassian officer. Madred tortured Picard for Starfleet tactical information. Picard resisted, but later confessed that the experience so brutalized him that he would have told Madred anything had he not been rescued.

The same occasion marked the only time a non–crew member was ever in command of the *Enterprise-D* during Picard's stint as captain. That individual was Edward Jellico, who took the captain's seat while Picard was in the custody of the Cardassians.

In 2354, Picard had been romantically involved with a

woman named Miranda Vigo during shore leave on Earth. Although Picard and Vigo attempted to keep in touch, he never saw her again.

In 2370, a Ferengi named Bok found Jason Vigo, the son of Miranda Vigo, and resequenced the boy's DNA to make it seem as if he were Picard's son. Bok, who had plotted against Picard before, planned to kill Jason in retaliation for the captain's supposed murder of Bok's son in 2355. Fortunately, the plot was exposed and Jason Vigo's life was preserved.

Beverly Crusher finally learned of Picard's feelings for her in 2370, when she and the captain were implanted with psi-wave devices so she could read his thoughts. To his surprise, Picard learned that his feelings were reciprocated, though the two opted not to act on those feelings for a while.

Picard enjoyed taking part in a series of hard-boiled holonovels featuring fictional twentieth-century detective Dixon Hill. On one occasion, a computer malfunction disabled the fail-safe mechanism that protects holodeck users, allowing a crew member to perish in the holonovel environment.

On another occasion, in 2365, a Sherlock Holmes holonovel gave rise to Moriarty, a villainous holoconstruct who tried to take over the ship. It took all Picard's powers of persuasion to convince the Moriarty construct to release his hold on the *Enterprise*.

The Moriarty construct appeared again in 2369. This time, Picard and Commander Data created a separate holoreality and outwitted the resourceful Moriarty into inhabiting it, forever unaware that he had not escaped the holodeck after all.

Tragedy and Triumph

Jean-Luc Picard was proud of his illustrious family history. One of his ancestors fought at the battle of

Trafalgar, another won a Nobel prize for chemistry, and a handful of Picards were among those who settled the first Martian Colonies.

On the other hand, Picard felt guilt over the role of another ancestor, Javier Maribona-Picard, who helped crush the Pueblo Indian Revolt on Earth in 1692. This became evident in the captain's dealings with a colony of Native Americans on Dorvan V.

For a long time, Picard wasn't confortable with children around him. In fact, almost from the moment he took command of the *Enterprise-D,* he foisted his child-related duties as captain onto his first officer, Commander William Riker. However, after being trapped in a turbolift with three young winners of a shipboard science contest, Picard came to appreciate children for their courage and optimism.

Still, he had no urge to start a family of his own. That is, until the tragic death in a fire of his brother, Robert, and his nephew, Rene—his only blood relatives, in 2371. At that point, the captain realized that he was "the last Picard," and regretted his earlier decision not to have children.

Picard's command of the *Enterprise-D* came to a premature end in 2371, when the ship was destroyed at Veridian III in an attempt to prevent Dr. Tolian Soran from destroying the Veridian system. Picard's partner in his effort to thwart Soran was James T. Kirk, captain of the original *Enterprise.* Kirk, who had been missing for some seventy-eight years following the launch of the *Enterprise-B,* was killed in the battle against Soran.

As captain of the *Enterprise-E,* Picard uncovered a Borg plot to go back in time and prevent Earth's initial contact with the Vulcans, thereby nullifying the formation of the Federation—and making the Borg's conquest of the sector in the twenty-fourth century a much easier task.

Picard took his vessel back in time as well and

thwarted the Borg scheme. However, he had to face his own inner demons in the process, coming to grips with the fear and anger that still plagued him as a result of his assimilation into the Borg collective.

As the captain of the fifth and sixth starships called *Enterprise,* Jean-Luc Picard will always be known as one of the great space explorers, scientists, and interstellar diplomats of the twenty-fourth century, a man whose considerable accomplishments were forged in the fires of wisdom, compassion, and conscience.

Look for STAR TREK Fiction from Pocket Books

Star Trek®: The Original Series

Star Trek: The Next Generation®

Encounter at Farpoint • David Gerrold
Unification • Jeri Taylor
Relics • Michael Jan Friedman
Descent • Diane Carey
All Good Things • Michael Jan Friedman
Star Trek: Klingon • Dean W. Smith & Kristine K. Rusch
Star Trek VII: Generations • J. M. Dillard
Metamorphosis • Jean Lorrah
Vendetta • Peter David
Reunion • Michael Jan Friedman
Imzadi • Peter David
The Devil's Heart • Carmen Carter
Dark Mirror • Diane Duane
Q-Squared • Peter David
Crossover • Michael Jan Friedman
Kahless • Michael Jan Friedman
Star Trek: First Contact • J. M. Dillard
The Best and the Brightest • Susan Wright
Planet X • Michael Jan Friedman

Star Trek: Deep Space Nine®

Star Trek®: Voyager™

Flashback • Diane Carey
The Black Shore • Greg Cox
Mosaic • Jeri Taylor

#1 *Caretaker* • L. A. Graf
#2 *The Escape* • Dean W. Smith & Kristine K. Rusch
#3 *Ragnarok* • Nathan Archer
#4 *Violations* • Susan Wright
#5 *Incident at Arbuk* • John Greggory Betancourt
#6 *The Murdered Sun* • Christie Golden
#7 *Ghost of a Chance* • Mark A. Garland & Charles G. McGraw
#8 *Cybersong* • S. N. Lewitt
#9 *Invasion #4: The Final Fury* • Dafydd ab Hugh
#10 *Bless the Beasts* • Karen Haber
#11 *The Garden* • Melissa Scott
#12 *Chrysalis* • David Niall Wilson
#13 *The Black Shore* • Greg Cox
#14 *Marooned* • Christie Golden
#15 *Echoes* • Dean Wesley Smith & Kristin Kathryn Rusch

Star Trek®: New Frontier

#1 *House of Cards* • Peter David
#2 *Into the Void* • Peter David
#3 *The Two-Front War* • Peter David
#4 *End Game* • Peter David
#5 *Martyr* • Peter David
#6 *Fire on High* • Peter David

Star Trek®: Day of Honor

Book One: Ancient Blood • Diane Carey
Book Two: Armageddon Sky • L. A. Graf
Book Three: Her Klingon Soul • Michael Jan Friedman
Book Four: Treaty's Law • Dean W. Smith & Kristin K. Rusch

Star Trek®: The Captain's Table